LIVING WITH JANE AUSTEN

Fanny Price, in *Mansfield Park*, tells her persistent suitor that 'we have all a better guide in ourselves…than any other person can be'. Sometimes, however, we crave external guidance: and when this happens we could do worse than seek it in Jane Austen's subtle novels. Written to coincide with Austen's 250th birthday, this approachable and intimate work shows why and how – for over half a century – Austen has inspired and challenged its author through different phases of her life. Part personal memoir, part expert interaction with all the letters, manuscripts and published novels, Janet Todd's book reveals what living with Jane Austen has meant to her and what it might also mean to others. Todd celebrates the undimmable power of Austen's work to help us understand the world around us, and our own minds and bodies, and to teach us about patience, humour, beauty and the meaning of home.

JANET TODD has been thinking and writing about books for more than half a century. She has been a biographer, novelist, critic, editor and memoirist. In the 1970s, she helped open up the study of early women writers by beginning a journal and compiling encyclopaedias before editing the complete works of Mary Wollstonecraft, Aphra Behn and Jane Austen. She has worked in English departments in Africa, the West Indies, the US and the UK. A former President of Lucy Cavendish College, Cambridge, she is now an Honorary Fellow of Lucy Cavendish and Newnham Colleges and a Professor Emerita of the University of Aberdeen.

Living
with
Jane Austen

JANET TODD

 CAMBRIDGE
UNIVERSITY PRESS

Shaftesbury Road, Cambridge CB2 8EA, United Kingdom

One Liberty Plaza, 20th Floor, New York, NY 10006, USA

477 Williamstown Road, Port Melbourne, VIC 3207, Australia

314–321, 3rd Floor, Plot 3, Splendor Forum, Jasola District Centre,
New Delhi – 110025, India

103 Penang Road, #05–06/07, Visioncrest Commercial, Singapore 238467

Cambridge University Press is part of Cambridge University Press & Assessment,
a department of the University of Cambridge.

We share the University's mission to contribute to society through the pursuit of
education, learning and research at the highest international levels of excellence.

www.cambridge.org
Information on this title: www.cambridge.org/9781009569316

DOI: 10.1017/9781009569323

When citing this work, please include a reference to the DOI 10.1017/9781009569323

First published 2025

Printed in the United Kingdom by CPI Group Ltd, Croydon CR0 4YY

A catalogue record for this publication is available from the British Library

A Cataloging-in-Publication data record for this book is available from the Library of Congress

ISBN 978-1-009-56931-6 Hardback

For Derek

CONTENTS

'How wonderful, how very wonderful the operations of time, and the changes of the human mind!'
Fanny Price, *Mansfield Park*

INTRODUCTION

Jane Austen is not my secret friend – although in my latest novel *Jane Austen and Shelley in the Garden* I made her a bothering companion to my heroine. Here in this book I try to stay with her writing, with her novels, letters and jolly tales – and control my desire for intimacy with their author.

I do, though, ask why her work makes so many of us want to open up to its creator, why she can tempt us into appointing her our comforter and advisor.

In *Mansfield Park*, Fanny Price tells her persistent suitor, 'we have all a better guide in ourselves … than any other person can be'. Sometimes, however, we crave another person to guide us and, when this happens, we could do worse – I think – than attend to Jane Austen. On the internet and in self-help books she has become therapist and guru to millions.

Over many decades I've read and used Jane Austen. Her work has appeared differently to me at different times of my life. Sometimes her 'advice' – her moral message – has seemed obvious, sometimes vexing, often painfully right. Yet I've also sensed that Jane Austen in her work and in life was irritated at those who presumed to proffer advice. In her letters she gave suggestions when consulted about writing; when she was asked about more personal matters, and especially when her advice was sought on affairs of the heart, she tended to hang back with a joke.

Advice fares poorly in her plots. In 'Edgar and Emma', a mischievous tale from her childhood, a footman, forced to be his lady's confidant, struggles to avoid the role of advisor; in 'Love and Freindship', a 'noble Youth' boasts of never having followed advice if given by his father 'in the least trifling Particular since the age of fifteen'. And so on, all through the six novels. In the last, *Persuasion*, Lady Russell, misunderstanding the passionate heart of her young charge, gives advice that delivers years of misery.

I should tread lightly, then, and remind the reader that what I write are my thoughts inspired by Jane Austen. I impute nothing to her. The thoughts come from different decades of my life and rely on memory, a sly faculty that spews up events and times I don't always wish to recall, which distorts and often colours outrageously – and repetitively.

MY MEMORY

Memories of my life are entwined with memories of reading, memories of thoughts about reading and thoughts others have thought that have bled into mine. Plagiarism in reminiscence is a rickety concept for the elderly.

Beyond books, my life was solitary, lacking siblings and close relatives, with too many moves to retain friends. Very little can be verified and my tales of the past have probably grown taller. Few are entirely 'serviceable' or 'obedient', to use Fanny Price's words; some memories are bewildered through the very act of repetition.

My father was a great raconteur of Second World War stories, of sea disasters and land invasions, mostly delivered in cheery humorous mode. He had no doubts about what he did or what the nation demanded of him. Captain Wentworth of *Persuasion* regales young women with tales of the sea. They're half in love, attentive to what would bore them from an older, ill-looking man. Jane Austen knew her readers: deprived of such presence, they need hear little of these tales – of daring, yes, but also of butchery and thieving, for what is prize-taking but sanctioned purloining at sea?

Like her ambitious naval brothers, Francis (she called him 'Frank') and Charles, Jane seems to have no problem with the custom of looting ships. Her sister authors, Frances Burney and Maria Edgeworth, were critical of warring men enriching themselves with spoils, but Austen takes the war and its chances with equanimity, even pride; the navy is just another, more heroic, profession. From a letter of Frank's she inferred that he was 'guiltless' of prizes. The word might suggest uneasiness – more likely it indicates her regret that poor Frank has failed to nab a prize; her sentence concludes by balancing his guiltlessness of prizes with his 'ignorance of promotion'.

What really happened out there in those hot islands and on cruel seas? I'll look at the warrior's return in Chapter 9 when I discuss Jane Austen's feelings about the war – and England.

My father's naval tales were rarely echoed, his comrades mostly unspeaking or dead (my father lived to be 100). One tale he told was of the sinking of the *Lancastria*, which he delivered as a flailing mass of 5,000 drowning oily men in freezing water. In 1940 Churchill hid the monstrous catastrophe from a nation wanting only victories in that gruesome time. Many years after when few really cared about it, the event was authenticated and entered history. An annual dinner was held for survivors and my father attended, now well into his nineties. I imagined the ageing guests speaking all at once, so little time left to tell their stories.

Outside the war, my father's other memories were even less easy to check. That long country walk to school alone in dark winter mornings when he was tiny. Six or seven miles, he said: how many was it really? All the way from the leaning magpie cottage to the little Shropshire town. I measured it once in a car – the distance was shorter than he claimed. Distances depend on the length of legs.

I was late in discovering Jane Austen. She wasn't my childhood passion. For many years I mixed her up with Jane Eyre, assuming them to be the same 'book'. By the time I reached my mid-teens, I'd grown away from the only serious work of 'fiction' found in every mid-Welsh house I knew, John Bunyan's *The Pilgrim's Progress* – as scary a vision as any Gothic thriller. Curiously – at least I find it curious – Bunyan seems to have had no significance for Jane Austen. When I got round to reading *Mansfield Park*, that most 'serious' of her novels, I expected to meet *The Pilgrim's Progress* in the virtuous

Fanny Price's library of books, and even more to find it intruding into Sotherton. The Wicket Gate through which Pilgrim passes to all sorts of temptation in life must surely, I thought, resonate with the locked iron gate to the wilderness that Maria Bertram and Henry Crawford climb over. But not a trace. Instead the naughty lovers flirt outrageously by quoting suggestive bits from Laurence Sterne's *Sentimental Journey*.

Possibly Bunyan's severe Protestant piety would destroy the balance between Maria's selfish treatment of Mr Rushworth and her erotic longings, and Austen's portrayal of the real constraints of a spirited woman with little social choice. Or maybe Jane Austen just didn't like Bunyan.

The novel that later penetrated my flesh and crept in behind my eyes, the novel that overwhelmed me as totally as *The Mysteries of Udolpho* excited young Catherine in *Northanger Abbey*, was Dostoevsky's *The Brothers Karamazov*. I found it alien and thrillingly intimate. I read, gorged on, dreamed with, fantasised through, and moved my mind and developing body into it. I didn't understand all the hard words or daring ideas but was exhilarated by what was perplexing. Such a dramatic picture of adult living and loving it painted!

Looking back on the events of my life, I'm aware that Grushenka and Dmitri were not ideal models of grown-up love for a naïve teenager. How much better to have passed from girlhood to semi-womanhood with Elizabeth Bennet and Mr Darcy – even better with Elizabeth alone. To have had her in mind as I met young men for the first time and felt the strange necessity of flirting. Sadly, *Pride and Prejudice* and I were not then introduced. Otherwise, I might have learnt about irony rather earlier.

Trying to recapture that 1950s teenager, ignorant as no girl can be today, I see that the Austen book I should have read was (of course) *Mansfield Park*. For Fanny Price and I shared an experience of abandonment.

We were both deposited like badly wrapped parcels in alien territory. She was ten when the carriage trundled her from Northampton towards Mansfield Park with grim Aunt Norris; I was eleven when I set off from Sri Lanka for boarding school 6,000 miles from home in a building that looked, against the bare mountains, like Wuthering Heights. After a year my parents tried to cheer me from afar by sending a coconut with my name painted in black on its green husk. It bemused the matron, who carried it away in a towel.

A 'small thick rain' was always streaming down the windows.

In 'Tiroconium', a rant against boarding schools, Jane Austen's favourite poet William Cowper imagined an opponent angrily responding to him:

> Oh barb'rous! would'st thou with a Gothic hand
> Pull down the schools – what! – all the schools i' th' land?
> Or throw them up to liv'ry-nags and grooms,
> Or turn them into shops and auction-rooms?

It's a thought.

The acute homesickness which Jane Austen describes in *Mansfield Park* and which I experienced in life was as real and disabling as my childhood asthma, born of compulsory milk and coal-dusted rooms. Cowper caught it when he imagined the boy being sent off: 'With what intense desire he wants his home.' Never mind if that home was shifting, in my case, or slovenly in Fanny Price's.

Jane Austen imagined or remembered homesickness. She was twice sent off to school, albeit with a beloved sister, and she suffered the custom not only of wet-nursing but also of care out of the house for the first eighteen months or so. Describing grief after her little nieces had lost a mother, she remarked: 'One's heart aches for a dejected mind of eight years old.' The sentiment serves for exile as well as bereavement.

Child-moving was common across the classes. The Austens took in an aristocratic child as young as five for tutoring and found him 'very backward of his Age', unlike those clever Austens – except for the second son George, born mentally defective and unmentioned in early biographies of Jane; he was cared for outside the family by poorer people.

To homesick Fanny in *Mansfield Park*, Jane Austen allowed the self-pity no other (older) heroine should wallow in. It was staunched by a cousin's kindness – and therein hung the plot.

In the early 1950s, girls' boarding schools aped boys', adopting the prefect system of placing unripe children over smaller ones: Mrs Norris and the Bertram sisters combined. Oh for a Miss Hamilton (later Mrs Smith) of *Persuasion*, already in the school when motherless Anne Elliot arrives at the age of fourteen. The older girl – no prefect system here – 'had been useful and good to her in a way which had considerably lessened her misery'. It's no wonder that, at the novel's end, Anne's man helps Mrs Smith get back her inheritance. Presumably it comes from slave plantations. In the past slavery was largely ignored as a context of Austen's writing, but, in recent years with our cultural emphasis on race and African slavery, it has come very much to the fore in critical comment. So now I can't help noticing the source of Mrs Smith's wealth. Nothing is simple in Jane Austen if you scratch a surface.

Poor Fanny grew up to be demolished by the twentieth-century novelist Kingsley Amis as the 'killjoy' of the Austen canon. But she's so much more: an image of painful, struggling, isolated goodness in a harsh diminishing world. I'd like to have contemplated her under the bedclothes before my torch and hot water bottle – and my coconut – were confiscated: I might have understood that masterpiece even then. But with her 'self-denial and humility' she'd have been no model for an adolescent girl like me, who had 'insubordinate' stamped on every termly report.

Besides, I didn't read books to find but lose myself: I read them to become other people, to live the lives I wasn't living. When a little more sophisticated, I read them both to recognise myself and my world and to feel estranged.

Not many childhoods are described in Jane Austen's novels. Little children on the periphery are spirited, rambunctious, noisy, eager: the Gardiners in *Pride and Prejudice* rushing out to smother returning parents; the unruly Middleton children of *Sense and Sensibility* demanding constant attention from guests; the small Knightleys wanting aunt Emma to tell the story of Harriet and the gypsies over and over; the little Perrys gobbling up Mrs Weston's wedding cake; and the excited Musgroves in *Persuasion* gladdening their doting parents' hearts while grating the nerves of fastidious Lady Russell. There's less of adolescence, of teenage years, about which young Jane reveals so much of herself through her glorious little notebooks of stories and plays. Within the novels, the portrait of childhood becoming youth I love most (now the boarding-school years have finally faded) is Catherine Morland's in *Northanger Abbey*.

Delivered with heavy-handed spoofing of Gothic romance, it allows us to see around the mockery to the girl growing up among a mass of siblings in the worthy rural rectory. Up to puberty, young Catherine plays cricket, rolls down the green slope at the back of the house, is bored out of her tiny mind by dull books of history and wearied with trying to make even younger ones learn their letters. But then at fifteen she begins fussing about her looks, memorising sayings from *Elegant Extracts* and curling her hair. A fresh young person with curiosity and no vanity.

Off she goes to Bath for adventure – with the most wholesome maternal advice in all Jane Austen:

> I beg, Catherine, you will always wrap yourself up very warm about the throat, when you come from the Rooms at night.

How wise was that where colds were rampant and could turn life-threatening! Better than worrying about seducing baronets. Better too than sending a daughter through the rain to catch a cold and pursue a husband, as Mrs Bennet does in *Pride and Prejudice*.

Of course it works out for the very best: *Pride and Prejudice* is the most joyful of Austen novels.

GENERATIONS

Before breaking off my excursion into autobiography, I must say a little of the generation to which I belong. I am not a 'baby boomer' – not a product of that indecorous explosion of a million post-war wombs. Neither am I from the heroic War Generation of my parents, who fought or swaggered through that big defining exhilarating event (if not mown down or mutilated). I am of the generation *dominated* by that War, the children of mothers who, finding their conscripted wartime roles denied in peace, were shunted back to wifehood and home-making. (Cinema, fashion and romances aimed to make the move glamorous – and did so for many.) To work out of the house was to shame demobbed men. Motherhood was not central to these women, but they – at least in the lower middling ranks – felt it right to teach daughters to marry well-off men. Preferably professional.

Men accepted the principle. In *Emma*, traditionalist Mr Knightley remarks, 'A man would always wish to give a woman a better home than the one he takes her from.' Emma considers the notion of leaving her father as a 'sin of thought'. Jane Austen resolves this most beguiling of novels by *not* taking the woman to 'a better home'. Emma is already at home. Her husband comes to *her*.

The narrator of *Pride and Prejudice* fixes Mrs Bennet as a figure of fun in the very first chapter. Yet her desire for her daughters to marry 'well' is no different from that of most mothers who gave birth during the Second World War. The need to 'elevate' oneself with a husband (to quote Emma) was consuming – as if no woman had melded chemicals or driven a Fordson Model N tractor in those six extraordinary years.

Like Mrs Bennet, these 1940s mothers had a point. For, without that high-earning, wife-keeping man, you found yourself working right through pregnancy, childbirth and childcare.

So that's what I did. If you wanted a man's job, you had to act like a man.

I've checked with Google what my generation is called. I'm from the Silent Generation.

Jane Austen didn't marry or bear children; she became 'an old maid'. Emma may have believed that it was 'poverty only which makes celibacy contemptible', but her creator didn't share the sentiment, and neither does Emma's counterpart Miss Bates, described as 'neither young, handsome, rich, nor married'. In his *A Memoir of Jane Austen*, Austen's nephew and biographer James Edward Austen-Leigh claimed that Jane and Cassandra accepted spinsterhood and early on 'took to the garb of middle age'. Just clothes – for thrift and convenience? – or something more basic? A stab at agelessness? A freedom? In a letter from her brother's mansion at Godmersham, Jane wrote:

> By the bye, as I must leave off being young, I find many Douceurs in being a sort of Chaperon for I am put on the Sofa near the Fire & can drink as much wine as I like.

Growing up, I assumed the maturity of those war-inflected mothers awaited us girls. But then the culture started changing for the better, and women could, if they wished, toss off that antiquated glamour and dress like little girls in short skirts and frolic in newly naughty ways – the pill, you know, and the washing machine and black-and-white television. Did Jane Austen choose clothes to wear in refusal of an old norm? Is there something childlike and excessive there despite that middle-aged garb?

She and her sister lived with their mother their whole lives and would always be the 'girls'. Jane had been a precocious, diverting child; as an adult she went on writing little spoofs and funny letters to entertain her nieces and nephews, now that her brothers were grown into professional men. So, in her late thirties she was enjoying the ebullient silliness of her thirteen-year-old self, remembering with pleasure other times and audiences. It's an inspiring example – to be amazed, amused, and to laugh while choosing to wear just what you wanted.

MARY WOLLSTONECRAFT

In this book I've given Jane Austen a companion, an alter ego. Appropriate I think, for she wrote during the flowering of women's writing, when female voices were heard more clearly than ever before in English history. It's worth remembering that, although extraordinary, Jane Austen was not alone.

The feminist Mary Wollstonecraft, author of *A Vindication of the Rights of Woman*, was born fifteen years before Jane Austen. Those years made all the difference. To be born in 1775 not 1759 is to hear of the French Revolution and the Terror it spawned when still a child and to know that ideals are dangerous and utopias likely to morph into dystopias, that getting through life needs detachment and cynical good humour, and that the best hope for society and government is pragmatism. Wollstonecraft couldn't have anticipated this.

After her early death at thirty-eight, her husband William Godwin lovingly wrote a memoir to celebrate her life. His admiring pages taught a shocked world that female sexuality, education and independence led to illegitimacy, abandonment and suicide. The 'rights of woman' became horribly wrong.

Jane Austen and Mary Wollstonecraft are geniuses, and both knew it, but, where Jane Austen privately enjoyed the sense of her own talent, Mary Wollstonecraft shouted out her distinction. She paid the price, of course. She was a signpost pointing the road for others: through her daring exploits in life and work she was, she claimed, 'forced to stand still … amidst the mud and dust' to be splattered and dirtied by women as well as men in changing times.

Those fifteen years' difference, as well as different trajectories and temperaments. Had I been born fifteen years later, I would have been a baby boomer. See the difference it makes?

Possibly Jane Austen read Godwin's candid memoir and responded sympathetically by creating Marianne in *Sense and Sensibility*, who nearly comes to such grief as Mary Wollstonecraft. She is saved – by an older man and a loving sister. The pathetic ones, the two Elizas, sad dying mother and disgraced daughter, are confined to an inset tale. Jane Austen never allows such women print-room again: other pens must dwell on guilt and misery. But you feel she knew of both.

While I was writing my biography of Mary Wollstonecraft, I thought of *Pride and Prejudice*. I brought the two momentarily together, life and fiction. It's one reason why I found myself critiquing the beautiful estate of Pemberley and why I discovered darkness in the hero of this most sparkling of novels. I give my views in Chapters 1 and 2.

In life, Jane Austen and Mary Wollstonecraft didn't meet. Had they done so they're unlikely to have become friends or even much impressed each other. Austen might have written amusingly of the meeting to her sister, while keeping mum in front of the woman whom Horace Walpole dubbed 'a hyena in petticoats'. With her tendency to talk over others, as Godwin noted on their first meeting, Wollstonecraft would hardly have noticed her auditor.

Virginia Woolf feared an encounter with Jane Austen:

> an atmosphere of perfect control and courtesy mixed with something finely satirical. Which, were it not directed against things in general rather than against individuals, would be almost malicious, would, so I feel, make it alarming to find her at home.

THE BOOK

I hope that in what follows I can convey a little of the excitement that still overwhelms me as I go on reading Jane Austen. I'm noticing more and more of the quality that the discerning critic and novelist Walter Scott called the 'exquisite touch which renders ordinary commonplace things and characters interesting from the truth of the description and the sentiment'. But, like her first readers, mainly family and friends, I also find myself dwelling now on the comic, the ridiculous characters, from vapid Lady Middleton to Diana and Susan Parker and above all brash Mrs Elton. Also, being old, I can't avoid noticing ailments, so I devote two chapters to them, and another to dying.

I'm now twice the age Jane Austen was when she died and I'm still listening to girls who will always be twenty.

Personal writing, memoir, autobiography or life-writing is now common, in fact necessary in this Wild West of media cacophony, which shares what was once private with whoever can be persuaded to read and click on 'Like'. But, although I'm inserting myself into this book, I can't quite slough off a sense of the unseemly – what would Jane Austen think of such indecorum?

In David Lodge's *Changing Places*, the American Austen scholar Maurice Zapp, whose ambition is to write everything that could possibly be written about Jane Austen, astonishes the bored students in his English class: he first describes the scene in *Persuasion* where Captain Wentworth lifts the Musgrove toddler from Anne Elliot's shoulders, then he exclaims: 'If that isn't an *orgasm*, what is it?'

Writing or talking about Jane Austen – it's easy to embarrass yourself.

Happily, I can step back from full frontal exposure. The mantra of Second Wave Feminism was that the personal was political, but for me the personal has been the professional. To atone for the bad luck of a life of intermittent illness and an adolescence with the wrong novels, I must set one piece of ravishing good luck, that from the age of twenty-two to seventy-two I was paid to read books – among them the six novels, funny tales, absurd poems and quirky letters of Jane Austen.

JANE AUSTEN ON MEMORY

Before I set off on my backward journey, let me remind you what Jane Austen herself said of memory and tale-telling.

In *Mansfield Park*, Henry Crawford remarks of Shakespeare's work:

> It is a part of an Englishman's constitution. His thoughts and beauties are so spread abroad that one touches them every where, one is intimate with him by instinct.

Edmund elaborates: 'His celebrated passages are quoted by every body.' What was true of Shakespeare is just as true now of Jane Austen. Her image and her books are at the centre of a community of memory that we enter whenever we encounter someone who's read *Pride and Prejudice* – or seen the film. Mention the name of Mr Darcy and people respond.

Austen frequently dwells on the magic, instability and puckish-ness of memory. In *Pride and Prejudice* Elizabeth Bennet claims it can be brought under control. She tells Darcy. 'Think only of the past as its remembrance gives you pleasure.' She's used to being the smartest female in her raucous house and tends to declare what later needs modifying. Does she believe what she says is possible?

Darcy does not: 'Painful recollections will intrude, which cannot, which ought not to be repelled.'

But Elizabeth continues in declarative mode, explaining later to her bemused sister how to respond to an abrupt change of love object: 'in such cases as these, a good memory is unpardonable'.

Either be careful what you remember or watch what you say you remember.

Fanny Price sees memory as a faculty of wonder and trick-ery. When foolish Mr Rushworth can't learn his lines for a play which the lively Crawfords and Bertrams are delighting to stage in Mansfield (the patriarch conveniently absent), Fanny, always alive to a victim, tries 'to make an artificial memory for him'. The play's demand for memorising taxes her further when beloved cousin Edmund and Mary Crawford use their need to learn lines as an excuse to invade her private East Room.

They arrive severally and, instead of making her a fellow-actor – probably now, having listened to so many rehearsals, she's the only one who knows the whole soon-to-be-burnt script by heart – the pair reduce her to a prompter. This is the role she's forced to play outside her special room as she watches preparations for what promises to be for her a 'suffering exhibition'.

In one of those odd little rhapsodies that are both endearing and unsettling for the reader, Fanny Price ponders the strange-ness of memory:

> How wonderful, how very wonderful the operations of time, and the changes of the human mind! … If any one faculty of our nature may be called *more* wonderful than the rest, I do think it is memory. There seems something more speakingly incomprehensible in the powers, the failures, the inequalities of memory, than in any other of our intelligences. The memory is sometimes so retentive, so serviceable, so obedient—at others, so bewildered and so weak—and at others again, so tyrannic, so beyond controul!—We are to be sure a miracle every way— but our powers of recollecting and of forgetting, do seem peculiarly past finding out.

If intended to impress its hearer, this quaint speech is ill-timed. Mary Crawford is as inattentive as the least teachable student in the giggling back row. Do we readers take advantage of the latitude for reflection Mary rejects? Are we struck by what Fanny calls 'the inequalities of memory'?

The passage is not just subverted by Mary Crawford's boredom, but later by Fanny herself. When she sets off for Portsmouth, she forgets the friskiness of memory. She has in mind a home completely different from the one she left.

When it was first suggested that a child from Portsmouth be offered a place to live in Mansfield, she was the nameless 'child'. She would be accommodated but not adopted by her relatives. Jane's brother Edward was whisked away to a grander house, chosen to fill the needs of an estate, not removed like Fanny to relieve a burden from a needy family. Fanny goes from Portsmouth because Mrs Norris invites the eldest girl. The choice surprises Mrs Price 'when she had so many fine boys', especially since the chosen girl 'was somewhat delicate and puny'. Fanny wouldn't have known what her mother thought of her, but a sensitive child of ten has eyes and ears and must have laid down some memory of hurt.

Despite musing on the trickery of memory, Fanny goes to this Portsmouth home filled with beguiling hopes. Had she forgotten what Cowper wrote in 'Tiroconium'? That there's no going back to the same place, that the boarding-school boy, returning home at last, has been chilled by absence. He steps into his house as an 'alienated son'.

Swiftly disillusioned in greasy Portsmouth, Fanny finds respite in renovating her memories of Mansfield Park. Readers have seen her despised, ignored and exploited during eight long years. Now she recalls only 'happy ways' in a house of 'elegance, propriety, regularity, harmony', of 'peace and tranquillity'. Every hour of the day she 'remembers' this elysian place darkened only by the 'trifling' shadow of Aunt Norris. She recollects a 'regular course of cheerful orderliness', failing to note that this 'orderliness' is maintained only under the authority of Sir Thomas. It breaks down once his heavy hand is withdrawn.

What is this ductile, tricksy memory that has so little regard to 'truth'? The *Lancastria* did indeed sink with the loss of 5,000 men but, if they were hidden from the country that sent them to their death, where lay the 'truth' in those years when it lived only in my father's (and other unknown men's) memory?

Sir Thomas sends Fanny to Portsmouth to make desirable memories of Mansfield – and in the squalid household learn the value of money. His plan works.

Persuasion is a novel about memory as a master and as a site of mourning. It begins with Sir Walter Elliot living in his book of family and ancestors, the *Baronetage*. Then it moves to his second daughter, the neglected Anne, who exists on the memory of a summer when, out of boredom, two young people, a handsome young sailor and a lonely motherless girl, fell deeply in love.

Now in the present of the book seven years on, Anne Elliot has met the beloved again. She's appalled and bewildered to see so little love coming her way when she has hoarded hers with such care. She looks at Wentworth, remembers and forms new memories, seeing also her 'silent pensive self' – not for nothing is she Sir Walter's child.

She is about to leave her relatives the Musgroves in Uppercross, where she has reconnected with the Captain but only in a way to disconcert. She fears he may soon be lost to her again:

> a small thick rain almost blotting out the very few objects ever to
> be discerned from the windows, was enough to make the sound
> of Lady Russell's carriage exceedingly welcome; and yet, though

desirous to be gone, she could not quit the mansion-house, or look an adieu to the cottage, with its black, dripping, and comfortless veranda, or even notice through the misty glasses the last humble tenements of the village, without a saddened heart.—Scenes had passed in Uppercross, which made it precious. It stood the record of many sensations of pain, once severe, but now softened; and of some instances of relenting feeling, some breathings of friendship and reconciliation, which could never be looked for again, and which could never cease to be dear. She left it all behind her; all but the recollection that such things had been.

The dripping, comfortless veranda under rain and the humble tenements express the pain of alienation, of exile from happiness. Anne forces these items to clutch at that golden time so long past, now replaced by thin but still blessed memories: 'some breathings of friendship and reconciliation, which could never be looked for again'. She has overlaid the precious summer with dull November, fusing old and new yearning into renewed pain, but also a kind of comfort.

Elizabeth Bennet would have had no truck with memory turned into such sensitive lacerating introspection.

I've left *Emma* to the last because it alone discusses memory as a topic swinging free of the characters while also resting within them. Emma is not as sure about memory as Elizabeth, nor as curious as Fanny, nor so overwhelmed as Anne Elliot. 'Perfect happiness, even in memory, is not common' is a sentiment delivered in that slippery free indirect style for which Jane Austen is famous. The 'style' allows Emma to appear to think worthy thoughts while not quite being mistress of them in Elizabeth's manner. The sentence follows her visit to the inferior Coles in Highbury. She feels she's condescended beautifully, but all is not quite 'perfect': her treatment of Jane Fairfax perhaps, that clever, handsome woman whose vulnerability she never grasps.

By the end of the book, Emma's memory is even more disturbed. 'Seldom, very seldom, does complete truth belong to any human disclosure' intones that soothing, ambivalent Emma-ish voice; memories must stay where they are or be wrenched into new forms:

> seldom can it happen that something is not a little disguised, or a little mistaken; but where, as in this case, though the conduct is mistaken, the feelings are not, it may not be very material.

'Something' is a little dishonest here, but the honey-toned voice softens the edge. It makes her lover's belief that he can speak 'nothing but truth' just a touch ridiculous.

When I first saw Jane Austen on the £10 note, I rejoiced that her image adorned precisely the amount of money she received for the first book she sold to a publisher, the novel published after her death as *Northanger Abbey*. I cringed at everything else: that prettified picture instead of Cassandra's sardonic, perhaps grumpy, sketch; in the background the great house where she never lived instead of the cottage she loved; the quotation – 'I declare after all there is no enjoyment like reading' – an opinion spoken by foolish Caroline Bingley in *Pride and Prejudice* while trying to interrupt and capture the indifferent hero.

For a British banknote declining in value and representing the country's past and present, surely a better aphorism would be that line from *Emma*:

> Seldom, very seldom, does complete truth belong to any human disclosure.

CHAPTER 1
The Brightness of Pemberley

I understand the seduction of property. I grew up in rented houses and my mother let her eyes trace pictures in *Country Life*. So did I – so do a lot of others. They call it property porn. I've found the magazines piled up in the bathrooms of very respectable people.

How much more compelling is property if it comes with a handsome proprietor. I must remember, it's fantasy.

THE PEDIGREE OF PEMBERLEY

In her great Enlightenment feminist work *A Vindication of the Rights of Woman*, Mary Wollstonecraft showed how thoroughly women colluded in their subordination, how much they embraced their state as overgrown irrational children. She led up to her pioneering book by reviewing a great deal of women's writing for a new radical magazine, the *Analytical Review*.

Her opinion stated in review after review was clear: novels snare and delude weak-minded women who turn to fiction because they can't face reality. As peddled by female authors, romance encouraged a corrupt love of glamour, a thoughtless feminine surrender to the insinuating gallantry of men. The pernicious fantasy allowed middle-class women to imagine themselves fine ladies and all women to believe they could exercise more than fleeting power over sexually desiring men.

With what? Temporary beauty? A little liveliness perhaps, a meaningless skill like dancing or singing? Beneath this illusion lay the naked reality of patriarchy: the legal, social and economic subordination of one half of humanity to the other.

Wollstonecraft's was a frontal attack on the romantic genre which Jane Austen was about publicly to enter. What would she have thought of *Pride and Prejudice* if she'd had a chance to read it?

Perhaps her method of looking at works closely would have let her see that this particular novel was no ordinary run-of-the-mill 'romance', which she compared to a 'whipped syllabub'. She'd have agreed with the idea expressed in Austen's original title 'First Impressions', that women should be warned against trusting intuition over reason. In *A Vindication of the Rights of Woman* she held firmly to the need for her sex to be rational, to judge with consideration and care, and not to believe, with Marianne Dashwood of *Sense and Sensibility* that, if something *feels* good, it's right.

'Oh why is virtue always to be rewarded with a coach and six' – or a great estate? – Mary Wollstonecraft exclaimed after reading yet another romantic novel 'by a Lady'.

If she *had* so exclaimed over *Pride and Prejudice*, would she have been wrong? What is it but a sophisticated fairy tale (albeit infused with reality), in which a rude frog magically becomes a polite prince, and in which his bride, a Cinderella from beyond the prince's circle, becomes princess of Pemberley, so for ever escaping her (step)mother. Surely no other ending is quite so comfortable and jolly as this: it concludes the first novel Austen published as 'author', no longer just 'a Lady'. (Just as well since by 1813 'be a Lady' seemed rather old-fashioned.)

Through cinematic translations, Darcy's estate of Pemberley has been multiplied: a boon to England's National Trust and other stately homes. Houses often attract visitors by advertising a glimpse of filmic Pemberley, if a scene was set there. Their shops sell candles, lavender pillows, home knitted scarves and prettily bound versions of *Pride and Prejudice*. Other items suggest entry into genteel life: Regency nightdresses, cookery books of trifles and plum puddings, kits for the needlepoint Austen's leisured ladies do in their patterned drawing rooms.

Near where I live is Wimpole Hall, a National Trust property. It was once owned by the daughter of Rudyard Kipling, author of 'The Janeites', a tale in which soldiers from the First World War become a fellowship through familiarity with Austen's novels. So it was no accident that, while I was strolling round the Wimpole grounds, I was thinking about Jane Austen and Pemberley, especially its lineage. I'm personalising because for me Pemberley is as much a character in *Pride and Prejudice* as Wuthering Heights in Emily Brontë's novel. But the estate of Pemberley is better bred.

Here's how I see its ancestors. From the Renaissance onwards, the English country-house poem loudly praised rustic manly virtue and pitted the austere but comfortable and harmonious against the flashy and luxurious, the kitsch tastelessness of the (usually) newly rich against the innate good taste of the well-born and -bred. Estates featured in these poems were real, inhabited by noble men and women making dynastic marriages and eager for praise in portraits and poems about themselves and their properties.

The realist novel emerging in English in the eighteenth century made this poetic country house its own. It kept many details; above all, it let the house and gardens embody the dignified and virtuous owner. Examples include Henry Fielding's Paradise Hall in *The History of Tom Jones*, Samuel Richardson's Grandison Hall in *Sir Charles Grandison* and Tobias Smollett's Brambleton Hall in *The Expedition of Humphrey Clinker*. All of these are rich, fertile, hereditary estates whose proprietors must be worthy or they couldn't possess them.

How can you doubt the worth (if not always the sagacity) of an Allworthy of Paradise Hall, any more than a Knightley of Donwell Abbey? (I wrote – or the Word programme insisted on writing – Downton before Abbey, not Donwell. The trope persists.)

Women writers were quick to enter the novel in the delusive (and deluded) way Mary Wollstonecraft deplored, and, along with many exploiting men, they tweaked the formula. In their stories, the socially equal bride is replaced by a woman from a lower (but not too lowly) sphere, virtuous and remarkable for beauty, wit and gentility. The progress is followed by Monimia in novelist and poet Charlotte Smith's *The Old Manor House*, by Fanny Price in *Mansfield Park* – and by Elizabeth Bennet in *Pride and Prejudice.*

Austen was not enthusiastic about *Tom Jones*, with its sexy roistering hero: she presents it as a man's book approved by boorish John Thorpe in *Northanger Abbey*. Instead, according to her first biographer, her much-loved brother Henry, she admired *Sir Charles Grandison*.

Before I became an enthusiast for Jane Austen, I read Samuel Richardson's earlier novel, the huge, tragic *Clarissa*. I was overwhelmed, finding it an English equivalent of that wonderful Russian *Karamazov*. In *Clarissa*, the virtuous heroine, after being tormented almost out of her mind, is raped: she prefers death to marriage with her rapist and life in a world that includes such men.

I was so moved by this extraordinary novel that, spending a university holiday with my parents in a Shropshire village, through the local library I ordered up the seven volumes of Richardson's next work *Sir Charles Grandison*. They arrived in a small van from Ludlow, I think – or Shrewsbury. I was unprepared for how interminable a novel it turned out to be. (Stupid really since Henry Austen had qualified his statement of his sister's admiration by declaring that her 'taste secured her from the errors of his prolix style'.)

Appalled to find that many readers, especially women, had been impressed rather than horrified by his villainous but wittily entertaining rapist, Richardson set out to write a book that illustrated the good *man*, as *Clarissa* had displayed the good woman. By the time I reached Volume 5 and realised nothing much was going to happen, I'd understood that virtue needed suffering to display itself. With her vulnerable body, a woman of any rank could be distressed and tormented with ease, but why should a man with money, status and health suffer except in some self-inflicted way through poor judgement? Why should anything dark descend on so splendid a man as Sir Charles?

Half a century has elapsed after my encounter in the village library, wondering how many more volumes I could push myself to read.

Now appreciating Jane Austen, I marvelled at her admiration for anything about *Sir Charles Grandison*. I felt I should return to the book and this time concentrate on its estate rather than its owner and his interminable virtues.

I settled on a few details out of the enormous number Richardson provides – quite outdoing poor Mr Collins listing the trees and fields around his modest parsonage. Unlike Mr Collins and Richardson, Jane Austen knew that readers cared little for trees and fields presented to no purpose. But there it was: she admired *Grandison* – and presumably Grandison Hall.

After much puzzlement, I concluded that the main reason for admiration was Richardson's mastery of intricate communal scenes *within* a house, competing conversations and views. Jane Austen could well have learnt from this. As for Grandison Hall, despite the tedious description, it *is* rather like her Pemberley.

Grandison Hall stands in a 'spacious park' and has fine avenues: its owner thinks it 'a kind of impiety to fell a tree, that was planted by his father'. The park boasts lawns and 'a winding stream … abounding with trout and other fish'. It has a well-stocked library offering views from its windows 'as boundless as the mind of the owner'. Almost half a century separates *Grandison* from *Pride and Prejudice* and by the 1790s unbroken lawns had fallen out of fashion: oaks and chestnuts are scattered on Darcy's large expanse of green.

All is elegant inside but 'not sumptuous' and Sir Charles is surrounded by worthy servants, grateful tenants and a very admiring housekeeper. (You can see where I'm going.)

Richardson described Grandison Hall so minutely to display Sir Charles through his property. But by the time we reach it, there's no need; we gain the perfect place after we've already waded through thousands of pages praising the virtues, manners and demeanour of Sir Charles.

Jane Austen would avoid this pitfall since, initially, her hero is not faultless, and because he's not so repeatedly and mono-thematically revealed, Darcy needs Pemberley as Sir Charles doesn't need Grandison Hall. Pemberley, the reduced version of Richardson's stately pile, serves to reveal Austen's hero as a good man as nothing else can.

As I walked towards the folly on the other side of the man-made lake in the grounds of Wimpole, I also came to think that Jane Austen might have derived another notion from reading the thousands of pages of *Grandison*. As well as the skilled handling of multiple conversations and the depiction of the Hall, might she not have noticed the overall absurdity of the book and thought that she could achieve the Richardsonian effects in far more succinct a manner, by judicious lopping and cropping? In which case, she could make something better, more readable and more brilliant than her predecessor – so becoming (in echo of her acquisitive heroine) – 'mistress' of the new form of the novel.

I was pleased with the thought as I tramped across the ha-ha avoiding sheep droppings, mainly because I find it hard to bear the fact that Jane Austen died before she knew of her extraordinary fiery fame.

Like Sir Charles Grandison, Fitzwilliam Darcy is defined by his large house, symbol of power in and on the land. Master of his world, he commands people's lives, preventing and arranging marriages. Comically considering Mrs Bennet's eagerness to marry her daughters well, it's Darcy who brings about the weddings of three Bennet girls. After his first insulting proposal, Elizabeth subdues him with her sharp tongue but, although both are humbled by the other's words, Darcy's letter proves most potent. However, if her seduction (and reformation) begins with the letter, Pemberley finishes the business, as Elizabeth (playfully) admits to sister Jane, who asks when her attraction began:

> I believe I must date it from my first seeing his beautiful grounds at Pemberley.

The estate modifies her understanding of its owner, of his social power, and, above all, of his goodness, his virtue. In Meryton, Darcy is out of place, so rude as to be almost comic. Unlike Anne Elliot, he never learns 'our own nothingness beyond our own circle'. Like his future bride, he needs Pemberley.

THE GILPIN WAY

In presenting this transforming estate, Austen has an advantage over Richardson: she was steeped in the writing of William Gilpin, that great authority on and promoter of the picturesque manner of looking. Gilpin is so significant because he offers a way that an outsider, a visitor, may experience the gardens and grounds of *someone else*'s great property.

In his tours through the land describing and sketching scenes of 'picturesque beauty', Gilpin, a parson from Hampshire like Jane Austen's father and brother, is the observer, never the owner, and he takes the reader with him as observer too. He sees his landscapes less as possessions than as imaginative stimuli available to anyone who has learned how to look.

When he arrives at a house, Gilpin checks for symmetry and elegance, complaining when an owner has overlaid nature with 'tawdry ornaments' or achieved an 'incoherency'. Sometimes when gazing at a mansion and judging it inadequate for his mode of aesthetic looking, he imagines the owner standing beside him – and then he worries he's being too severe: he doesn't want to disturb the man's innocent tastelessness. If an owner is dead and a property opened to public viewing, it becomes fair game.

I'll return to Gilpin when I look at Jane Austen's view of nature in Chapter 7. Here he's primarily the observer of stately piles and improved grounds, a judge of what the rich have done to the earth.

All Austen's major characters are aware of Gilpin's books. Young Jane mocked their popularity in a skit called 'A Tour through Wales'. One sister sketches (an activity much praised by Gilpin for its power to concentrate the viewer's mind on details) while the other sprints beside her mother on a galloping pony. A single pair of satin slippers is divided between the sisters, who – alliteratively – 'hopped home from Hereford'.

In the more serious, later childhood tale 'Catharine, or the Bower', ignorance of Gilpin exposes a lack of taste. 'We are going to the Lakes,' declares trivial Camilla Stanley, while boasting, 'I know nothing of the Route, for I never trouble myself about such things'. Heading for the same Lakes, Elizabeth Bennet passes the Gilpin test:

> We *will* know where we have gone—we *will* recollect what we have seen. Lakes, mountains, and rivers, shall not be jumbled together in our imaginations …

Austen fails to describe the route Elizabeth and the Gardiners follow, but she can assume its stopping-places are known to Gilpin readers: Oxford, Blenheim, Warwick and Kenilworth. These are all real halts on the trail to Derbyshire.

Gilpin was one of the first to promote the wild charms of Derbyshire and to connect them with 'fiction and romance'.

Just as she reduced Grandison Hall, so Jane Austen 'lopt & cropt' the Gilpin tour in Elizabeth's and the Gardiners' journey northwards. But Gilpin is resplendently present when Elizabeth arrives at Pemberley.

As the August sun shines on the great estate, she approaches it (to my mind) almost book in hand. We know she's versed in Gilpin from her earlier naughty reference to his view that three cows form a picturesque group whereas four do not. She parodies the preference when at Netherfield she remarks that she won't make a fourth with Darcy and the Bingley sisters in their walk, for she would spoil the scene. By such comment she lightly mocks the rude Bingley women, as well as Gilpin in prescriptive mode.

Like modern Rosings, Pemberley stands on rising ground and is backed by woody hills. It's an uncommon position for a supposedly ancient house. *Emma*'s Donwell Abbey is built in a sheltered spot without wide views, while the placing of ancient Sotherton in 'one of the lowest spots of the park' in *Mansfield Park* 'excluded the possibility of much prospect from any of the rooms'. In the unfinished last novel 'Sanditon', Mr Parker's old manor house lies in a hollow, whereas his new one, built for a sea view, sits on an exposed clifftop.

Pemberley's imagined Derbyshire site allows the visitor to arrive and be surprised in the way Gilpin suggested a landowner try to arrange, using a curved and sweeping driveway and strategic trees. Elizabeth and her relatives fully experience the sudden excitement when a great house comes into view – as its master will similarly surprise them later:

> the eye was instantly caught by Pemberley House, situated on the opposite side of a valley, into which the road with some abruptness wound.

In the late eighteenth and early nineteenth centuries, Derbyshire was famous for deep coal mining, which in turn led to the construction of canals of the sort Jane Austen and her family opposed when one threatened the pristine beauty of her brother Edward's large estate in Godmersham. Mining and communications brought prosperity to the middle classes and great wealth to the upper, but at the expense of land and labourers. In Derbyshire in particular poor workers turned militant and tried to sabotage the new industries that were taking their livelihoods. But signs of industrial activity, as well as of protest, were largely hidden from the mansions of those who benefited most. (The National Trust now notes a property's connection with slavery, but seems less eager to stress its exploitation of local workers.)

As fantasy, Pemberley exists beyond capitalist enterprise and is untouched by the rape of northern lands. The 'amorous effect of "brass"', to use W. H. Auden's phrase about Austen's work, is as strong in *Pride and Prejudice* as in money-obsessed *Sense and Sensibility*, but Pemberley has no monetary value nor is it scrutinised for its yield. A negative point, but difficult not to notice in the context of other Austen novels.

Pemberley will always be what it is. Kellynch in *Persuasion* becomes a rental and the smaller manor of the Parkers in its cosy hollow near Sanditon may be turned into a hospital. Pemberley will neither be let nor transformed.

Its landscaping needs no improvement. No payment has been made to a fashionable gardener like Humphry Repton, mentioned by name in *Mansfield Park*. The association of beauty and money clear to Maria Bertram and urban Mary Crawford is absent here.

As Gilpin disliked signs of ostentation in a house, so he disapproved 'embellishments' in the grounds: temples, obelisks, hermitages, summer and tea houses. Happily, Pemberley lacks modish garden furniture. It has only a 'simple bridge', rather than the decorated oriental structure Gilpin so abhorred at flashy Chatsworth nearby. No mention even of hothouses: Austen often uses them to represent the flamboyance despised in country-house poetry. General Tilney in *Northanger Abbey* has an array of greenhouses, while the shabby John Dashwoods in *Sense and Sensibility* intend to erect one at Norland Park.

So where did those 'beautiful pyramids of grapes, nectarines, and peaches' Darcy and his sister offer their guests come from? (At least they provide no un-English pineapples. Only extravagant General Tilney has a pinery.)

As with garden bric-à-brac, so with animals: none sullies Pemberley's lawns or gravel. Jane Austen's letters are full of middle-class life among ducks and working donkeys. Not even classy hunters and pointers disturb Pemberley's turf. In common with virtually all young squires, Darcy shoots, but here in the time of the novel, he simply fishes. A suitable pastime he can share with the middle class; he and the trading Mr Gardiner may enjoy it together.

(Poor old fish, so unappreciated – and funny – is it the word or that strange sad face? Such commotion and campaigning against fox-hunting on snorting steeds, such silence about fishing with a cruel hook. Mammal privilege?)

Since Gilpin demands that an estate give a viewer an aesthetic experience, he upbraids landowners who draw attention to expense and artifice. A visitor will judge an owner through what he has made of his land.

Elizabeth follows the line. Aunt Gardiner sets up Pemberley as special before they arrive, remembering that it has the finest woods in the county. Duly instructed, Elizabeth 'admired every remarkable spot and point of view'. The point is not the detail, which is scanty, but that Elizabeth is delighted:

> She had never seen a place for which nature had done more, or where natural beauty had been so little counteracted by an awkward taste.

This is prelude not to a Romantic spiritual experience, where the viewer is taken out of herself within nature, but to Gilpin's picturesque 'transport'; it leads to the great moment when Elizabeth knows, as an outsider freed for once from her vulgar family, 'that to be mistress of Pemberley might be something!'

She fits this place, and, once over the first wonder of being there, feels none of the surprise of Mary Crawford finding herself happy in a parsonage garden. Nor indeed of Jane Austen herself, who described in a letter how she paraded 'about London in a Barouche' '& was ready to laugh all the time, at my being where I was'.

When the party reaches the house, they stand in the hall as middle-class tourists, very much as we do when we pay and enter a stately home to observe and wonder at its splendour and learn of the alien ways of past or present owners. Like us, they need guides, the housekeeper within, the gardener without. But, when they next enter, they won't be like us on our paid-for visit; they'll be translated into guests. They'll pass through the hall to the saloon and look out to those woods they'd first admired as tourists.

As in Grandison Hall, elegance, taste and grandeur combine in Pemberley but are left uncatalogued. Elizabeth has had her fill of stately-home visiting and is bored with carpets and curtains – as, dare I say, we often are as we traipse round a house, ordered to stay off Persian rugs and stick to plastic covered walkways. The house interests only as it embodies Darcy, no longer the boorish outsider of Meryton, but now the very model of a landowning country gentleman.

With growing interest Elizabeth sees him in the stones of the house, on canvas and in what might be called the Reynolds portrait, the housekeeper's glowing account of perfect master and landlord (echoing the flattering paintings Sir Joshua Reynolds made of his grand sitters). Now Elizabeth has the daring thought, 'of this place … I might have been mistress!' – a step into the fantasy of personal *ownership* with the man as conduit. The desire for social elevation and acquisition is blatant – and lovable. How easy it is to understand!

After encountering Darcy, Elizabeth explores the gardens, not quite as a stranger now, for she has met the master. Her eye has 'power to wander' and, as she takes the circuit walk, her Gilpin experience is tied to growing feeling for Darcy who, through the landscape of his grounds, is revealing different images and different prospects. She enters a deep romantic gully of the sort Gilpin describes in his *Remarks on Forest Scenery* and longs to explore.

Have we at last got a fictional metaphor for sex, often delivered during less raunchy times than ours by excursions into deep, dark and wooded valleys? If so, the moment passes.

Out of politeness to her aunt, she hangs back – she's not now, if she ever was, like thrill-seeking Marianne. The compensation for demureness is another abrupt view of the master, whose silence and awkwardness she's imitating. No more wicked repartee to make him tongue-tied. Elizabeth regrets 'every saucy speech' of the first part of the book, which paradoxically has been what first attracted him – and us. She's shed the conceited independence Caroline Bingley (rightly) once discerned in her. She's already in training for mistress-ship of Pemberley.

Propriety to property.

In darker *Sense and Sensibility*, there's no question of the heroine Elinor becoming mistress of a great estate, just an indifferent parsonage. She has no such fantasy desire. Hers is a more difficult aim: 'I *will* be mistress of myself.'

Pemberley is the married place, and property for a woman comes with marriage. Elizabeth and Darcy *have to marry*. In Elizabeth, marriageability is based first on sexual power – the Gardiners easily see that it's Darcy rather than their niece who's 'overflowing with admiration' – and second on the change wrought in her by Pemberley. For the first time in the book, the author refers to her as 'the lady' while Darcy is 'master of the house'. The interrupting episode of Lydia scandalously running off with Wickham confirms these identities. When Elizabeth hears the dreadful news – dreadful for silly Lydia but also for the whole clan of Bennet girls – her response is ladylike: she collapses in tears.

If we needed a way to distinguish her from Mary Crawford of *Mansfield Park*, who at first seems to share so much of her quick wit and repartee, we see it here. Mary fails entirely to respond as prim Edmund expects when she hears of his sister's adultery. Not a tear shed.

Lydia's foolish elopement will also in time confirm Darcy's masculine and financial power. What cannot this man do and fix?

In *Sense and Sensibility*, the barbed conversations that form some of the delight of *Pride and Prejudice* take place between women, between Elinor and Lucy Steele and sometimes between Elinor and her sister. *Persuasion* ends with a sort of duet with Anne Elliot and Captain Wentworth singing out their love. But, except perhaps occasionally with Emma and Mr Knightley, the sexy sparring of man and woman meant for marriage does not happen again in Austen's novels.

PEMBERLEY AND THE NATION

When I think of a great property in Jane Austen, I think first of Pemberley. Yet I'm a little uneasy. Possibly it's because I'm so steeped in the work of Mary Wollstonecraft and her lifelong engagement with English politics.

Pride and Prejudice is not a political allegory and it makes no loud ideological point. We wouldn't love it so much if it did. But it *was* drafted in the 1790s, that revolutionary decade of clashing ideas: might it say something of the time in which it was first created?

In 'Catharine, or the Bower', young Jane Austen mocked popular didactic writers like Hannah More and Jane West, who blamed domestic vices for the corrupt political state of the country and urged social reform. Startled by observing a man passionately kissing her niece's hand, the aunt in 'Catharine' reacts in horror, turning the sexual scene into a national catastrophe:

> I plainly see that every thing is going to sixes and sevens and all order will soon be at an end throughout the Kingdom.

To which young Catharine moderately replies:

> upon my honour I have done nothing this evening that can contribute to overthrow the establishment of the kingdom.

The aunt reiterates her point:

> You are mistaken Child … the welfare of every Nation depends upon the virtue of it's individuals, and any one who offends in so gross a manner against decorum and propriety, is certainly hastening it's ruin.

It's funny, and we're on the niece's side as she tries to negotiate her way through her own sexual feelings within a context of severe disapproving aunt and encroaching young men. Nonetheless, the aunt's view, though humorously exaggerated, is not uncommon. Edmund Bertram in *Mansfield Park* will echo it when he connects private to national morals.

Before the French Revolution had turned bloody, the liberal Irish writer and politician Edmund Burke took a stand against the radical politics of Wollstonecraft, Godwin and others. His was a conservative vision of a stable England contrasted with a France he believed must become chaotic once its revolution progressed.

In *Reflections on the Revolution in France*, he thundered into the acrimonious English debate on state and society by giving a positive definition of the word 'prejudice'. This, he asserted, is something greater than private reason; it's a kind of communal belief that binds and secures a nation, makes it a community. For Burke the state and its history form an ancient edifice whose 'deficient parts' may be 'regenerated' but, if civilised society is to exist, this edifice must be preserved. Any great building saturated with its owner's virtues will echo the structure of England. At the apex is a land-owner, in place through hereditary succession – and ultimately, however deficient the incumbent may be, the Crown.

I find this structure implied in Pemberley. Darcy isn't quite an aristocrat, but with his Norman-sounding name and suitably high-born mother – daughter of an earl – he's the nearest to an aristocrat of any Austen hero. This identity lends itself to the alluringly archaic aspect of *Pride and Prejudice*, so different from *Persuasion* with its absurd and exhausted nobility.

Initially of course Darcy isn't perfect – I labour the point in Chapter 2. With his old-fashioned, self-sustaining arrogance in sex and society, he lacks a sense of enlightened civic duty to the wider nation. Burke grafts this onto the idea of hereditary power. 'I am ill qualified to recommend myself to strangers,' Darcy boasts. 'We neither of us perform to strangers.' But, in a hierarchical civic society that hopes to avoid the kind of revolution agitating France, no citizen is a 'stranger'. Darcy will learn.

Here I take Mary Wollstonecraft as spokesperson for what William Walter Elliot of *Persuasion* called the 'unfeudal tone of the present day'. She called Burke's image of the great estate an airy 'Chinese erection'. It was 'a folly', symbol of the 'property of the rich': 'when was the castle of the poor sacred?' she demanded. Across the Channel not long before *Pride and Prejudice* was drafted, great landowners like Darcy had been beheaded, their property confiscated. 'Remember that we are English,' says *Northanger Abbey*'s Henry Tilney to Catherine Morland, addled by Gothic fiction set on mainland Europe.

As Jane Austen began both *Northanger Abbey* and *Pride and Prejudice*, the French Revolutionary War was being fought in part to keep intact such English country estates as she describes. In seaside Brighton the militiamen kick their heels, but Darcy raises no militia and is himself neither soldier nor sailor. Austen's other heroes work for a living as clergymen, sailors or farmers. Darcy of Pemberley is simply the otherwise unoccupied master of land. It's for him that *others* fight and work. Perhaps it takes what Burke calls the 'moral imagination' to accept this idea. Even had she admired *Pride and Prejudice* – and it's hard to imagine anyone with her acute intelligence not seeing its cleverness – Mary Wollstonecraft surely would have recoiled from this aspect of the book.

CAMBRIDGE IN 1961

Over sixty years ago, when I was the age of Jane Austen as she began *Pride and Prejudice* and made a heroine the same age as herself, I became the first in my family to go to university – indeed to stay on in school past fourteen. I became a student at Cambridge University. There I encountered judgements of the sort I'd not met before. Criticism goes round and comes round, and now, after so many decades, I know how much we make our authors what we want: our eyes as culturally trained as any eighteenth-century Gilpin tourist's. One generation seems as antiquated to the next as it in turn will seem to its successor – round and round we go.

My time at Cambridge as a wonderfully naïve and unprepared student was dominated by two male critics. Both were antagonistic to the English heritage aesthetics of the country house which *Pride and Prejudice*, if not all Austen's novels, have inadvertently promoted. The first critic was F. R. Leavis.

In those austere post-war years of the 1950s and early '60s, Leavis proclaimed his dislike of the country-house dream to which England is addicted, its frivolity and immaturity; he saw it summarised by the mandarins of culture, Bloomsbury and its pretty arty houses, by snobbish Virginia Woolf and her dilettante 'high-brow' companions: Rupert Brooke and E. M. Forster among others, cavorting at Grantchester just down the road from serious Cambridge. Admiring Jane Austen, he found her greatest novel not *Pride and Prejudice* but *Mansfield Park*, with its failed gentry and flawed house.

As an undergraduate I felt Leavis ideologically coercive with his one-line putdowns of authors, his ridicule of those he disliked. If earlier on I'd had more formal cultural education, perhaps I'd have felt less antagonistic to what he preached and those who helped him do it. However, I wasn't reading English Literature to find a new religion, but to discover more of the joy I'd already had from it. I came in time to see Leavis as the arch Mandarin himself telling me from on high not to love what I loved and to see as he saw or be damned as trivial. Yet his method of sensitive close reading stuck with me – it's a good way to begin experiencing any work.

The second was Raymond Williams, whom I found more congenial. But he wasn't the dominant force in my female college – colleges were segregated then and 'girls' were a small minority in the university. His popularity made it difficult to get close to him: my friend and I tried to insert ourselves into one of his groups, but they were big and male and we slunk away again. I loved and still love his books although, in contrast to Leavis, he didn't often engage closely with a thrilling text. His work made Austen an historian of an acquisitive capitalist society: good income and good conduct were rarely connected, he mused. To support his claim, he cited *Emma*, *Persuasion* and *Mansfield Park*, but, like Leavis, he avoided *Pride and Prejudice*, leaving it to settle among the old fictions that let the upper rank rejuvenate itself by absorbing energy and virtue from below. Its country-house world appeared to him simplified.

He has a point. Pemberley's tenants and servants are mere attributes of the good landowner. Of Darcy, Elizabeth exclaims:

> As a brother, a landlord, a master, she considered how many people's happiness were in his guardianship!—How much of pleasure or pain it was in his power to bestow!

Power, mastery, pleasure and pain, Darcy of Pemberley is a heady mix. Mary Wollstonecraft would have choked. Nobody should wield such awful, hereditary power through this coalescing of birth, masculinity, arrant privilege and property. Raymond Williams certainly thought not.

The cultural worries of my youth are very different from those rocking the nation now, but neither dominates *Pride and Prejudice*. For – I hope the point is worth repeating – the book is *fantasy*, a nostalgia-tinged past sweetened by a deliciously clever romance of the brightest, most sparkling sort. Read against the grain, naughty Wickham might appear the Austen equivalent of the bastard Edmund in *King Lear* or Heathcliff in *Wuthering Heights*, the bitter, cunning outsider who destabilises order and beauty from within (with Mrs Bennet perhaps the truth-telling 'fool' in this counterfactual scenario). But those great works were tragedies, this is romantic comedy. Here Wickham is merely expelled, sent even further into the alien north of England.

I'm urging the conventionality of *Pride and Prejudice* and the closeness of Pemberley to Fielding's and Richardson's great houses. But there's a big difference: outside English literature courses we don't read *Tom Jones* or *Sir Charles Grandison* – rarely the latter even in the most traditional of colleges. What's distinctive in Austen's book?

The succinctness, the minimalism, the delicious irony and wit. Something else?

Of course: the *something* is Elizabeth Bennet, with her open glee of possession. Unlike Austen's other heroines, she has no anxiety over dispossession; despite what her mother thinks of the entail on Longbourn, her second daughter lacks any sense of the precarity that begins so many novels. She rejects her home cheerfully – indeed she did so when she refused Mr Collins. Likewise, while her sister Jane and Bingley take a house only thirty miles away, she's happy to live far from the rest of her family. With entry into Pemberley, she fulfils that famous comic and tipsy opening that declares a rich man 'the property' of some young woman:

> However little known the feelings or views of such a man may be
> on his first entering a neighbourhood, this truth is so well fixed
> in the minds of the surrounding families, that he is considered
> as the rightful property of some one or other of their daughters.

Real property as land, Elizabeth will not own, but she can and does bag the 'property' within her grasp: the man of property. To be mistress isn't to be master, but the next best thing, and, despite any shady gender politics, I'm with her as she gaily enters that classy house.

Similar journeys will be made by the steely governess in Charlotte Brontë's *Jane Eyre* and the unnamed companion in Daphne du Maurier's *Rebecca*: they end with the masters indeed, but only when their houses are in ruins. Pemberley is intact.

Is there *any* mockery of Pemberley, any of what the astute nineteenth-century novelist and critic Mrs Oliphant called the 'quiet jeering' that distinguishes Austen's work? Is there any subtle critique in its exclusions?

In her later novels, where Austen perfects her 'free indirect style' of letting us see simultaneously the mind of the central characters and the narrator's knowledge of her mind, some 'jeering' may be discerned. But I can't find it here. Pemberley seems to me to exist without irony.

In what may still be called 'canonical' literature, the pattern, the old archetype, stops here with Darcy and Elizabeth. *Pride and Prejudice* is the last 'classic' novel to bring social and individual so resoundingly together, making a narrative of fusion, male and female, upper and lower, North and South, stability and energy. It allows a hero to unite civil and semi-feudal society as best master and landlord in a denouement that provides complete happiness for the heroine – and her readers.

In life of course, man and house rarely connect so sweetly. The only known marriage proposal Jane Austen received was from Harris Bigg-Wither of Manydown Park. She accepted it, then the next day changed her mind. His house was a fine mansion desirable for any parson's ageing second daughter, Bigg-Wither apparently less so. Did Jane, even for just a day, choose a house over possible romance? She'd left Steventon and moved to Bath, where she was never quite at home. Surely at such a time the temptation must have been great. But she resisted.

She was writing 'The Watsons', in which, as far as one can tell, the heroine will refuse a lord and his castle – although there's a hint she'll end up in a parsonage. The fragment is bleak, far from the fairy tale tone of *Pride and Prejudice*. The woman of 1804 in her transplanted life knows more than the stationary girl of the 1790s. Then in 1811–12 the adult, securely settled with mother, sister and friend in an all-female household, will revise but not modify that gleeful youthful vision of 'First Impressions'. By then, she knows where to find such delight herself. In a letter of September in the year she published *Pride and Prejudice*, she describes herself sitting 'alone in the Library' of her brother's great house of Godmersham, 'Mistress of all I survey'. Reading books.

Yes, of course, *Pride and Prejudice* is as gratifying, comforting and indulgent as the fiction Mary Wollstonecraft lamented. Famously it proved an escape for Kipling's lower-class soldiers in the First World War in 'The Janeites' and to Winston Churchill in the Second, and, since then, in so many guises, to countless readers from Kettering to Karachi. It may indeed be escapist, glamorous pap to prevent girls and women seeing the restricted, degraded role of their sex in society and to keep the lower classes in their place with fantasy of entry into a privileged sphere. Perhaps its formula nurtures popular romance of Harlequin and Mills and Boon and allows nostalgia for a supposedly less complex era called 'the Regency'. But it's more – we all know it is, and I can't finish my first chapter by denying that I feel its seduction. Such a happy laughing book!

CODA

In the novels published after *Pride and Prejudice*, Jane Austen will give her heroines many comfortable homes, though none so grand as Pemberley. In the last, *Persuasion*, however, she lets her heroine be married with no home to go to at all.

Anne Elliot has refused the marriage that would have restored her to her family estate of Kellynch Hall and chosen instead a beloved, unpropertied man. In this novel, the distinction is clear at last between a home and a house: the sailors can make a home on a boat, or in a rental for a few months in Lyme Regis, but Anne's father, the landowner Sir Walter, can't make one anywhere, not in his ancestral Kellynch Hall nor in his gaudy rooms at Bath. Anne Elliot understands that people are more important than property, and that they are not at all the same thing.

CHAPTER 2

The Darkness of Darcy

PATRIARCHY AND ME

Perhaps it's because I came to *Pride and Prejudice* through the Karamazov brothers and Heathcliff that I saw darkness in Mr Darcy. Or perhaps I allowed him to be darkened by a context unfair to foist on the nation's favourite romance. However it happened, many years ago, I looked for a shadow and found it. Embedded in the light and sparkling novel I saw traces of an attraction to something – how can I put it? – deeply masculine, violent and powerful, which, if acted out rather than contemplated from an armchair, would be, at the least, disturbing.

Not long after I emigrated to America I encountered Kate Millett's *Sexual Politics*. I read the book with eyes and mouth wide open. I couldn't imagine anyone English, anyone I'd ever met, writing anything like this. I was looking into a mirror for the first time and seeing myself and my surroundings *together*. The Cambridge of Leavis and Williams seemed very far away.

For Millett, literature became a series of brutal misogynous texts – Henry Miller, Norman Mailer and D. H. Lawrence of course – but in gentler mode misogyny included novels by women colluding with patriarchy: Charlotte Brontë and Jane Austen. Once my astonishment at Millett subsided (just a little), I noticed how far her analyses strayed from the texts – hers was no Leavisite close reading – but no matter: you have to exaggerate to make a point, you have to simplify to make a revolution.

Millett led me to look from a female point of view at works once seen only through male critical eyes and taken as simply 'aesthetic' objects. Now I saw in them aggression of the physical and psychological sort. Years after Mary Wollstonecraft proclaimed the civil *rights* of her sex, her life experiences as a vulnerable woman taught her forcefully of the deeper sexual and psychological *wrongs* created by a patriarchal system. I investigated her shifting ideas in the biography I wrote of her; then again in my first novel *A Man of Genius*, partly based on Wollstonecraft's later life and on the powerful Romantic idea of the supreme (male) genius, so irritating to Kate Millett in its misogynous narcissism.

Cultural attitudes I remember from my young years in the 1940s and '50s support Millett's analyses. Rape, if not especially violent, was tolerated: a girl should cope with it and not tell. It was in any case because she'd 'led the man on' or, if she hadn't, it was because she was 'frigid'. Unwed mothers were a disgrace. Shotgun weddings tied a woman to a man perhaps disliked or hardly known. Masculine power was normal and girls did best in life who accepted, tamed and exploited it. Sweep the rest under the cultural fitted carpet.

Now much more in the open than in 1970, let alone 1950, with a series of movements and rebrandings from #MeToo to the notion of 'gaslighting', the subject will go on demanding to be analysed and combatted. But it was my memories of harsher times as well as early feminist reading that let me see the shadow of Mary Wollstonecraft's life falling on Jane Austen, not only in the portrayal of passionate Marianne in *Sense and Sensibility* but also the depiction of love in *Pride and Prejudice*.

I'm old now, and the posturing of those with (temporary) physical or political power seems more comic than disturbing (angry Kate Millett warned us against humour – but her warning was of *male* humour used against women). So as a woman in her eighties, I want now to bat away the Patriarch and quote Shakespeare at him:

'Truly, thou art damned like an ill-roasted egg, all on one side.'

Perhaps it's the nature of old age to find life funnier, more absurd – and brighter – than it once seemed; life's full of surprises, not all good! I might even take another look at Bunyan and see if his burden is as terrifying as it felt to a six-year old. (Now I think of it, I probably conflated the images of Pilgrim and Sinbad the Sailor, with the Old Man of the Sea on his back. Rather different tales, since Pilgrim loses his burden through severe virtue, Sinbad through getting the Old Man drunk.)

AUTHORS AND THEIR BOOKS

Margaret Atwood wrote of a book, 'You enter it, but then you must leave: like the Underworld, you can't live there.' The novelist must write 'the end', and only readers should go on if they dare. The Modernist novelist and playwright Samuel Beckett said he knew nothing of his characters beyond what he'd written. He never waited for Godot at the train or bus station, or sanctioned anyone else to do so.

This austere response is not Jane Austen's. James Edward Austen-Leigh wrote that his aunt:

> took a kind of parental interest in the beings she had created, and did not dismiss them from her thoughts when she had finished her last chapter … She would if asked tell us many particulars about the subsequent career of some of her people.

She said very little of Mr Darcy.

Like Sherlock Holmes, Darcy jumps right out of the book that gave him birth: in Sir Arthur Conan Doyle's words, he lives 'in some fantastic limbo of the children of the imagination, some strange

impossible place'. 'Strange' indeed: he turns up now as a character in spinoffs, mashups, theatre plays and amdrams everywhere,
especially throughout the English-speaking world. He goes to
the Wild West and Venice, becomes a vampire and werewolf. He
attends Regency balls and themed *Pride and Prejudice* weddings –
who or what do brides think they're marrying?

I confess, this almost febrile exploiting makes me uneasy. It's
part of our present habit of cutting up our literary forebears and
their works to serve as funny consumer items, as if the old high
culture were at the end of its tether, close to its demise, good only
for dressing up in clownish clothes or mocking with a winking
kind of knowingness.

Is that too starchy? Possibly. My discomfort makes me uncomfortable. What's my attitude but a yearning to hold onto those old
elite (male, white?) aesthetics that made some literary and artistic
works almost sacred? Well, that ship has sailed (as a character in
a recent film of *Persuasion* remarked with anachronistic aptness
about Captain Wentworth). Mashups, sendups and spinoffs are
the mode.

As perhaps they always were. Aristophanes makes fun of
Euripides and parodies Homer; Mrs Noah swings free of the Bible.
Didn't young Jane spend her childhood spoofing the sentimental
novels the grownups were reading? Indeed so, but the literature
she mocked was second rate. That was the point.

Enough polemics. I'll stay a while with Darcy in his book, then
look at the darkness he's (inadvertently) promoted in the following
centuries – and in the mind of my younger self.

Am I doing a kind of historical mashup?

MR DARCY IN *PRIDE AND PREJUDICE*

Jane Austen's Darcy enters her novel with every advantage of
person – tall and handsome – and of possessions – a round £10,000
a year and a large house. Boorishness ruins the impression made by
his assets. He's morose and fastidious. Mrs Bennet has his measure
(as he has hers): she accuses him of lacking a 'right disposition'
in company, of being one of 'those persons who fancy themselves

very important and never open their mouths'. He has no respect for 'the convenience of the world'.

In an earlier, more brutal age, such a man might express disdain in physical violence, a whip from a high horse; here in the civilised moment as the eighteenth turns into the nineteenth century, he has only words and looks. He is rude to everyone, even his close friend Bingley: did he choose him because he was shorter and less well-born, not just, as Elizabeth Bennet surmises, because he was pliable? Rank matters: Darcy is restrained before his aristocratic aunt, Lady Catherine de Bourgh. He resembles her: she's formidable in words, he in silence.

The Darcy of the early chapters is so bad he's almost comic. In 'Jack and Alice', a tale Jane wrote age fourteen, Charles Adams is 'of so dazzling a Beauty that none but Eagles could look him in the Face'. At a ball the fierce beams darting from his eyes ('infinitely Superior' to the sun's) force everyone to huddle in a corner to escape his inconvenient effect. Darcy believes his glance elevates any girl 'with the hope of influencing his felicity'.

Darcy and Charles Adams expect a lot from a woman – especially a future wife. Darcy thinks she should be elegant, graceful and accomplished in all arts and languages, having improved 'her mind by extensive reading'. Charles Adams is more succinct:

> I expect nothing more in my wife than my wife will find in me — Perfection.

In keeping with his lordly attitudes, Darcy's first movement towards Elizabeth is mastering. He stares at her, then eavesdrops: he has a right to look, to overhear and to perplex. No woman seeking marriage could act so. Women watch men in Austen novels, but not with such impudence. (Joe Wright's film continuously tracks Elizabeth's gaze, but Keira Knightley is acting in 2005.) There is, however, a fine example of a woman reducing a man to his body in *Persuasion*. Demoted from being mistress of a mansion to a hostess in Bath, Elizabeth Elliot looks at her sister's once despised suitor appreciatively: she understood 'the importance of a man of such an air and appearance as his. … Captain Wentworth would move about well in her drawing-room'.

Elizabeth Bennet responds to Darcy's condescension with 'easy playfulness'. The word 'archly' catches her tone: the equivalent Darcy adverbs are 'gravely' and 'coldly'. When she cheats him of 'premeditated contempt', he falls in love, then blames her for his predicament: he's been 'bewitched' – as Henry VIII believed himself to have been by clever Anne Boleyn. He grows even more silent and conflicted. He shares none of his feelings with Bingley, his friend. Only worldly-wise Charlotte, standing in the wings at Netherfield Park, notices what's going on. Perhaps in time she'll facilitate an affair that can benefit herself and her new husband. As Mr Bennet later acidly remarks to Mr Collins, the proprietor of Pemberley will have Church livings in his gift.

Then out of the blue comes that passionate statement of love that redeems Darcy for just about every reader. The words emblazon T-shirts, tea-towels and coffee-mugs.

> In vain have I struggled. It will not do. My feelings will not be repressed. You must allow me to tell you how ardently I admire and love you.

Yes, yes, but is it enough?

That concludes the first part of *Pride and Prejudice*. Then the book morphs into another tale: the taming of Darcy – and Elizabeth.

Darcy's passion is difficult to convey. On film it can be given physical expression. In the most famous adaptation, of 1995, Andrew Davies has Colin Firth jump into the Pemberley pond and emerge with that wet shirt clinging to his torso (the shirt, now dry, was recently sold for £20,000). This vivid cinematic act has skewed our attention, certainly mine.

In the novel, when the narrator slips into Darcy's head, she exits promptly. Only in an early work does Austen linger inside a male mind. In the novella 'Lady Susan', we see a man wrestling with himself and his disapproving family: he's fallen in love with a woman who is sexually more assertive and verbally more agile than he is. A little like Darcy with Elizabeth?

In this second part of the book, Austen must make Elizabeth – and her readers – unthink with dizzying speed their first impressions. Without the erotic physics of cinematic ponds, she uses the letter. Darcy takes a verbal dip into his inner life. He writes to explain himself to himself, as much as to the woman he presumes he's lost.

Delivered with 'haughty composure', the letter begins a change in hero and heroine. From now on emphasis is not on Elizabeth's effect on Darcy but on his effect on her. She becomes diminished in individual and personal consequence, but her *social* consequence is inflated. First impressions, the intuitive, the 'indescribable', the treacherously subjective – so often associated with the feminine – are overwhelmed.

On first reading Darcy's words, Elizabeth sees 'pride and insolence', a swaggering masculinity. On the second she's mortified but mortified by *herself*: 'her sense of shame was severe'. With one letter this 'squeamish youth', to use Mr Bennet's resonant phrase, makes her thoroughly ashamed of a family of lawyers and tradespeople she'd lived by and laughed at – and with – for nearly twenty-one years.

In another youthful production, 'The History of England', young Jane insists that no historical document is without bias. Darcy's letter is taken as truth, a correct account of once disputed events. Revision or re-vision becomes fact. Elizabeth moves swiftly from a first exclamation – 'This cannot be!' – to secure acceptance that it must be and is.

'Till this moment, I never knew myself,' she declares. Later heroines will be more doubtful, avoiding anything so final. Self-knowledge will be a work in progress.

The letter weakens Elizabeth's once egalitarian views. Earlier she noted that Wickham's guilt seemed equal to his humble descent, and, musing over Darcy's treatment of her sister Jane, explained it as a result of her 'having one uncle who was a country attorney, and another who was in business in London'. After the letter and a sight of Pemberley, Elizabeth declares she's a gentleman's daughter, not the niece of a tradesman, though the tradesman is more honourable than the gentleman.

With knowledge of his virtues comes a change of attitude towards Darcy and his discourtesy. Jane Austen shares with her sister authors, Frances Burney, Maria Edgeworth and Charlotte Smith, all like her born into the middling ranks, a dislike of a kind of aristocratic grandee wonderfully exposed in *Letters Written by Lord Chesterfield to his Son*, private letters published posthumously in 1774. In them manners were severed from morality and made into a tool for worldly success in the upper orders: Lord Chesterfield explained how to interpret and use social codes to one's advantage. For the public at large the *Letters* revealed how smooth manners could be a veneer for manipulation and entitled hedonism. Charming and easy, that is, but below the surface, cunning and controlling.

Austen's heroines, Elizabeth, Elinor, Anne and Emma (most of the time), have easy manners and use them to smooth society. It's different for men. They shouldn't be downright rude, like Darcy on first appearance in Meryton, but nor should they be *too* smooth. Look at the other Austen heroes: awkward Edward Ferrars of *Sense and Sensibility*, tongue-tied Edmund Bertram of *Mansfield Park*, blunt Mr Knightley of *Emma*, whose incivility is a recurring theme, though he was supposedly Jane Austen's favourite leading man.

Easy manners mark disreputable Wickham with his 'very pleasing address' and 'happy readiness of conversation'. They mark Austen's other shallow men. Before he arrives in her village of Highbury, Emma imagines Frank Churchill as 'universally agreeable', adapting himself to the desires of everyone. Mr Knightley dismisses such a man as a 'practised politician'. In fact, Frank uses his arts less as a politician than as a mischief-maker, hurting the woman he supposedly loves in secret and staining Emma's reputation. Finally, in *Persuasion* comes that wily gentleman of charming address, Mr William Walter Elliot, on first appearance 'a man of exceedingly good manners', 'so polished, so easy, so particularly agreeable'.

So it's no disgrace that Darcy never achieves much 'polish'; he's not in danger of becoming too courteous. He improves in response to Elizabeth and her worthy relatives, but when he arrives at the Bennet household as Elizabeth's future husband he fails to make small talk. Mr Bennet remarks of his soon-to-be son-in-law: 'He is the kind of man, indeed, to whom I should never dare refuse any thing, which he condescended to ask.' Comic of course – but 'dare' and 'condescend'?

Perhaps, as in *Emma*, the hero shows courtesy in acts not words: Mr Knightley saves rejected young Harriet from the scorn of the vicar by asking her to dance; rich Mr Darcy saves the Bennets from disgrace by paying off Wickham. Mr Darcy shows the greater generosity, but Mr Knightley's kindness is more heart-warming.

MR DARCY ESCAPES THE BOOK

Begun in the 1790s, *Pride and Prejudice* was published in 1813. Its context is both Gothic and Romantic.

Accepted 'queen' of Gothic fiction, in the 1790s Ann Radcliffe authored novels so sensational that they turned the heads of more sensible and mature people than *Northanger Abbey*'s young Catherine Morland. The Radcliffean heroine of learning and delicacy resembles the accomplished female imagined by Darcy, but, instead of attracting a husband in country-house drawing rooms, she's deposited in mouldering monasteries and dilapidated palazzi around hot Catholic Europe. In such un-English lands, marauding, raping, thieving men repeatedly threaten her, but she never loses her powerful virginity or her composure. When menaces are at their most extreme, she faints and becomes surprisingly inviolate.

The embodiment of threatening evil is the Gothic villain: moody, mastering and – although Mrs Radcliffe is at pains to prevent him being so – fascinating to the watching heroine and to the reading girl. Montoni, the villain of *The Mysteries of Udolpho*, is so magnetic that his victim gazes at him but is at a loss to know why she does so. Readers are disappointed when he's shunted off in a sentence. Other authors will give him more latitude.

Lord Byron admired Mrs Radcliffe. He confessed he saw Italy through her eyes when he first visited it – as she'd never done. Lacking Radcliffe's diffidence, young Byron took her Montoni and other alluringly wicked villains and made them his own on paper and in life. He created the image of a new man, the dark Romantic hero, the Byronic hero (Byron quickly became an adjective), something similar to the Radcliffe villain but more intentionally sexy and more English in his classy arrogance. Jane Austen met the character in one of Byron's phenomenally popular 'Turkish tales'. She marked the occasion with the memorable line: 'I have read the Corsair, mended my petticoat, & have nothing else to do.'

She might mock, but 10,000 copies of this swagger poem were sold on the morning of publication.

Was she intentionally mocking? The tying of 'The Corsair' to a petticoat is inconclusive: her letters all jump about and she may not have meant to belittle the haughty hero. Later she copied out Byron's poem 'Napoleon's Farewell', fascinated perhaps by the author and his imperious subject.

Byron admired Radcliffe and Burney, but apparently missed out on Austen – although the London publisher John Murray whom Lord Byron and Jane Austen shared sent Byron and his half-sister Augusta Leigh a copy of *Emma*: 'Tell me if M[rs] Leigh & your Lordship admire *Emma*?' he asked. Byron probably didn't read the novel. It arrived at an especially trying time for him when he was indeed being 'mad, bad and dangerous to know' – at least for his newly married wife. Such behaviour as he exhibited was time-consuming. But after Austen's death Byron certainly knew of her, for he appreciated as 'full of fun and ferocity' a skit written by Walter Scott's son-in-law, in which as his moody *alter ego* Childe Harold he's accosted by female characters from *Emma* and *Mansfield Park* chattering about his marital problems:

> Perhaps her Ladyship was in the wrong after all—I am sure if
> I had married such a man, I would have borne with all his little
> eccentricities ... Poor Lord Byron!

However mocked, the posturing Byronic hero stalked Britain and
the Continent, buttressed by colourful tales of his creator, the
dashing Lord who combined intellectual power with depravity.
From him derives a whole line of stern, powerful, self-obsessed
and wickedly alluring men, in whom I see something of the early
Darcy – in potential.

With a little temporal leeway, mightn't we find the potent
fantasy-figure emerging from the interaction of Jane Austen's
imagination with her cultural moment? If so, it might not be too
huge a leap to think of Darcy as well as Byron and Byron's heroes
as some of the ancestors of Emily Brontë's Heathcliff in *Wuthering
Heights* and Charlotte Brontë's Mr Rochester in *Jane Eyre?*

Are you with me?

Let me take another jump to du Maurier's Maxim de Winter
(and, less plausibly, to Bram Stoker's Dracula). These 'men' share
with Darcy the 'implacability' of resentments and his 'unforgiving
temper'. There are differences: the arrogance of Austen's hero isn't as
thoroughly assaulted and humbled as that of most of his successors –
many ending up dead or mutilated. Also they have women who love
their tyranny, and each, from Mr Rochester to Maxim de Winter, is
encouraged in his sadism by experience with a first angry, masochistic
or 'mad' wife. (I saw this when I read Millett's enraged prose – and
that most disconcerting of spinoffs, Jean Rhys's *Wide Sargasso Sea*,
which introduced us to the misery Mr Rochester hides in his attic.)

Few of Austen's first readers noticed Darcy. They enthused over
her heroine and the minor comic characters. An exception was
Annabella Milbanke. She found the interest of the novel 'very strong,
especially for Mr. Darcy'. Like poor Isabella Linton, who, irre-
sistibly attracted to the would-be abuser, becomes Mrs Heathcliff
in *Wuthering Heights*, Annabella paid for such 'interest' when she

married rather than fantasised about such a man. She lived out the rest of her life as the estranged Lady Byron.

The line of avatars has insinuated itself into cinematic history. Laurence Olivier, who played Darcy in the 1940 adaptation, was also Du Maurier's Maxim de Winter in the same year; in the previous one, he played Heathcliff. In the 1952 BBC adaptation Darcy was Peter Cushing, best known for his roles in Hammer Horror vampire films. In the book Mr Darcy startles Elizabeth by emerging from the stables just as she's leaving his house, but the encounter with wet Colin Firth draws also from Heathcliff's emergence from the shadows and of Jane Eyre's first sight of Rochester, galloping into sight on his horse, his great white and black dog running with him. Firth's Darcy is Austen out of the Brontës.

I was too old to enjoy 'Darcymania' in 1995. I didn't view Laurence Olivier's Darcy at the right time either. Besides, for me the old ham was always Richard III, a portrayal I venerated from the moment I saw it aged seventeen. Josephine Tey's *Daughter of Time* had already made Shakespeare's hunchback villain a misunderstood 'outsider'; Olivier added those magnetic eyes to the macabre mix. Had I read *Pride and Prejudice* then, it would have been tame fare beside this Grand Guignol.

The fantasy I'm struggling to describe is largely female. Darcy prompts desire in women. The American critic Lionel Trilling noted 'man's panic fear at a fictional world in which the masculine principle, although represented as admirable and necessary, is prescribed and controlled by a female mind'. Dated in expression – but some truth there. Austen's novel has spawned a thousand romances read primarily by, answering the desires of and controlled by women. Two waves of modern feminism with their different emphases on gender fluidity and equality have made no dent in this established industry of desire. Think of E. L. James's Christian Grey.

There is, though, an antidote: humour. In the 2008 mini-series *Lost in Austen*, Darcy was teased through time-travelling. Translated to twenty-first-century London, he became bewildered. How long could Darcy stay in a modern city before being diminished into modern man, the knitted-jumper-wearing protagonist of *Bridget Jones's Diary* (also played by Colin Firth of course)?

Her death in 2022 interrupted Hilary Mantel's proposed spinoff of *Pride and Prejudice*. She had surmised that, behind all that moody silence, Darcy was simply not very bright, whatever the narrator claims of his cleverness. The silence of Fitzwilliam Darcy was not, she believed, a sign of superior sense and deep thought but rather a symptom of his mental torpor:

> A solemn countenance, a grave manner, a pre-occupied frown; these suggest to us a mastering of life's perplexities born of a habit of deep reflection, and vigorous examination of every fact and circumstance. Yet, but what if the frown means nothing but ill humour? If the grave and pre-occupied air means nothing but insufficiency in the face of whatever circumstances present? What if the long silences, so intimidating to my sex, are merely the consequence of having nothing to say? What if that prevailing solemnity results from a simple failure to see the joke? Reader, to think it is to know it: Darcy was a more harmless soul than we had imagined, and replete with good intentions; his silence in company proceeded, not from a conviction of natural superiority, but from a solid, sterling stupidity, such as an English gentleman alone dares display.

Isn't this delicious? With this man, poor Elizabeth in the gilded Pemberley cage will have a lifetime of giving witty answers to 'witless questions'. She might have had an easier time in the Hunsford parsonage with Mr Collins.

A DARKER VIEW WITH MARY WOLLSTONECRAFT

In *Mansfield Park*, Jane Austen turned her pen away from 'guilt and misery' while knowing of both. Is it perverse to find darkness in her most 'sparkling' work? Hilary Mantel was a baby boomer, a decade younger than me. She cuts Darcy down to utilitarian size. I fear I've been trying to inflate him.

While thinking off and on about Jane Austen, I was writing my biographies of the troubling figures of Mary Wollstonecraft and her sad daughter Fanny, whose unrequited love for the poet Shelley I speculated about in *Death and the Maidens*. I found in both mother and daughter a kind of obsessive self-destruction borne of childhood (and cultural) experience too strong to be overcome by rational political arguments. Each suffered a mental breakdown under the wounding of hearts that had given away too much care.

In rationalist mode in her *A Vindication of the Rights of Woman* Mary Wollstonecraft believed that patriarchal culture infantilised women. They should break free from victimisation and strive for self-reliance. In society as then constituted, passionate erotic love was a snare: women would be safer as human beings, especially as mothers, by combatting it.

But Enlightenment rationalism was faltering. Ideology was no match for historical injury in nations or individuals. The French Revolution that Wollstonecraft left England to witness had clung on to past resentments and, from ideals of Equality, Liberty and Fraternity, was creating Terror and Empire; soon Britain and France were at war.

Despite remarkable exertion and much resilience, the suffering and neediness she'd experienced as child and young adult haunted Mary Wollstonecraft. She fell 'irrationally' in love in the way she'd warned women against in *The Rights of Woman*. She couldn't apply to herself and her experience her book's harsh prescription: that sexual desire, when obsessive, must be rationally combated or it would destroy.

Let me explain a little more of my portrayal of Wollstonecraft and so suggest my sense that her life might cast a flickering light on one of the world's most famous romantic heroes. Strange perhaps, since Wollstonecraft's lover Gilbert Imlay had nothing of the grandeur of Darcy-Heathcliff-Rochester. But my business here is not with the man but with the woman.

She was thirty-four when she met Imlay – call him adventurer, speculator, war-profiteer or just *l'homme moyen sensual*. In his very ordinariness he was unworthy of this commanding intellectual, and quite unprepared for the abjectness that lay below the liberated surface.

Biology took its course. Wollstonecraft bore a daughter, Fanny (who, as a sensitive exploited carer among egoists, wasn't unlike Austen's fictional Fanny Price). Imlay took time to abandon mother and child in cold chaotic France, lonely Scandinavia and disapproving England. Wollstonecraft responded with begging letters, one suicide attempt, then another. (Her daughter Fanny succeeded where her mother failed: she killed herself at twenty-two.)

Even in *The Rights of Woman*, Wollstonecraft had exempted the 'grand' romantic passion from her rationalist advice, this will o' the wisp of literature. Hers with Imlay became such a one. With him, she accepted the romantic belief that a sexual encounter had special, almost transcendental meaning. Holding to utopian hope, she'd trusted that sexuality, so potentially degrading to women in the old scheme of things, could somehow be imaginatively transformed.

Unhappily, the real-life relationship resolved itself into a tussle of domination and subordination, which she, the woman, could only lose in this man's world. Lurching from abjectness to futile attempts at self-assertion, she never asked the question Godwin asked in his *Memoirs*: 'Why did she thus obstinately cling to an ill-starred unhappy passion?' His answer was: 'Because it is of the essence of affection, to seek to perpetuate itself.'

Now, erotic obsession has been medicalised as OCD. A lot of literature would disappear if it had been diagnosed earlier, and if it could be treated and cured.

Beyond temperament there were other constraints. What every woman knew, but a few tried to doubt in the heady revolutionary days of equality and liberty, what Jane Austen tells us directly more than once: the sex act was one thing for a man, another for a woman. Maria Rushworth in *Mansfield Park* is condemned to exile, whereas her lover walks abroad unscathed. Had Wickham not been bought off, he'd have sailed on to seduce again, while, without Darcy's bribe, sixteen-year-old Lydia would have blighted her own life and her family's forever. Wollstonecraft noted that woman's reputation was confined to 'a single virtue—chastity'.

'Fallen', she needed Imlay more than he needed her. A woman may get a man with what Lady Catherine calls 'arts and allurements' but, after sex, he'll always hold the whip in his upper hand.

Look at that famous opening phrase of *Pride and Prejudice*, ignoring for a moment the humour:

> It is a truth universally acknowledged, that a single man in possession of a good fortune, must be in want of a wife.

To me, it's poking fun not just at pompous male pronouncements but also at the language of Enlightenment, truth and universal rights – including that of *The Rights of Woman*.

It's intended as funny, of course, but that need of a woman to marry which underlies the claim – that sense that marriage is worth any misalliance or selling of girls, that men of power and money attract erotically as well as financially – just might give a bittersweet tinge to the happy ending of *Pride and Prejudice*.

When first Elizabeth encounters Darcy's arrogance, she refuses to leave it alone. She makes it into a funny story to amuse her family and friends. Later she listens attentively when she first hears of Pemberley. Is it possible that the masculine package of privilege is already exerting a pull? As it does for the reader; no one familiar with romance could doubt from the first that Darcy and Elizabeth were meant to be together, after suitable disturbance.

All the characters in the book are interested in Darcy. Everyone talks about and desires him, from his aristocratic aunt and her sickly daughter to the ordinary folk of Meryton who want him to notice them and speak. When he refuses to fulfil their desires, they still talk about him: they can't help themselves. In the old feminist terms of the 1970s, is Darcy not Patriarchy itself, with all its glittering, merciless, unequal glamour?

Am I making too much of this? Or is there something here that Austen herself understood – and would touch on again in *Persuasion*? Did she feel a little of what I'm describing, and so seek to undermine it?

Look at Darcy's long-winded explanation, that rhetorical *conformatio* that follows his proposal. The thrilling declaration of love is in direct speech, but what follows is in the free indirect manner that always allows some tinge of narrative irony, some absurdity to escape from and around the words.

> He spoke well, but there were feelings besides those of the heart to be detailed, and he was not more eloquent on the subject of tenderness than of pride. His sense of her inferiority—of its being a degradation—of the family obstacles which judgment had always opposed to inclination, were dwelt on with a warmth which seemed due to the consequence he was wounding, but was very unlikely to recommend his suit.

Surely for a supposedly 'clever' man to give such a scathing description of the inferiority of his beloved's family during a proposal is beyond belief.

Jane Austen executes a similar manoeuvre with sophisticated Mary Crawford in *Mansfield Park*. Socially discerning, Mary knows how to deliver well-judged, appropriate compliments. However, towards the end of the book she writes a letter fantasising about Tom Bertram's death – to humourless, virtuous Fanny Price! Had Mary become too attractive to fit the plot?

I've mentioned Jane Austen's naughty habit of letting her fictional characters live beyond the books. When once visiting London she sought likenesses of her creations at the Society of Painters Exhibition in the Spring Gardens. She was pleased 'particularly … with a small portrait of Mrs Bingley, excessively like her'. She'd hoped to find Elizabeth but 'there was no Mrs Darcy'. She proceeded to Somerset House and the exhibition of Sir Joshua Reynolds's paintings. Once again she looked but 'there was nothing like Mrs D. at either'. She added: 'I can only imagine that Mr D. prizes any Picture of her too much to like it should be exposed to the public eye.—I can imagine he w^d have that sort [of] feeling—that mixture of Love, Pride & Delicacy.'

I can imagine too.

AFTER DARCY

Jane Austen would never again unite such power and glamour in a hero. Her next two leading men would be unassuming, diffident Edmund Bertram and worthy, taciturn George Knightley. Darcy was left to her Gothic sisters and their descendants. But there *are* characters other than protagonists. After revising *Pride and Prejudice* Austen wrote *Mansfield Park* and created Sir Thomas Bertram.

Sir Thomas is another patriarch in a big house frightening the vitality out of his dependants. Could he be Mr Darcy grown older, if he'd been foolish enough to marry Caroline Bingley instead of Elizabeth Bennet?

In Sir Thomas Bertram, the slightly unsavoury potential of the Darcy character is clearer through his association with African slavery. It also emerges in the strange possessive gaze he turns on the female body. Darcy had looked at Elizabeth in an overbearing way; Sir Thomas follows the habit with his niece Fanny Price.

Returning from the slave island of Antigua, he stares at the young girl in his house in such a way that, when she hears of it, she cringes. When she was a humble child, he failed to notice her, but now he imposes his intrusive physical admiration on her pretty girlish body.

'[Y]our uncle never did admire you till now—and now he does,' declares her obtuse cousin. He notices her 'complexion', her 'figure'. Edmund thinks her silence in company with her uncle simply shyness; perhaps, considering what she feels here about this powerful man, she finds even social questioning a kind of unwelcome flirtation.

Sir Thomas gives his blessing and patriarchal power to his surrogate Henry Crawford, who also invades Fanny's vulnerable body. His pursuit in the drawing room at Mansfield Park is called 'a grievous imprisonment of body and mind' and, when finally Henry has to move, it feels like an emancipation: 'She was at liberty, she was busy, she was protected.' It's comedy at Fanny's expense, adding to the overall impression that everyone in this spacious modern house feels hemmed in. But, for all the irony of the scene, I think we may feel uneasy with Fanny.

As we do in the ball for her coming out. Until she revealed her attractions to Sir Thomas and was sought by a man of means, nobody could tell whether she was 'in' or 'out'; she was simply growing up like the Bennet sisters, without parade. She hadn't been 'brought up to the trade of *coming out*'.

Mary Wollstonecraft deplored the custom:

> what can be more indelicate than a girl's *coming out* in the fashionable world? Which, in other words, is to bring to market a marriageable miss, whose person is taken from one public place to another, richly caparisoned.

Now, commodified and constrained, Fanny fears the approaching ball that supposedly will change her from child to nubile woman. Characteristically, she's watched by the man who arranged it:

> Sir Thomas himself was watching her progress down the dance with much complacency; he was proud of his niece ...

He's given her good manners, he muses, though he stops short of taking credit here for her body – her new 'beauty'.

In this instance Sir Thomas is observed by a shrewder eye than his son Edmund's: Mary Crawford's. Mary is courting Edmund by making herself agreeable to everyone in the house – a latter-day Lady Susan in her ability to charm (until she fails with Fanny). She sees Sir Thomas's 'complacency' about his niece and uses it to compliment him. Earlier, on learning of Sir Thomas's return, she imagined him like one of the 'old heathen heroes, who, after performing great exploits in a foreign land, offered sacrifices to the gods on their safe return'. The most obvious sacrifice will be his daughter Maria, from whose inadequate marriage he hopes to increase his consequence in the district, but, since Mary also knows the standing of Fanny in the household, perhaps she might proleptically see Fanny as the sacrificial lamb?

Maybe, too, she understands something more about this uncle-niece relationship, for she and Fanny – though Fanny would never allow it – have much in common. Both live in an uncle's house like orphans: Mary with a 'vicious' Admiral and Fanny with a more ambiguously threatening landowner.

The near masochism forced on Fanny through most of *Mansfield Park* is set against the unpalatable self-absorption and glitter of pride in the rest of the inmates of the great house, but, even when rebranded as humility, it has its problematic side. In *Emma* Jane Fairfax, when she begins to doubt that the marriage she's been promised will ever take place, dreads the dependence of working in a family; Fanny has been acting as companion to Lady Bertram for many years, correcting her needlework and reading to her, and she runs errands for any demanding adult. She will in the end be a wife, not governess or companion, but as the book-burning patriarch Sir Thomas shuts the gates of the Mansfield estate and parsonage he congratulates himself on 'a great acquisition in the promise of Fanny for a daughter'. Living in the rectory she will have lifelong external 'protection' while continuing to serve the house. She will be always within its 'view and patronage'.

'Acquisition': that's clear enough. Fanny will be 'protected' but will she ever find herself 'at liberty'? Mr Darcy is not Sir Thomas and the tie of husband and wife is more equal than that of uncle and niece. Yet in both cases and in the other works I've cited, the man of power and property has a dominance that is hard to ignore. Elizabeth will benefit Pemberley, for Darcy has given his estate the mistress it has long lacked – and Elizabeth will enjoy the status. But the fact that as readers we delight in what both Darcy and Elizabeth have gained through the great property is the smudge of darkness I find at the heart of this lightest and brightest of novels.

CHAPTER 3

Talking and Not Talking

'Whom are you going to dance with?' asked Mr Knightley.

She hesitated a moment, and then replied, 'With you, if you will ask me.'

Perfect.

~⟁~

He proposes.

What did she say?—Just what she ought, of course. A lady always does.—

GETTING IT WRONG

When I open an Austen novel, I feel pleased and expectant. But I realise that for *Emma* I'm now beginning another chapter with 'uneasiness'. It must be a sort of tic that happily passes as I go on writing. Still, for the moment there it is. I revere *Emma* but something disturbs me about the heroine and her novel.

Anyone who fears she might be an interloper, the not-quite-proper arrival in a new place will understand my point. Mrs

Elton dropped abruptly into Highbury: loud Mrs Elton, not quite 'a lady'.

As a child I changed schools incessantly before landing at that Bastille of a boarding school. As an adult, I moved jobs and continents at a similar wild rate. So I suffered not once but repeatedly the transplanting Mrs Elton declared 'one of the evils of matrimony'. I know what it is to be out of place, to get it wrong in language, gesture, opinion and intellectual notions. To overcome the awkward, inevitable deep-down shyness in school, academia or new town, what is there to do but try to assert yourself and jiggle the old regime to make it let you in. No chance of course, you'll overegg the pudding. But it makes you feel – occasionally – a whole lot better, like a perky mouse fidgeting among complacent cats.

I'll preface fictional Augusta Elton with real-life hapless James Stanier Clarke, a man who, with the best intentions, also got it famously wrong. Despite his voluminous writings on religion and the navy, he lives for posterity only as the butt of Jane Austen, his position the more compromised by association with his employer, the Prince Regent.

Jane Austen particularly disliked the Prince, whose treatment of his wife Caroline shocked and entertained the nation. She wrote of the Princess, 'Poor woman, I shall support her as long as I can, because she is a Woman, & because I hate her Husband.'

None the less, the Prince Regent had his uses. At the suggestion of Clarke, Austen dedicated *Emma* to him with all the flattering fol-de-rol required. She was irritated when she realised that, in addition to the flattery, she must provide a special, expensively bound copy with crimson leather and gold tooling for the royal library. It's doubtful whether, after all that, the dedication helped sell many books. Publicity is always a matter of chance.

Given Jane Austen's private opinion of the Regent, it was especially ironic that Clarke should express his admiration for her by making a further proposal. Over the years this has caused even more hilarity among Austen fans than the fulsome princely dedication.

With the approaching marriage of the Regent's daughter and heir Charlotte to the German Prince Leopold in mind, Clarke suggested that, instead of more *Emmas*, Austen write an 'Historical

Romance illustrative of the History of the august house of Cobourg'. She replied that she'd die laughing if she tried (and persisted in trying) any such thing. She was mocking the genre of historical romance – but surely also Clarke and the royals. Rather an impertinent response in the circumstances.

In fiction it's the turn of Mrs Elton to err egregiously and in the process entertain Jane Austen readers. 'Mrs E.' from Bristol with her middle-class background and ways desires to make a splash or just to be accepted in the tight-knit society of Highbury. She enters a strange place and wants to be thought well of, to avoid the gentry condescension she's astute enough to know will come her way. What weapons has she but a sister who married up and her own immense energy – 'vivacity' she calls it – for organising? Poor Mrs Elton. It is and will continue to be a rough ride – even when, or perhaps especially when, the rich Sucklings finally 'explore' to Highbury in their barouche-landau.

Take the strawberry-picking party at Donwell Abbey. Mrs Elton wants to organise the event like a modern entertainment, a community visit to a theme park. She's nothing if not modern, a visitor not only from Bristol but also from the future.

> It is to be a morning scheme, you know, Knightley; quite a simple thing. I shall wear a large bonnet, and bring one of my little baskets hanging on my arm. Here,—probably this basket with pink ribbon. Nothing can be more simple, you see. And Jane will have such another. There is to be no form or parade—a sort of gipsy party.—We are to walk about your gardens, and gather the strawberries ourselves, and sit under trees;—and whatever else you may like to provide, it is to be all out of doors—a table spread in the shade, you know. Every thing as natural and simple as possible.

Then she exclaims:

> I wish we had a donkey. The thing would be for us all to come on donkeys, Jane, Miss Bates, and me—and my caro sposo walking by.

What a delightful mishmash of errors to offend a traditional country squire! To be over-familiar with the owner of Donwell Abbey is, as far as Emma is concerned, a scandalous failure of tact. (Her own formality derives from childhood memory of an older man, one who's been in undeclared love with her since she was thirteen – best not look through contemporary eyes here.) The informality extends beyond and below Mr Knightley; Emma is jolted when Mrs Elton uses Jane Fairfax's Christian name without her title 'Miss'. She protests: 'Heavens! Let me not suppose that she dares go about Emma Woodhouse-ing me!'

Then there are the plans Mrs Elton makes for the day – so very 'French'. The English believe strawberries a quintessential *English* fruit, the 'wholesome berries' described in Shakespeare's *Henry V*. Yet, describing types, Mrs Elton gives the fruit a Continental aura: 'hautboy infinitely superior—no comparison'.

A prominent beauty at the court of Napoleon, Madame Tallien, was famed for bathing in the juice of fresh strawberries. She used 22 pounds per basin; presumably she didn't bathe daily. Her luxurious doings were much reported and tutted over in primmer England. As for the play-acting, there's no avoiding an echo of the guillotined French queen. In her ascendant days, Marie Antoinette enjoyed a *fête champêtre* or picnic garden party at her retreat of the Petit Trianon while pretending to be a shepherdess tending perfumed sheep.

The British royal family also indulged in role-playing. Queen Charlotte and George III, before madness irrevocably descended, went about with decorated pitchforks and floppy hats on their farm near Windsor, so eagerly that King George earned the nickname 'Farmer George'. The soubriquet wasn't affectionate. Then there were the recent birthday celebrations for the Prince Regent in Bexhill. In August 1811 the *Sussex Weekly Advertiser* recorded a 'gipsey party' with big hats, baskets, donkeys and 'an elegant cold PICNIC collation … on the grass'. Strawberries would have been served, for the Prince adored them. A royal model for Mrs Elton's proposed alfresco 'gipsy party' at Donwell Abbey?

Especially comic is the detail of the donkeys. They were not as lovable then as they are to us. The Austen ladies kept two in

Chawton to use with their trap. During her last winter, Jane noted how little she and her mother had recently employed them: the animals had had such a long 'run of luxurious idleness' that they'd probably forgotten much of their 'Education'. Mrs Elton's imagined donkeys are not like these working beasts, but part of pastoral kitsch. She's led up to them through her variety of props: hats, baskets and pink ribbons.

(One day perhaps someone of means will donate a donkey and trap to the Chawton cottage museum for Jane Austen re-enactments. It would be an attraction, though, like Willoughby's proposed horse for Marianne Dashwood, possibly too expensive a gift to accept. There used to be gorgeous Shire horses at Chawton House until their upkeep proved too costly.)

Mr Knightley had invited people to Donwell to eat his strawberries in a conventional manner. Mrs Elton is trying to contrive a middle-class appropriation, turning the rigid Abbey entertainment into a modern country fête with outdoor eating and fun. Mr Knightley's response to her vision is withering:

> My idea of the simple and the natural will be to have the table spread in the dining-room. The nature and the simplicity of gentlemen and ladies, with their servants and furniture, I think is best observed by meals within doors.

In opposition to the owner of Donwell, Mrs Elton wishes to fashion the estate into something other than it is, what perhaps it would become if no more heiresses married into it and a Knightley descendant acted as fecklessly as Sir Walter Elliot in *Persuasion*: that is, a tourist centre.

For the tourist, the world must be remade as a caricature of itself so that it can be easily understood and assimilated. Just after the time when Jane Austen was writing *Emma*, there were sight-seeing trips to the battlefield of Waterloo, begun even before the bodies of the dead had decomposed. Visitors showed extraordinary *sang froid* as they contemplated hands and legs sticking out of the mud, hunted for souvenirs and purchased (possibly fake) pickled fingers and other memorabilia from commercially minded locals. They were much criticised (but undeterred) by the more refined, including the patrician Duke of Wellington, who saw them reducing this great defining battle to a public spectacle.

Vulgar though tourism might seem, Mrs Elton and the battlefield scavengers represented the future in a way Emma, Mr Knightley and the Iron Duke did not. In less than thirty years' time, Thomas Cook would begin his tours to beauty spots and national monuments in Britain and on the Continent, allowing the middle and lower classes to see what their betters on the Grand Tour had long been seeing and buying – and, like the mercenary Belgians in 1815, giving locals the opportunity to exploit the trade by creating what the visitors had come to see. When after the Second World War death duties began to pinch (temporarily) and some British aristocrats made their houses into tourist attractions, they were immeasurably helped by Jane Austen, who by then had become the unacknowledged patroness of the stately home and National Trust.

Mrs Elton desires to give Highbury a makeover. Having travelled first from commercial Bristol to the resort of Bath and then to rural Surrey, she longs to be a projector as much as Tom Parker, the entrepreneur in 'Sanditon', though, being a woman, she lacks his opportunities. She knows that a place has to be constructed for public enjoyment and that people need to be persuaded into new roles to fit it. Mr Parker entices visitors to his resort through typical nineteenth-century advertising.

Mrs Elton contrasts with Elizabeth Bennet in *Pride and Prejudice*, who, fearing that she and her trading Cheapside relatives will be taken for what they are, middle-class tourists at the stately home of Pemberley, is profoundly relieved when the landowner rescues them and turns them into guests. But for both Mr Parker and Mrs Elton, the world has begun its unstoppable shrinkage into a series of described and packaged spaces presented through the growing number of guidebooks telling 'you' where to go and what to see. Mr Knightley insists on the strawberry party being an old-fashioned visit to his country property, not a tripper's day out. His putdown of the new manner of being, seeing and speaking has momentary power, but the Mrs Eltons will triumph in the end.

Yet, even if we give Mrs Elton her due, in the time and place of the book we're left with the fact that the play-acting in the strawberry beds, if it came off, would *not* have been decorous. What Mrs Elton suggests invokes the uneasy make-believe of the tripper who's not at home in the real world of the country house and who can't know enough about what she's seeing no matter where she goes. It's an anxiety that continues, felt by those who travel and yearn to belong, to be more than tourists.

THE RIGHT WORDS

In the twentieth century when only the upper orders had training in conversation, the late Queen's lady-in-waiting Lady Glenconner remembers being taught when and what to say and when not to speak. In *Sense and Sensibility*, Lady Middleton mentions the weather, which remark spares Elinor further teasing embarrassment about a lover with the initial 'F':

> Most grateful did Elinor feel to Lady Middleton for observing at this moment, 'that it rained very hard,' though she believed the interruption to proceed less from any attention to her, than from her ladyship's great dislike of all such inelegant subjects of raillery as delighted her husband and mother. The idea however started by her, was immediately pursued by Colonel Brandon, who was on every occasion mindful of the feelings of others; and much was said on the subject of rain by both of them.

In her childhood writings, young Jane shows how the civility and clichés of polite society are designed to mask adult cruelty, which flares out when formalities are dropped. In 'Frederick and Elfrida', the heroine addresses the 'amiable Rebecca' in genteel language before gliding into honest comment on her squint, greasy hair and hunchback. In 'Jack and Alice', Lady Williams swerves from courteous language to remark on Alice's red-faced drunkenness.

Moderation in everything. Lady Middleton is trivial; you can be *too* conventional, too superficial. Pre-packaged phrases, learnt from life or novels, are a necessary part of social existence, but need skill and some integrity to use. Conventional speech about the weather or any other subject learnt from conduct books may become absurd, as it does with foolish Mr Collins of *Pride and Prejudice* when dealing with a young woman who rejects convention. So, in his marriage proposal he insults Elizabeth's intelligence.

As does Mr Darcy, making the opposite error. Instead of properly engaging with the rules and language of courtship, he ignores them entirely by abusing the family into which he proposes to marry. He claims to feel the 'apprehension and anxiety' expected of a suitor, but without conviction. (Knowing the 'established mode' Elizabeth is aware *she* should express 'a sense of obligation' but simply can't.) Both men, Mr Collins and Mr Darcy, are wrong-footed in their proposals by Elizabeth's uncharacteristic silence. This reduces her usual conversational advantage at the moment when it would be most useful. Later she proceeds in un-conduct-book fashion to reject both suitors with minimal ceremony.

On the second occasion, Darcy has learnt the form. He declares, as a proposing man should, that he 'thought only of' Elizabeth. Mr Elton in *Emma* will use the same words but in his inebriated state they affect his haughty listener very differently.

Young Jane loved hyperbolic, silly and sentimental language; she scattered verbal absurdities all over her childhood tales. Men are 'Horrid and Shocking'; youths are 'beauteous and amiable'; minds are 'exalted'. In *Northanger Abbey* Henry Tilney mocks young Catherine for the trite language of 'amazing' and 'horrid' picked up from reading Gothic novels lent by her new 'intimate friend' Isabella Thorpe. Her common-sensical mother at home in the parsonage speaks very differently. The pedantry Henry shows in trying to stop the language from changing – through popular usage, 'nice' was expanding from the single meaning of 'neat' – is gently teased by the narrator. But he has a point in suggesting that sloppy use of words inhibits serious thought.

I often feel like Henry Tilney. I wince when people say 'stood' for 'standing' and 'sat' for 'seated', 'disinterested' for 'uninterested' and 'lay' for 'lie', and forget the earlier meanings of 'awful' and 'wicked'. *My* problem of course. But in *Sense and Sensibility* we're expected to catch Lucy Steele's lapses in grammar, exhibited to us as so many pinned specimens of her illiteracy.

In the anxious 1950s I was on the other side: the divide was class not education, although Evelyn Waugh once remarked, 'There are subjects too intimate for print. Surely class is one?'

In 1955 Nancy Mitford playfully separated the English lower middle from the upper middle class by the words they used. Like 'lavatory' or 'toilet', 'napkins' or 'serviettes', 'pudding' or 'sweet', 'drawing room' or 'lounge', 'sofa' or 'settee'. Settled in England, my parents and I acquired a settee for our lounge: we sat on it with serviettes eating a sweet. If Nancy Mitford or anyone of her rank had visited and cringed, we'd have felt like the poor sisters in 'The Watsons' about to eat their 'quietly-sociable little meal' when Lord Osborne and snobbish Tom Musgrave pay their inconsiderate call.

Hilarious really, these small differences: so narcissistic to notice for those on the right side.

'Women believe it betrays a want of feeling to be moderate in expression': they're 'often transported beyond what the occasion will justify,' thought Hannah More, a prolific religious and moral writer of poems, novels, plays and pamphlets; she had a huge influence over the middle and lower classes during the French wars. While Austen recoiled from More's strident didacticism, she agreed with many of her moral and social opinions. Marianne's rhapsody on dead leaves in *Sense and Sensibility* might fit More's stricture, for she mocks the use of 'rapturous epithets' especially loved by ladies who talk in superlative mode. Hannah More also deplores 'violent intimacy' in friendship that declares its shallowness in gushing emotive phrases. The depiction of false Isabella Thorpe in *Northanger Abbey* supports her point. In *Emma*, the narrator praises the verbal and physical restraint of the Knightley brothers who, on meeting, neither embrace nor exchange endearments. Emma appreciates 'tenderness of heart', but she and the author wish it to be subordinate to 'clearness of head'.

Austen and Hannah More might be addressing our own time. In a fairly recent habit we now routinely use hyperbolic vocabulary. 'Absolutely', we say; 'totally', 'amazing', 'fabulous', 'passionate', 'fantastic', 'ecstatic', 'gorgeous' and 'brilliant', we declare about the most ordinary things and events. In many circles, too, we've fallen into the operatic 'luvvie' vocabulary of 'dearests', 'darlings' and 'precious ones'. To accompany the words, we've started embracing each other even on first meeting, of air-kissing from side to side in the way once mocked as Continental. The poet Lord Tennyson had a dream that Prince Albert kissed him; when he woke, he remarked, 'Very kind, and very German.'

The habit of such physical contact was interrupted during the Covid lockdown years, and there was much lamenting at its loss. The nation was deprived of 'hugs'.

THE WAYWARD PLEASURE OF WIT

Wit depends on language not gesture, on cleverness not sentiment. While being admirable when it demonstrates quickness of mind, it can also be mere showing off, sometimes for cruel purposes. Samuel Johnson deplored the latter use and, as so often, Austen is with him here.

Her oeuvre is a kind of fugue. After creating one type of heroine, she investigates not quite an opposite but an alternative; then back she swerves to repeat subtly what's been done in the novel-but-one before, to reprise that quietly thoughtful or that witty, sprightly young person.

Elizabeth and Emma share wit or a quickness with language, a 'velocity of thought' to use *Emma*'s phrase. Although they're of similar age, twenty, the creator of the first was also twenty, the creator of the second a mature woman in her late thirties. For Elizabeth Bennet, Jane Austen didn't worry about outside judgement. She told Cassandra:

LIVING WITH JANE AUSTEN

> I must confess that *I* think her as delightful a creature as ever appeared in print, & how I shall be able to tolerate those who do not like *her* at least, I do not know.

Compare this with a reported statement about her later heroine Emma:

> I am going to take a heroine whom no one but myself will much like.

Between these two, the first so beloved of readers, the second not so much, lies naughty Mary Crawford of *Mansfield Park*, just as quick or witty as either but without their luck and moral frame: that background of louche uncle and metropolitan ways has ruined her. In a book devoted to meek Fanny Price, Mary is transfixed by the narrator's crushing judgement: that her cleverness emanates from a mind 'darkened, yet fancying itself light'. Mary takes 'light' as the opposite of 'heavy'; Fanny and the narrator contrast it with 'dark'.

All her life Jane Austen relished silly novels. She laughed over them with her niece Anna, who brought back volumes from the circulating library for them both to enjoy and ridicule. She even wrote out a spoof recipe for the kind of woman other novelists were creating:

> Heroine, a faultless Character herself.—perfectly good, with much tenderness and sentiment, & not the least Wit.

Exactly. The virtuous lack wit. The witty have temptations to err which are closed to the dullard.

'Wit' or cleverness in women was a repeated topic in conduct books, as well as in contemporary moralistic novels of the sort Austen delighted to mock. In *A Serious Proposal to the Ladies* (1694, 1697) Mary Astell declared that to be called witty is only complimentary for a woman when associated with feminine graces. Otherwise, she's 'impertinent', a word Elizabeth Bennet uses for herself, and Caroline Bingley employs to denigrate her.

'Impertinent' has been largely dropped from the modern lexicon of discipline. It was much used in my school days when anyone 'answered back'. For nubile girls of the past, it was best not to reveal too much quickness or knowledge and to let boys shine without competition. (I found this injunction complicated when I got to Cambridge in the early 1960s and discovered that girly reticence didn't impress. Looking contemptuously at us as my friends and I from our single-sex college sat together writing away, one lecturer declared that girls took notes and regurgitated while boys sat proud and tall, assimilated, rejected, thought and spoke cleverly. Girls peaked at eighteen, boys went on and on. Those 'brilliant minds', you know.)

In the eighteenth century the 'Bluestocking' provoked horror, much as the 'hairy-legged feminist' would do in the twentieth, the one descending from the other. Elizabeth Montagu, 'Queen of the Blues', was an influential woman of letters who held a salon for conversing and thinking people of both sexes. Nonetheless, she made a point much anticipated and echoed:

> Wit in women is apt to have bad consequences; like a sword without a scabbard, it wounds the wearer and provokes assailants.

In his *A Father's Legacy to his Daughters*, Dr John Gregory advised his girls, if they wished to be happy, to conform to society. If they had wit, they should be cautious in displaying it and, if they had learning, they should conceal it. Such advice disgusted Mary Wollstonecraft, who responded that Gregory's idea of female upbringing was a system of 'dissimulation': why shouldn't women improve themselves until they 'rose above the fumes of vanity; and then let the public opinion come round', she cried. 'This desire of being always women, is the very consciousness that degrades the sex.'

Most advice-givers followed Gregory rather than Wollstonecraft. In *Essays on Various Subjects, Principally Designed for Young Ladies*, Hannah More wrote that the clever young girl should suppress the lively, caustic remark, especially if true. Wit should be kept under wraps. In her *Rural Walks: in Dialogues. Intended for the Use of Young Persons,* Charlotte Smith urged her readers always to watch their language. Whatever they think of the company, they should, like Hannah More's model lady, check 'that flippancy of remark, so frequently disgusting in girls of twelve or thirteen' – even worse in grown women aiming to appear 'fashionable'.

Most female novelists agreed with the advice-givers and ensured that the witty or verbally quick heroine came off badly: she was almost invariably deprived of the hero or damned by the plot. Even Frances Burney, so witty in herself, made quickness with words dangerous in her heroines. An extreme example of a novel turned admonitory, and damning a woman at first allowed an attractive wit, is *A Simple Story* by Elizabeth Inchbald, translator of the German play *Lovers' Vows* that causes such mayhem in *Mansfield Park.*

Composed over many years, the novel begins by displaying a high-spirited and sexually passionate young woman, rather like bold, independent Elizabeth Inchbald herself, admirer and friend of Mary Wollstonecraft, though later disapproving of her irregular life. The novel brings the heroine to a sad end, her verbal flightiness leading inexorably to moral and physical flightiness. Her tongue-tied, even abject daughter points at the moral of the book through her virtuous, miserable but ultimately rewarded life. The novel screams Inchbald's ambivalence, the pull she feels towards independence and radical beliefs and the equal tug of social respectability and acceptance.

Knowing how they must write to sell, other clever female authors like Burney and Edgeworth couldn't bear not to create characters a little resembling themselves, and they gave unusual verbal freedom to peripheral women, usually older than the heroines and unmarried or widowed. These speak a great deal more than the story demands – and don't triumph. Burney's last novel *The Wanderer* gives the anti-heroine page after page of unanswered feminist rhetoric in Wollstonecraft style, then leaves her lonely and rejected. In Austen, the peripheral (if we exclude Mary Crawford) are *not* witty – Mrs Elton declares herself to have 'vivacity' not 'wit' – but her heroines, though taken down, are allowed much latitude on their journey to maturity and marriage.

Elizabeth Bennet and Emma Woodhouse must both have been readers of 'novel trash' rather than more serious literature: Elizabeth goes out of her way to declare she is not a great reader and she joins her father in mocking the serious student of the family, the less favoured sister. Mary Bennet has been sympathetically treated in a spinoff novel by Janice Hadlow, but she receives precious little sympathy from Jane Austen. She's despised because she takes time to formulate her thoughts and can't speak with the speed demanded by this sparkling work. She's also a little stupid.

Mr Knightley notes Emma's lists of worthy books that remain unread, while the plan of serious study with Harriet fails almost before it begins. It's hard to imagine Emma settling down with *Some Account of the Public Life and a Selection from the Unpublished Writings of the Earl of Macartney* in two large volumes, as Fanny Price does in her cold upper room in Mansfield Park. Both Emma and Elizabeth Bennet are presented less as students of literature and more as storytellers who have learnt some of their skill from Gothic and sensational fiction, as well as from popular plays.

Emma makes characters of the people around her, then imposes her imagining onto them: aristocratic birth for Harriet Smith, the usual revelation for the unknown orphan in romantic fiction; and a naughty liaison for handsome, secretive Jane Fairfax, common in contemporary light drama. She sees neither for what she is: a vulnerable young woman for whom, in this society, suitable matrimony offers the best chance of happiness. Neither has Emma's handsome fortune nor, though the book hardly endorses it, her opportunity of singleness. The indelicacy of Emma's patronising interference with Harriet is underlined by its closeness to what Mrs Elton is doing with equally vulnerable but brighter Jane Fairfax.

Although imagining more for others than for herself, Emma faintly echoes the infatuated girls created by Charlotte Lennox in *The Female Quixote* and Eaton Stannard Barrett in *The Heroine*.

Enthralled by romantic reading, these misconstrue the real world and exaggerate their own significance until brought to reason and social submissiveness by wiser men. Jane Austen admired both books and created Catherine Morland of *Northanger Abbey* in the mode. The tradition might just include Emma Woodhouse.

Elizabeth Bennet differs from Emma in being more of a danger to herself than to others with her dramatising. She fashions a tale from the incident at the Meryton assembly where she was publicly snubbed by Darcy. Her hurt feelings are soothed by telling it 'with great spirit', for she delighted in 'any thing ridiculous'. This habit allows her to judge simplistically. She ridicules her awkward cousin Mr Collins and can't understand her friend Charlotte regarding him as other than the butt of her jokes and anecdotes. Privy to Charlotte's assessment of Mr Collins's advantages, we readers understand that it wouldn't have been altogether absurd to keep the heir of Longbourn attached to the family, as Mrs Bennet wished – serious Mary, we are told, would have had him, but her willingness is lost in the general hilarity of Elizabeth and her father.

Like Emma, Elizabeth flattens mixed characters, so that either Wickham is good and Darcy bad or the reverse. She makes quick sketches of people and then is trapped by them. Rarely does she check how a fact might be corroborated later. She believes and endorses Wickham's story of Darcy's ill-use when she notes Wickham's interest in her, then, as trustingly, knowing Darcy to be in love and Wickham to have moved on, she believes Darcy's letter of explanation. From evidence in the novel, we see that Wickham is indeed a gold-digger, but his enjoyment of the company of two Bennet girls suggests this isn't his exclusive character. A bad egg, but a little more unknowable than Elizabeth allows. As for the past, that boyhood rivalry with Darcy for his father's notice – it's interesting.

Elizabeth savours her abilities. She was created by a youthful author who'd just finished writing her indecorous juvenilia. Despite the psychological realism of the portrait, cheery Elizabeth is some-times close to the pert and sprightly heroines of these teenage years, to Laura of 'Love and Freindship' or Eliza in 'Henry and Eliza', as Darcy is to radiant Charles Adams in 'Jack and Alice'. Elizabeth enjoys and prepares her sallies. She tells Charlotte she *intends* to be cheeky with Darcy and she relishes getting the better of him. Usually, it's the young man who discomfits or quizzes the lady, but Elizabeth has learnt the technique from her father, who, surrounded by silly wife and younger daughters, has made her his companion in poking fun at a family he should have sought to guide rather than mock. Her teasing is self-conscious, seductive and clever.

The point needs a leisurely quotation and I choose the passage where Elizabeth addresses Darcy through the third person of his cousin Colonel Fitzwilliam. 'You mean to frighten me, Mr. Darcy, by coming in all this state to hear me? … My courage always rises with every attempt to intimidate me,' she begins. Then she tells the often-rehearsed tale of their first meeting, revised for a fresh auditor:

'You shall hear then—but prepare for something very dreadful. The first time of my ever seeing him in Hertfordshire, you must know, was at a ball—and at this ball, what do you think he did? He danced only four dances! I am sorry to pain you—but so it was. He danced only four dances, though gentlemen were scarce; and, to my certain knowledge, more than one young lady was sitting down in want of a partner. Mr. Darcy, you cannot deny the fact.'

'I had not at that time the honour of knowing any lady in the assembly beyond my own party.'

'True; and nobody can ever be introduced in a ball-room. …'

'Perhaps,' said Darcy, 'I should have judged better, had I sought an introduction, but I am ill qualified to recommend myself to strangers.'

'Shall we ask your cousin the reason of this?' said Elizabeth, still addressing Colonel Fitzwilliam. 'Shall we ask him why a man of sense and education, and who has lived in the world, is ill-qualified to recommend himself to strangers?'

'I can answer your question,' said Fitzwilliam, 'without applying to him. It is because he will not give himself the trouble.'

'I certainly have not the talent which some people possess,' said Darcy, 'of conversing easily with those I have never seen before. I cannot catch their tone of conversation, or appear interested in their concerns, as I often see done.'

'My fingers,' said Elizabeth, 'do not move over this instrument in the masterly manner which I see so many women's do. They have not the same force or rapidity, and do not produce the same expression. But then I have always supposed it to be my own fault—because I would not take the trouble of practising. It is not that I do not believe *my* fingers as capable as any other woman's of superior execution.'

No wonder Mr Darcy proposes, and no wonder Elizabeth (at first) refuses him.

THE DOWNFALL OF WIT

Elizabeth for the most part exercises her talent for mockery within the family, unlike Emma, who enjoys ridiculing the sillier women whose situations shadow hers: Mrs Elton and Miss Bates. That is, of course, until she misconstrues both subject and audience and is taken to task for her self-indulgent jest on Box Hill. She never behaves so unkindly to her selfish father and so preserves what Mrs Smith in *Persuasion* calls 'the smooth surface of family-union'.

The Box Hill outing is meant for pleasure, but the town community suffers 'a languor, a want of spirits, a want of union, which could not be got over'. Frank Churchill intervenes to liven things up, making languor into distraction. He singles out Emma for praise, thus vexing Mrs Elton as the watchful outsider. What follows is a painful scene, with some similarities in minor key to the flirtatious one quoted above of Elizabeth, Darcy and his cousin. It uses a triangular structure of Frank talking as Emma – before she interrupts his drama with her own self-conscious play-acting tone, not so distinct from Elizabeth's but horribly misjudged.

'[Emma] only demands from each of you either one thing very clever, be it prose or verse, original or repeated—or two things moderately clever—or three things very dull indeed, and she engages to laugh heartily at them all.'

'Oh! very well,' exclaimed Miss Bates, 'then I need not be uneasy. "Three things very dull indeed." That will just do for me, you know. I shall be sure to say three dull things as soon as ever I open my mouth, shan't I?—(looking round with the most good-humoured dependence on every body's assent)—Do not you all think I shall?'

Emma could not resist.

'Ah! ma'am, but there may be a difficulty. Pardon me—but you will be limited as to number—only three at once.'

Miss Bates, deceived by the mock ceremony of her manner, did not immediately catch her meaning; but, when it burst on her, it could not anger, though a slight blush showed that it could pain her.

'Ah!—well—to be sure. Yes, I see what she means, (turning to Mr. Knightley,) and I will try to hold my tongue. I must make myself very disagreeable, or she would not have said such a thing to an old friend.'

Emma should have expected Miss Bates to be discomfited, but her eyes have been on coquettish Frank Churchill. She's wrong to speak. Anne Elliot of *Persuasion* has cutting thoughts – they're unavoidable – but, like the exemplary conduct-book girls, she doesn't express them. Thinking to please Wentworth by showing the strong will and determination he declares he admires, her rival Louisa Musgrove insists against his advice in jumping off the Cobb and giving herself concussion. Perhaps now Wentworth might question his prejudice against a persuadable temper, Anne muses. She says nothing aloud.

Anne Elliot, Elinor Dashwood and Fanny Price are aware of the constant compromise necessary between self and society which, at the outset of their novels, Elizabeth and Emma have yet to learn. They do learn, of course: from men. After reading Darcy's letter, Elizabeth completely accepts the truth about her indecorous family. Only now does she extend their flaw to herself, for she too has been loose-tongued and loose-eared. Emma fully understands her error at Box Hill only when chided by Mr Knightley.

Self-esteem for girls is now much prized, no one is accused of being 'forward' or a 'show-off' as in the tutting 1950s. No young person (so I understand) is pushed to answer the unanswerable question so prevalent in my childhood: 'Who do you think you are?' Nonetheless, is pertness encouraged? Is there still a gender divide in wit and quick repartee?

I can't answer for the present or future but I recall two witty women I wrote about years back, Aphra Behn and Mary Carleton. Both were in a way brought down by repartee, the one immediately, the other in reputation.

In the 1660s, Mary Carleton faked being a German princess and got away with the deception for a long, lucrative time. For her final trial she dressed elaborately as for a show in an Indian striped gown, silk petticoat, and white shoes laced with green and with hair fashionably frizzled. Thus coquettishly prepared, she took the stand and couldn't resist answering pertly back.

She was hanged at Tyburn in 1673.

I felt some fellow feeling, having also been in a court (for divorce rather than counterfeiting and not arrayed in such stylish attire) and given a flippant answer to a malevolent judge. The consequences were serious but not life-threatening. I was dismayed but not hanged.

Aphra Behn was impressed by the show Mary Carleton put on and used it for the ending of her clever tale 'The History of the Nun', where the protagonist also ends on the scaffold fashionably dressed.

One of the most brilliant writers in English, Aphra Behn strode the Restoration stage of the 1670s with more performed plays to her credit than any other playwright, man or woman. There had been no professional women dramatists before her and she assumed that the sexes wrote with the same conventions and language. It was a strange time in English history, when a libertine court dominated the stage and allowed sexy, amoral comedies to amuse an audience by displaying witty men and women triumphing over the foolish and lumpenly virtuous.

As ever, there was backbiting between rival authors and personal slurs were common. Aphra Behn's success provoked envy in many and it became useful to attack her as 'a woman' writing loosely – and wittily. Stung, she wrote an angry defence:

> All I ask, is the Priviledge for my Masculine Part the Poet in me, (if any such you will allow me) to tread in those successful Paths my Predecessors have so long thriv'd in, to take those Measures that both the Ancient and Modern Writers have set me, and by which they have pleas'd the World so well. If I must not, because of my Sex, have this Freedom, but that you will usurp all to your selves; I lay down my Quill, and you shall hear no more of me, no not so much as to make Comparisons, because I will be kinder to my Brothers of the Pen, than they have been to a defenceless Woman; for I am not content to write for a Third day only. I value Fame as much as if I had been born a Hero; and if you rob me of that, I can retire from the ungrateful World, and scorn its fickle Favours.

Not really being a 'defenceless Woman', she didn't lay down her pen or go away. She continued writing witty risqué plays as well as extraordinarily powerful prose works. She had the 'Fame' she wanted in her time, but her time was passing. The court wasn't the whole society, and soon a reactionary, more puritanical and sentimental culture came to dominate the country, a culture that regarded the courtly ethos of wit and excess as irreligious and corrupt.

As her cultural moment receded, Behn's reputation sank. Gender difference was reasserted and it would prevent women writing with the same freedom as men for many centuries to come. From now on, women authors were constrained to wield a 'purer' pen and treat more modest subjects than men. As the eighteenth century progressed, Aphra Behn became a terrible exemplar of female wit, repeatedly reviled as 'Amazonian' – an epithet thrown at Mary Wollstonecraft a century later. Then she was silenced or, if remembered, remembered only to be condemned. Walter Scott deplored her 'manners' and 'language'. It's unlikely that Jane Austen knew of her brilliant transgressive work. But these two surpassing authors are associated in my mind.

Neither Jane Austen nor Aphra Behn had children but both, as professionals, thought of their work as their imaginary offspring: Austen called *Pride and Prejudice* her 'darling Child', while Behn dispatched her first published work with the epigraph 'Va mon enfant! prend ta fortune.' Both made a point of acknowledging their lack of formal training, of being ignorant of masculine learning, and hinted they were the better for it. Both knew their worth and what they were about: 'I studied only to make this as entertaining as I could,' Behn declared in an Epistle to her play *The Dutch Lover*, suggesting that learned men often failed in this first rule of play-writing. Austen made her most forceful claim in *Northanger Abbey*, provocatively displaying her excitement about her creative power and, like Aphra Behn, asserting the value of her female pen:

> Oh! it is only a novel! … only some work in which the greatest powers of the mind are displayed, in which the most thorough knowledge of human nature, the happiest delineation of its varieties, the liveliest effusions of wit and humour are conveyed to the world in the best chosen language.

Woman's work is (here) entertaining, skilful, and useful, especially when set beside the culturally approved 'serious' writings of learned men, apt to be sadly derivative and dull.

MODERATION AND MARRIAGE

In her fiction Jane Austen portrays clever women reformed and to an extent silenced by men's rebukes. One reason for this is surely that, in a narrative context – as in drama – wit or verbal cleverness tends to be *too* attractive. For proof, we have Lady Susan, protagonist of Austen's youthful unpublished novella.

Aware that eloquence is the greatest asset a woman can have, Lady Susan intends to exploit it to control men's desire. Under cover of feminine performance, she pursues the traditionally masculine aim of seducing to enjoy sexual and, even more, psychological mastery: 'There is exquisite pleasure in subduing an insolent spirit,' she remarks. Before she comes to understand him and herself better, this might foreshadow Elizabeth's attitude to Darcy.

Elizabeth and Emma Woodhouse justify rather than judge themselves for their linguistic quickness. Elizabeth knows she's witty at other people's expense but declares, rather unconvincingly, that she doesn't laugh at what's good. Perhaps not, but we see her laughing at others before understanding them. She outwits Caroline Bingley while having no sympathy for this young girl and her awkward hankering after Darcy, and she mocks Miss de Bourgh, comparing her arrival at the rectory to the escape of pigs as a source of excitement. She feels no compassion for the ailing daughter of a dominating mother. At home, she sneers at her studious sister Mary.

As aware of rank as snobbish Emma, Elizabeth takes an opposite tack: where Emma disparages those beneath her – the Martins, Coleses and Eltons – Elizabeth mocks the ranks above her, initially siding with Wickham against Darcy and taking pleasure in besting Lady Catherine.

Much has been written about the 'social butterfly', youthful Jane Austen, flirting with Tom Lefroy, who was whisked away once he showed interest in this almost portionless girl. In her letter to her sister, Jane makes a comic tale of the farewell:

> At length the Day is come on which I am to flirt my last with Tom Lefroy, & when you receive this it will be over—My tears flow as I write, at the melancholy idea.

Without a break follows news that 'Wm. Chute' had called and been very 'civil'. What could it mean, she wonders.

Indeed, what could it, when William Chute, of no particular interest, comes hard on the heels of Tom Lefroy, about whom biographers, critics and fanfic authors have made a mountain?

Austen's Elizabeth and Emma (like their creator) enjoy flirting with charming young men. But, in the time span of the book, they begin to have marriage on their minds. Elizabeth is open to it – or she'd not have needed the warnings of Aunt Gardiner against dallying with unreliable Wickham or gone to the Netherfield Ball intending to subdue his heart. When Colonel Fitzwilliam makes it clear at Rosings he has no intentions towards her, she declares she doesn't mean to be unhappy about him – so she *had* imagined him as suitor.

The jauntiness of young Jane Austen and her two heroines over vanishing young men could be papering over real romances, true heartbreak of the sort Marianne Dashwood endures. What did Elizabeth Bennet really feel when she heard that Wickham was paying court to Miss King? What she says to her aunt seems of a piece with her usual gay wit, but may there be some bitterness? Emma too. She and Mrs Weston have both fantasised about her union with Frank Churchill. Emma duly flirts with him when he appears, making a public show of it, as in the embarrassing scene on Box Hill. She must do some self-searching to discover how much she's affected by this long-awaited visitor. Was there erotic involvement or, as she later suggests, mere identification of two self-dramatising characters in this small Highbury pond?

Initially Elizabeth and Emma felt no urgency in finding a husband, mainly because each holds a peculiar place in her family. Mr Bennet gives 'the preference' among his daughters to quick Elizabeth, and Emma knows she'll never be more important to anyone than to her father, or more mistress of a household. Yet both young women know their independence of manner is superficial. Compared with men, all women are dependent, whether clever or stupid. Colonel Fitzwilliam prates of being dependent, but Elizabeth interrupts him: 'the younger son of an Earl' won't know much about feeling inferior. Emma tells Mr Knightley that he can have little understanding 'of the difficulties of dependence', adding, 'You do not know what it is to have tempers to manage.'

Fanny Price and Anne Elliot become adult sexual and social beings requiring no moral reforming; Elizabeth and Emma, the sprightly heroines, need correction. Through *temporary* self-reproach, they give up intuition and self-dependence in favour of an external morality, channelled to them through a would-be male lover.

From a twentieth-century feminist perspective, this is not the happiest conclusion; hence in part the difficulty early feminist literary critics had with Jane Austen, unless they resorted to reading 'against the grain'. In the Austen resolution there's a lack of interest in empowerment which, after years when women's empowerment, emancipation and entitlement have been constant demands, can now seem rather refreshing. If feminism of the 1790s and of the twentieth century wanted women to find themselves and escape patriarchy – and so marriage and sometimes motherhood – Austen is giving us a wry, liberated alternative.

In the final pages of her novel, neither Elizabeth nor Emma is deprived of verbal spark, although the spark is restrained and, as I've already urged in the case of Mr Darcy, there's no sign their husbands will rise to their imaginative flair. In general, I find a sweetly traditional vision here, joined to a sceptical, wistful sense of wit and cleverness (when not too demanding) as part of the intelligent female self. Whatever happens in other women's fiction of the time, it is, as Emma declares, too late in the day for the Austen heroine to become naïve and simple, even if that way a gently unassuming virtue might be delivered. In *Persuasion*, Anne Elliot contemplates the pretty, merry young Musgroves and feels no envy:

> saved as we all are by some comfortable feeling of superiority from wishing for the possibility of exchange, she would not have given up her own more elegant and cultivated mind for all their enjoyments.

CHAPTER 4

Making Patterns

~·≈≍·~ ·~≈≍·~

AN ACADEMIC MEMORY

When I arrived in Florida in the late 1960s, I shifted from the close reading and judging that Cambridge had tried to instil in me and that, despite being largely impervious at the time, I had carried on when I took my first teaching job in Ghana in the early 1960s. In the US, while excited to encounter the wonderful writing of Flannery O'Connor, Carson McCullers and James Baldwin, I met clever scholars reading in the old-fashioned way, bringing into their study whatever knowledge they'd acquired of works, writers and their times. And, outside the classroom, I read Kate Millett.

I settled into what I liked best, the biographical, critical and literary combined, hearing people talking about authors as once living beings, letting the idiosyncrasies of their existence speak if they wished – without the moral and political patina of Leavis or Williams – and as time went by, without being completely over-whelmed by the angry interpreting of Kate Millett. But then, after a few more intellectual and geographical detours, I made another move, to New Jersey. Into the thick of it.

Women's Studies was getting under way. It continued to be acceptable to work on major women writers like Austen and the Brontës and increasingly Virginia Woolf, though now often with a 'feminist' slant, but still rather frowned on to be delving among the archives for the unknown: Mary Wollstonecraft was inching up into the hinterland of the canon, but wasn't yet quite within. Then, in the 1970s 'French Theory' exploded like a bomb over US Departments of English.

The celebrated French theoretician Julie Kristeva visited New York, strikingly stylish in appearance and excitingly impenetrable in 'discourse' – such a contrast to direct, angry, troubled Kate Millett. As well as with her beautiful clothes – I was in the scruffy feminist phase of no-nonsense dark jumpers, jeans, sturdy sandals and Afro hairdo – I was fascinated by her 'post-structuralist' critique of 'essentialized structures'. Now I learnt that to be 'essentialist' was as bad as being a note-taking dullard in Cambridge had been. (Before I'd quite seen the difference, I remember – with shame – giving Kristeva a copy of my journal devoted to early women writers, so totally misunderstanding the gulf between us. She kept it for a couple of nights then returned it with impeccable politeness, wearing different but equally beautiful clothes. Oh dear.)

'*Écriture feminine*' declared 'Woman' should write herself, her feminine body and the unconscious. It sounded a little like what happened in the eighteenth century, with its heavy re-gendering of body and mind after the strangely 'non-binary' period of Aphra Behn. Mary Wollstonecraft complained that women were pushed to act and write the irrational and intuitive, the 'feminine'. Now again, 'difference' was stressed. We mustn't inhabit the male 'symbolic': we were all recreating Patriarchy every time we opened our mouths. (A few years later, when she'd given birth, Kristeva stressed the significance of wombs and infant babbling; not immediately relevant to my life, but the emphasis on motherhood was handy. There was not a lot about children in early American feminism beyond advice to give little girls trucks instead of dolls.)

For a time I stopped beavering away at my 'minor' women and set about writing a book that would – and along with the 'gaze' this word had become modish – 'gesture' towards Theory, even if it failed to enter its world. I wrote *Women's Friendship in Literature*, a clever ruse, I thought, combining a feminist interest in the eighteenth century with something I hoped might be close to 'structuralism', if not its more fashionable 'post' variety. I wouldn't aspire to be a theoretician, but perhaps I could avoid being 'essentialist'.

I found patterning, interrelations and underlying themes – and with another 'gesture' to French Theory – in both English and *French* texts (the latter drawing lightly on my year as an au-pair in France where I'd picked up vocabulary suitable for the two-year-old I was supposedly minding). *Women's Friendship* was the nearest I came to embracing an academic 'ism' outside 'feminism', which never quite cut the mustard in elite English Departments, hence being speedily hived off into its own domain of 'Gender' or 'Women's' Studies.

The new way of looking took me back (almost) to the old Cambridge close reading of works other people decided were 'canonical'. To be on the safe side most were by men, but approached unconvention-ally through a critique of the patriarchal 'gaze': novels of Samuel Richardson, Jean-Jacques Rousseau, Denis Diderot, the Marquis de Sade and John Cleland, a heady mix declaring that, if I couldn't rise to the post-structuralist, I could at least be 'transgressive'.

Here in this book, for the first time, I brought in Jane Austen, while slipping in Mary Wollstonecraft and Madame de Staël among the also-rans. My subject was – and here I felt quite dar-ing – female relationships. They included the intimate friendships Jane Austen found so comic in her childhood tales, then mocked again in *Northanger Abbey*, and – more shocking – lesbian ties in Diderot, Rousseau and Cleland. I roundly asserted that my topic had been until this moment 'hidden by our critical biases and wilful blindness'. (It was, after all, rather more Millett than Kristeva!)

And yet – I find this amusing now – I couldn't quite achieve this new flipflop away from biography and history. Having finished and had the book accepted by a good university press, I added a 'Biographical Context'. To fit with the rest of the book and touch again on the fashionable transgressive, I made patterns in lives as well as works. I suggested that Jane Austen was afraid of presenting warm female relationships in the later novels in part because she and her sister Cassandra were *too* close for propriety, too much entwined with each other. I cited a passage in Cassandra's letter written after Jane's death:

> I loved her only too well … I am conscious that my affection for her made me sometimes unjust to & negligent of others, & I can acknowledge, more than as a general principle, the justice of the hand which has struck this blow.

I ended with this quotation, not spelling out what I was suggesting – a common habit of the semi-outsider in life and work – and I confess to still finding the statement strange, a daring appropriation of another's death for one's own spiritual journey. But I wouldn't go further now, as I didn't then. I let the idea lie along with all the other unknowable aspects of Jane Austen's life and writing.

So I never made it into French Theory. Indeed, I couldn't even define post-structuralism properly. I remember a visit to Cambridge when I had a Guggenheim Fellowship from the States and was invited to a college high table for dinner. Having presumably been primed, the Master stared down the long board at me, then declared that they had amongst the guests a literary scholar from America: would she tell them what post-structuralism was? Jane Austen doesn't give Sir Thomas Bertram's reply when Fanny asks him about the slave trade in *Mansfield Park*, and I no longer remember how I handled the Master's question – but I remember the preceding moment vividly.

My ignorance didn't prevent my being invited later to provide a couple of lectures on French Theory and Theoretical Feminism for the English department. 'Just think of that, eh Hedda,' as boring Tesman kept saying to the heroine of Ibsen's *Hedda Gabler*. I prepared a handout of extracts from Kristeva, Cixous and Derrida, taken from an anthology. (More about extracts in Chapter 8.)

Women's Friendship in Literature did well in the US. Its success allowed me to push on with my encyclopaedias, editions and literary histories in peace. It was less successful in England; Anita

Brookner, a novelist whom I admired, wrote a scathing review in the *Times Literary Supplement* declaring that the subject of female relationships should not be written about, for it undermined the romantic plot and the proper heterosexual tie.

When I needed to return to England and find a job (not my best 'career' move!), I took the book off my CV, listing instead my work on the hymns of William Cowper and John Newton (I'd written this while teaching in Puerto Rico; there were few books in the library but hymns were in my head, thanks to daily assemblies in boarding school). I found a modest job – so modest I needed to augment the salary by writing for money. I became a happy biographer of little-known women, including of course Mary Wollstonecraft and Aphra Behn.

FIRST AND LAST WORKS

My reason for this swerve into academic reminiscence is that, in recently re-editing Jane Austen and so reading the novels one after the other, I found that the habit of seeing patterns and connections across finished works and fragments was enjoyably returning. Never really 'structuralist', it's simply an observing of binaries and narrative conventions in the old manner: F. R. Leavis's wife Q. D. Leavis, for example, berating those who revealed the 'unprofitable attitude' of admiring Austen uncritically, insisted on the author's 'meagre' invention that meant patterns and character types were simply repeated and reworked. In my biographies I sought patterns and repetitions in lives: so, what follows is something like literary criticism informed, in my case, by the habits of a biographer.

Jane Austen wrote 'Sanditon' just before her death. She began *Northanger Abbey* at the outset of her literary career, though it was probably still in revision when she died. These two works may seem an odd pairing but there's one immediate superficial resemblance: 'Sanditon' is a fragment and *Northanger Abbey* is more full of fragments – scraps of paper, unfinished books and so on – than any of the other published novels.

To bring the two works together, let me begin with the arrival of *Northanger Abbey* in print after its long delay.

The first version was probably written in 1794 and a more complete text settled on in 1798–9. In May 1801 the Austens quit Steventon rectory for Bath. Late the following year, it's likely Jane was revising her work, possibly inspired by actually living in the town where much of her novel is set. The next spring, through an agent of her brother Henry, who dealt with the business side of her publishing, she sold the work to Benjamin Crosby's firm for £10 on the promise it would be published as early as possible. It was advertised but not printed.

It must have taken Jane Austen a while to realise the book wasn't coming out. Just before moving into her settled home in Chawton in 1809, she wrote to Crosby under the pseudonym Mrs Ashton Dennis (MAD) saying she'd send her work elsewhere if he'd lost interest. Crosby's son offered her the book back for the original £10. Perhaps she lacked the sum; whatever the case, she now concentrated on settling into the new house and publishing the other works begun so many years back in Steventon: *Sense and Sensibility* and *Pride and Prejudice.*

Northanger Abbey was still valued. It differed from these other novels in its *fairly* simple heroine and parodic intentions – more parodic, in fact, than the last of the childhood tales, 'Catharine, or the Bower' with its realistic depiction of the young heroine and of constrained female lives. In contrast to 'Catharine', *Northanger Abbey* employs the same kind of literary and social satire that runs through Austen's writings from early to late – through letters, comic poems and little literary spoofs – but was not given full rein in the other published novels.

In Spring 1816, Henry bought back the manuscript; Jane wrote a preface to explain that the original had been intended for publication in 1803 and that by now parts must appear 'comparatively obsolete'. We don't know what she meant – type of satire, Gothic mockery, literary and political references, style, clothes, hair?

There are no hints of how she might have updated the novel. Burney's *Camilla* is mentioned in *Northanger Abbey* as one of the novels to be admired; since *Camilla* came out in 1796, it might be considered rather old-fashioned. But the book is also mentioned in 'Sanditon', written in 1817; it rests on the library table in the new resort. Trains on dresses had been abandoned long before 1816, but they're still being pinned up in the Bath of *Northanger Abbey*. By 1816 muslins were so common that they weren't likely to interest even dress-obsessed Mrs Allen. Partly because of the rise of sea resorts like Sanditon round the coast, Bath itself was less smart than earlier. It had become the slightly unmodish town delivered in *Persuasion*.

The need for revision of little details suggests one way that *Northanger Abbey* differs from the other novels, a way shared with 'Sanditon'. Both take an interest in specific consumer items inessential for the plot, like the fashionable blue shoes and nankin boots in William Heeley's shop windows in Sanditon. Carriages travel through all the novels but perhaps work harder in these two. Take the gig. John Thorpe is proud of his, pointing out that it is curricle hung: the curricle being the more expensive vehicle. By 'Sanditon' in 1817 Miss Denham is embarrassed not to have anything grander than her 'simple gig': it reveals the sorry state of her finances.

' In both 'Sanditon' and *Northanger Abbey* items come alive. The laundry list and the farrier's bill seem to *mock* Catherine when she finally opens the Abbey's Gothic chest; the medicinal phials that accompany the hypochondriacs in Sanditon were 'at home' on the mantelpiece of the lodging house.

(Material items are prominent in Austen's other unfinished novel, 'The Watsons', which might suggest that, before she sent a manuscript for publication, she pruned such elements as would anchor a book in a precise time.)

Despite what she had once intended, when she received back the manuscript of *Northanger Abbey* Austen didn't seek another publisher. Henry, her usual negotiator, was much preoccupied. Also, perhaps by now, despite a little updating, she wasn't satisfied with the work, in which case it seems likely she'd be revising it further. She was writing 'Sanditon' from January to March 1817. Before she laid down her pen and pencil through ill health, she told Fanny Knight, her increasingly close confidante in fictional matters,

> Miss Catherine is put upon the Shelve for the present, and I do not know that she will ever come out.

It sounds as though she was still tinkering with this early novel – at the same time as writing 'Sanditon'. So, despite being separated by many years in conception, 'Sanditon' and *Northanger Abbey* may have shared the same ink.

After Cassandra's death, both works were at the mercy of her heirs and came to light with their help. Both were given titles based not on characters but on places, possibly – though not certainly – in opposition to the author's original intention. Jane Austen had latterly called *Northanger Abbey* 'Miss Catherine' and family tradition had her naming 'Sanditon' 'The Brothers' – as innovative a notion, considering her female-centred habits, as the sea resort itself.

I want to look at more similarities that are striking, I think, when the two works are brought together. Catherine Morland and Charlotte Heywood come from large families, there are ten Morland children and fourteen Heywoods. Both sets of fecund parents are commonsensical, down to earth, conservative and healthy. Both are reasonably well off through prudent management of earnings and income. Despite their large family, the Morlands can still consider giving their son James a living worth £400, as well as providing a dowry of £3,000 for Catherine, one of many girls. The Heywoods, with an even bigger family to launch, have married off their older girls, so presumably have a sufficiency, and Charlotte has enough for some retail enjoyment in Sanditon shops. In marked contrast to the Bennets of *Pride and Prejudice*, both sets of parents economise. They do so by (primarily) remaining stationary, hence the specialness of the first trips for the two young women that open the novels.

Charlotte and Catherine have good hearts, though they differ in strength of head. Both recognise beauty and grace in others without envy. Both are blessed with good health. Both are careful in what they say – Charlotte by design, Catherine by instinct – when not overwhelmed by novels. Unlike Emma Woodhouse, Charlotte can resist the comic putdown: for example, even when she discovers that Lady Denham, the great lady of Sanditon, is 'thoroughly mean', she 'keeps a civil silence'. She regards the trio of Diana, Susan and Arthur Parker as self-medicating fanatics or career invalids who've made ill health into their profession, but on the whole she remains polite.

The two young women are taken to holiday places, transitional locations (usually no one's primary and original home): spas and sea-side resorts set up for pleasure and well-being, very different from the hereditary fictional houses in other books. (Mrs Elton would be less out of place here than in Highbury: she loved Bath and recommended it to scornful Emma.) In the new locations, they are free of the constraints and responsibilities of relatives and domestic duties. In the opening of both works there's a comical sense of an adventure beginning. In Catherine's journey to Bath with Mr and Mrs Allen there's no 'lucky overturn to introduce them to the hero', where in 'Sanditon' the opening carriage ride begins with just such a lucky accident.

In both novels the sensible mothers bid farewell to their daughters without excessive anxiety. Mrs Morland gives no 'Cautions against the violence of such noblemen and baronets as delight in forcing young ladies away to some remote farm-house', letting her daughter set off with the minimal advice of wrapping up warm and keeping account of expenses in a little book. The warnings about the nefarious aims of men and the dire possibilities of sexual predation will reach both heroines through fiction alone. Charlotte in 'Sanditon' has read of abductions in *Camilla* and other romances, and Catherine is about to encounter them in Gothic novels. In life neither is abducted, though Catherine is taken on a carriage ride by John Thorpe against her protestations and she's at her most vulnerable in the trip home alone in a hack post-chaise.

In the 1975 continuation of 'Sanditon' by Marie Dobbs, Charlotte *is* abducted, but in Jane Austen's novel abduction remains a fantasy featuring the beautiful but poor Clara Brereton – a fantasy enjoyed by the literature-addled Sir Edward. He's as much preyed on by novels as Catherine Morland once was. He feels it *de rigueur* for a rakish person like himself to practise abduction, his purpose exaggerated and made silly by the difficulty of finding a location for the dastardly act that must crown it. Not common Ramsgate, Brighton or a remote castle, but distant 'Tombuctoo', though, being short of funds, he'd probably be reduced to taking his victim to his ordinary English country house or perhaps the tourist *cottage ornée* he's building on Lady Denham's land.

In both 'Sanditon' and *Northanger Abbey*, worthy families entrust their daughters to unsuitable chaperones. But the Heywoods and Morlands have an awful lot of daughters to get off their hands and may not be super-conscientious or imaginative, unlike lax Mr Bennet, who knows the perils of Brighton before Lydia sets off to court disgrace in *Pride and Prejudice*. Catherine and Charlotte are the *only* Austen heroines to be whisked off from home by people unrelated to them, to meet a future husband somewhere else. In the other novels, men enter, or are already in, the heroine's world.

Comically, the chaperones are unfit because foolish or weak, in contrast to the chaperones or older women of Gothic literature who try to wreck the young heroines' happiness through jealousy or greed. To conform, perhaps the dragon of Sanditon, Lady Denham will play the role. She's the last in Jane Austen's line of foolish or mean-spirited rich older women: Mrs Ferrars, Lady Catherine de Bourgh, Mrs Churchill, Lady Denham. Shades perhaps of Austen's own unlikable and probably pilfering Aunt Jane Leigh Perrot: women with independent means are unfailingly disagreeable in the novels. Could Lady Denham prove dangerous to Clara Brereton, if not to Charlotte? With a change of sex, we might see the General in *Northanger Abbey* as part of this line of volatile controlling older people. However, the *appointed* chaperones in both books lack spite or guile.

Seaside places are potentially dangerous in fiction. In *Pride and Prejudice* the near abduction or seduction of the heiress Georgiana Darcy by Wickham occurs at Ramsgate, and this despite – or perhaps because of – Lady Catherine de Bourgh's insistence that she be accompanied by *two* manservants. Jane Fairfax in *Emma* comes to grief – or did well, depending on viewpoint – in Weymouth. Rich mixed-race heiress Miss Lambe in 'Sanditon', we might suppose, will be as unguarded as Georgiana Darcy, although in the Austen fragment she's threatened only by the quack medicines favoured by her headmistress's family.

Catherine discovers that improperly digested fiction can cause mischief. After her humiliation in front of Henry Tilney (she's been snooping to see if she can discover if his father killed or imprisoned his mother), she rejects the Gothic as a guide to life. However, it was perhaps in part her novel-reading that led her to a correct sense of the rottenness in the centre of the Tilney house. The more educated, less impressionable Henry has long compromised with it at the expense of his poor sister.

Charlotte has read enough romances to enjoy imposing them on what she sees, but without being overwhelmed by her fancies. She's read *Camilla* carefully and realised that its warning against extravagance was once, but is no longer, applicable to her grown-up self. At times her refusal to be overwhelmed can make her seem prim, as when she rejects the passionate poetry of Robert Burns because of his unprincipled life. She makes some errors too: despite his ludicrous literary allusions, handsome Sir Edward requires *two* encounters to be judged soft in the head.

Without allowing her imagination to run away with her, Charlotte enjoys using her reading of romances to fashion novelettish outcomes for people she hardly knows. She imagines a disastrous destiny for lovely, vulnerable Clara Brereton because she seems the very model of a romance heroine:

> Her situation with Lady Denham so very much in favour of it!—
> She seemed placed with her on purpose to be ill-used.—Such
> poverty and dependence, joined to such beauty and merit, seemed
> to leave no choice in the business.

By contrast Catherine Morland has to be prodded by Isabella into seeing fictional plots in social Bath, though she's quick enough in an abbey under Henry's tutelage. Charlotte's manoeuvre is perhaps more like Emma's dangerous imaginings for Harriet Smith and Jane Fairfax, although she always seems more self-aware than Emma.

NARRATING

Literature in the form of popular contemporary novels and poetry is more prominent in 'Sanditon' and *Northanger Abbey* than elsewhere in Jane Austen's mature works. Unlike so many precocious juvenile writers, she'd been a parodist from her earliest years, a mocker of adult reading and writing styles, a ridiculer of the way literature enfolds life and life enfolds literature. It was her reading that first made her a writer. Austen was a critic, then novelist.

All her books refer to literature, but individual works aren't always named. Emma, the 'imaginist', for example, tends to impose drama on everyday events, whether gypsies in a lane or friends at the seaside. But we don't hear of particular titles she has read – only her wonderful lists. In 'Catharine, or the Bower', however, the heroine judges the triviality of her new friend by noting how little she appreciates Charlotte Smith's Gothic *Emmeline*. Catharine makes the mature remark that, 'if a book is well written, I always find it too short'. In *Northanger Abbey* and 'Sanditon' this use of specific works as a guide to conduct or as a method of judging others becomes comic: in the former, Mrs Morland proposes to cure lovelorn Catherine with a moralistic essay, and in 'Sanditon' the heroine picks up and puts down Burney's *Camilla* as no longer morally relevant to her; she does so in the local shop, so emphasising the fact that everything, including literature, is for sale in this town. In none of the three works does literature function to calm or control a mind in the way Anne Elliot in *Persuasion* uses poetry.

The notion of good taste being a sign of virtue was pretty much exploded in the twentieth century when the most despicable dictators celebrated great art: Hitler that of Wagner and Stalin that of Pushkin and Dostoevsky, although there's always been a line of wicked men with cultural capital in art and literature, like the murderous Emperor Nero. But to an extent the connection still worked for Jane Austen, even if she seasoned it with her usual trickling irony.

The direct mockery of famous Gothic romance in *Northanger Abbey* would be outdated by 1816. Only simple Harriet in *Emma* reads Mrs Radcliffe's *The Romance of the Forest*, the book behind Catherine Morland's imagining in the abbey, and no one reads Radcliffe in *Persuasion*. According to a comic account of contemporary popular fiction at the time, by the late 1810s the Gothic romantic heroine had been replaced by a sensible woman who does plain work. Yet the Gothic lingers in 'Sanditon' despite its contemporary satiric content.

At the end of *Northanger Abbey*, I feel the dead Mrs Tilney's ghost still haunting the abbey where her life has been uneasy. By sad chance, the ghosts of the dead husbands Mr Hollis and Sir Harry end 'Sanditon':

> Poor Mr. Hollis! It was impossible not to feel him hardly used; to be obliged to stand back in his own house and see the best place by the fire constantly occupied by Sir Harry Denham.

I see *Northanger Abbey* and 'Sanditon' as sharing similar inspiration. If true, their togetherness leads to a question. Could the spoofing treatment of Catherine in *Northanger Abbey*, quite different from the treatment of Austen's other heroines, have prompted a desire to create a work in which a heroine was less the observed than the observer?

Without sensible confidants, both Catherine and Charlotte have the potential to be watchers of other people, lookers-on in a new society. This characteristic is developed in Charlotte who becomes close to the satiric eye of an outsider, the alien who comes into a world with innocent eyes to record freshly. There's little evidence to me that 'Sanditon' was to be a coming-of-age story as *Northanger Abbey* is in many ways, though it might be argued that, even in the earlier novel, the places change more than the heroine. But Charlotte is often the observer of the absurdities of the flimsy town she's visiting.

She has one advantage over young Catherine; so far there's no intelligent and discerning character like Henry Tilney to overtop and intrude on her as ironic commentator. Of course we've seen very little of Sidney, the probable hero. From his reported comments on his hypochondriac siblings, he may well have been intended to exhibit some of the wit and dash of his bewitching predecessor.

Now I come to the most interesting similarity between the two novels: the bold, noisy narrative voice, more intrusive than elsewhere, though to different effects. In *Northanger Abbey* the word heroine is used more than twenty times, often prefaced by 'my' or 'our', most commonly when Catherine's place in the Gothic story is emphasised, while the narrator calls herself her 'biographer'.

The opening immediately establishes an intimacy between reader and narrator, who come together to look condescendingly at the young girl:

> [Catherine] never could learn or understand any thing before she was taught; and sometimes not even then, for she was often inattentive, and occasionally stupid.

Then we get general remarks from the older, presumably female narrator:

> To look *almost* pretty, is an acquisition of higher delight to a girl who has been looking plain the first fifteen years of her life, than a beauty from her cradle can ever receive.

So it continues, with interruptions of varying sorts and direct addresses, such as 'it may be stated, for the reader's more certain information ... that her heart was affectionate' until we reach 'her mind [was] about as ignorant and uninformed as the female mind at seventeen usually is'. We know exactly what the narrator means, we share the same reference.

We remain with this sardonic but affectionate narrator, except perhaps in Catherine's homecoming, by which time Austen has established her too much as a vulnerable young girl with consciousness and inner life to be comfortably subjected to narrative mockery:

> A heroine in a hack post-chaise is such a blow upon sentiment, as no attempt at grandeur or pathos can withstand.

The enjoyable conspiracy of reader and writer is however restored when the reader is reminded that we must all be 'hastening together to perfect felicity' because so few pages of the novel remain to be read.

In 'Sanditon', the narrator is not a participant in events, but rather an interested commentator. She is intimate both with the mind of the chief character and with the reader. She makes condescending remarks about Charlotte Heywood's youth – the way she responds to male admiration: 'at her time of life' she should want to please a handsome man; Sir Edward's 'title did him no harm' either. But, when her 'half-hour's fever' is over, 'sober-minded' Charlotte is back to being one with the narrator, who gives her a narratorial pat on the back.

The narrator comes across as a woman who's long outgrown her own youth, very like Prudentia Homespun, the interrupting gossip and narrator of Jane West's *A Gossip's Story* (a novel closely anticipating *Sense and Sensibility* in plot, despite Jane Austen's decision to be 'stout against any thing written by Mrs West'). It would have been fascinating to know how playful Austen's narrator would later be with the 'Sanditon' text she purports to be writing.

I find many similarities, then, between these first and last novels, especially in the use of parody and satire, and the intrusive narrator. For other elements, it depends on how you speculate about Jane Austen's practice. Did she begin with first-person letters, then move to omniscience of some sort, using free indirect discourse to fuse modes? Or did she sometimes make a narrative voice subservient to the characters' assumed personalities? Did she start in one genre and travel across others, occasionally arriving at eclectic social or psychological satire? We see she can transcend the genres of Gothic, parody and even anti-parody in *Northanger Abbey*: what this implies may work for 'Sanditon' too.

Or possibly, more mundanely, the realism of her published (and other unpublished) novels is a little at odds with the parody and satire of both *Northanger Abbey* and 'Sanditon'. The critic D. W. Harding, early promoter of the dark Jane Austen, saw in the former a disjunction between satiric Bath and Gothic abbey. He judged it the method by which Austen encoded her caustic sentiments, using a style that veiled their virulence. In this way she could express uncomfortable truths without offending satirised neighbours.

Apply the method to 'Sanditon' and we find that its broad farcical comedy might just be Austen's way of trying to avoid upsetting her ill self, as well as her reputedly hypochondriac mother, failed capitalist brother Henry and stingy aunt Jane Leigh Perrott.

(Might we go a step further and see Austen encoding herself as powerful author through the authoritarian narrator of *Northanger Abbey* and as the 'creative' comic entrepreneurs Tom and Diana Parker of 'Sanditon'?)

Austen's late revising of *Northanger Abbey* possibly triggered the whole project of 'Sanditon'. In which case, she'd be reversing the sexes: using the Henry Tilney–Catherine Morland dynamic to create (in the absence of Sidney Parker) the sober-minded Charlotte and fiction-addled, quixotic Sir Edward.

Unlikely though it sounds, perhaps, after the gentleman has been chastened and reformed rather than the lady, these two might make a match.

We'll never know.

CHAPTER 5
Poor Nerves

It was absolutely necessary that I should have the little fever &
indisposition, which I had;—it has been all the fashion this week
in Lyme. Miss Anna Cove was confined for a day or two, & her
Mother thinks was saved only by a timely Emetic ...

So wrote Jane to Cassandra.

'Fever' and 'fashion': the words in the same sentence tell us
a lot about Jane Austen's attitude to disorders of the body – the
non-contagious ones that nag but rarely kill.

The buzzword of the age was 'Nerves'. This will be a 'nervous'
chapter, darting about in honour of the nervous body and its power.
There'll be nervous men and women, real and fictional, and a
whole town created to serve them. I'll begin with Jane Austen's
letters– 'nervous' letters.

THE LETTERS

How could the creator of the perfect fictional sentence write those
tumbling-over-themselves letters? Marvellous, of course, but
helter-skelter and far from poised. Might they be called nervous
writing? In the best possible aesthetic and excited way? 'I could
lament in one sentence & laugh in the next,' Austen wrote to Fanny

Knight apologising for her erratic state and erratic style – for the nerves of writing.

I have become a fan of Jane Austen's letters, mischievous port-manteau accounts of a life filled with people – some too fat, some too short-necked, some just too nondescript for comment – and random things, from muslins and sofas to honey, cakes and wine. The letters are unpredictable, skipping from lace collars to a brace of pheasants, from ale to ailments. Austen displays in herself those little grievances we all have as duty bangs against desire, but she never stays long in irritable mode. Soon, she's off and away to green shoes or missing gloves.

The letters are captivating, with their spurts of excited or tremulous life. A niece has a 'purple Pelisse'; it may be a secret but not kept well enough to avoid the snooping of an aunt in the bedroom acting like a naughty, middle-aged Catherine Morland poking around Northanger. Not much escapes this aunt, not much is unrecorded. She's eager to share the most enticing trivialities.

Self-conscious too: 'I am going to write nothing but short Sentences. There shall be two full stops in every Line,' she once declared. Mostly the letters run straight on, lacking paragraphing or much punctuation beyond the ubiquitous dash, flying from topic to topic, and leaping from one event to quite another with differ-ent characters, so that some pages read almost like a modernist stream-of-consciousness novel by Virginia Woolf or Samuel Beckett.

Run-on because the mind does this.

> I wonder whether the Ink bottle has been filled. Does Butcher's meat keep up at the same price? & is not Bread lower than 2/6— Mary's blue gown!—My Mother must be in agonies

Of course they're not experimental in a literary way, and Jane Austen is not an ancestor of Beckett and Woolf: they're in part the result of a thrifty use of expensive paper. 'I am quite angry with myself for not writing closer,' she sighed on one occasion. But thrift is not the prime cause of her style. She's prepared to try for a 'Smartish Letter' while declaring she has absolutely nothing to say. She'll make something out of nothing. It's as if she were present at a social occasion when it feels rude to leave, although she knows she should.

The letter-writer becomes loquacious Miss Bates with added humour and self-consciousness. Comically, both Austen and her creation fixate on the 'petticoat'. Miss Bates does this so frequently that, when Emma mimics her to Mrs Weston, she highlights this most feminine of garments:

> 'So very kind and obliging!—But he always had been such a very kind neighbour!' And then fly off, through half a sentence, to her mother's old petticoat. 'Not that it was such a very old petticoat either—for still it would last a great while—and, indeed, she must thankfully say that their petticoats were all very strong.'

And in the letters:

> I will not be much longer libelled by the possession of my coarse spot, I shall turn it into a petticoat very soon.—I wish you a merry Christmas, but *no* compliments of the Season.—Poor Edward! ...

Most memorably for admirers of Byron there was that remark juxtaposing 'The Corsair' with mending a petticoat which I discussed in Chapter 2.

It becomes a tragicomic accident that, with Henry's posthumous help, Jane Austen's last recorded words in a letter concern a captain's wife and sister who, she hopes, 'have rather longer petticoats than last year'. With that hope, the collected letters of Jane Austen end.

Initially when reading the letters in Deirdre Le Faye's edition, I skipped back and forth from text to endnotes identifying second cousins and cousins much removed, trying to get my head round the convoluted marriages and remarriages of the spreading clan, the various parsonages and their changing inmates; then I'd switch to the glossary to learn about different carriages, about frocks and Church tithes.

Soon I saw that no modern reader could possibly come close to understanding all or much of what's there, however richly annotated. They were written for the eyes not of you and me but mostly of a sister who knew as much as anyone can of another being. She alone could read under and over Jane's words, catch the jokes, the buried or slithering humour that needed two to raise a laugh. I concluded it best not to look at the explanatory notes and glossary at all.

Try for a moment to imagine any of the novel heroines writing these letters. The mistress of Pemberley or Anne Elliot? We're in good company if we can't. When Fanny Knight wrote a letter to her aunt addressed as if to Georgiana Darcy, hoping for a reply in kind, Austen shut down the game:

> I cannot pretend to answer it. Even had I more time, I should not feel at all sure of the sort of Letter that Miss D.[arcy] would write.

Earlier, she enjoyed a game with niece Anna in which she invented a facetious note to a Mrs Hunter. She thanked her for a thread paper and described how she'd dissolved into tears over Mrs Hunter's rather clumsy novel which she, Jane, claims she'd been reading with sentimental enthusiasm. But this pretend letter concerned *another* woman's work, not a character from her own.

Writing half a century after her aunt's death, Caroline Austen didn't share my affection for Austen's epistolary style. She told her brother, James Edward:

> There is nothing in those letters that *I* have seen that would be acceptable to the public … they detailed chiefly home and family events: and she seldom committed herself *even* to an opinion—so that to strangers they could be *no* transcript of her mind—they would not feel that they knew her any better for having read them—

Her half-sister Anna was more of my opinion. She recalled that her aunt's talent for letter-writing 'was so much valued & thought so delightful amongst her own family circle'.

It's true the letters are not a 'transcript' of the mind of the novelist; if we want to savour that, we need only go to those novels. But they do brilliantly reveal a sentient being aware of weather, rain and wind on the body, of aches and pains, of other people impinging, and of a kind of agitation to record. The letters were written to inform and entertain Cassandra and fill time, hers and her sister's – did Jane fear a vacuum?

Caroline claimed that Cassandra burnt 'the greater part' of Jane's letters to her, those more intimate that told of inner life or unhappy family affairs. (The act has been dramatised in Gill Hornby's *Miss Austen*, where it's given imagined justification.) However, I'm suspicious.

If true, it's strange she left so much. Cassandra destroyed her own letters, an immense loss, but would she really burn Jane's when she so valued everything her sister wrote? Unlike Caroline and James Edward, she didn't try to make a rural saint of her sister, but, if she were worried about improprieties, wouldn't she have destroyed anything that might seem inappropriate? There's a lot left here that's unladylike. For correspondence that's supposedly been expurgated, it's remarkably uninhibited.

Caroline's first-hand account must be properly weighed. Cassandra is likely to have removed some letters that might have been hurtful to family members who were to receive them after her death. But is it possible that the famous incident when John Murray helped burn Byron's scandalous memoirs in his fireplace has influenced the Austen episode? Anecdotes have a tendency to migrate among celebrities.

When first published, the letters shocked many, including Austen's admirer, the novelist E. M. Forster. You can hear him spluttering over his morning coffee:

> her lapses of taste over carnality can be deplorable, no doubt because they arise from lack of feeling. She can write, for instance, and write it as a jolly joke, that 'Mrs Hall of Sherborne was

brought to bed yesterday of a dead child, some weeks before she expected, oweing to a fright. I suppose she happened unawares to look at her husband'. Did Cassandra laugh? Probably, but all that we catch at this distance is the whinnying of harpies.

The 'whinnying of harpies'! For that marvellous pair of sisters! The phrase is as memorable as the 'Hyena in petticoats' Horace Walpole foisted onto Mary Wollstonecraft.

Is the levity at Mrs Hall's expense unfeeling? Is it mocking the misery of stillbirth or miscarriage, or is it the jest of an outsider pointing to the comedy of mismarriage – and an ugly husband? Humour isn't universal; time and place affect it. You need only be an American in Britain or a Briton in America to discover that truth, despite our almost common language. Was humour different in the more robust 1810s than now?

If you haven't yet read the letters, I advise having a go and abandoning yourself to their charm. You don't need to interrupt enjoyment by flicking back and forth to glossaries and indexes. It's sufficient to keep in mind the main characters popping in and out as in a novel; the rest is wallpaper. The novels achieved their form from layers of revision, the laconic and terse possibly emerging from the once loose and erratic. The letters are unrevised and uncensored.

Wonderful, captivating, trivial, serious, everything, yes, but also 'nervous'. That need to go on and on, to catch at everything and nothing, not to stop even at the end of the paper, not to abandon that intimate recipient or leave her unentertained. Did entertaining demand some transgression? Is that why Mrs Hall of Sherborne is there? Such a remark, shocking to our sentimental age, would not have been made by an Austen heroine.

'Mrs Bromley is a fat woman in mourning.' Mrs Blount with her 'pink husband' has a 'fat neck'. The Miss Atkinsons are 'fat girls with short noses'.

There is something hectic and edgy in all this, something that wants to fill in space with whatever thought or observation comes to hand. In contrast to Wollstonecraft's letters, equally helter-skeltering, Jane Austen's avoid abstract ideas, as if thinking beyond the writing or momentary memory isn't to her point. The nervous haste is all about random people and things, a sort of phantasmagoria of the concrete.

I've wondered what could have brought about this nervous energy, this living in flux on paper.

Jane wrote most of her letters when Cassandra wasn't present. When Jane died, her sister confessed, 'I had not a thought concealed from her, & it is as if I had lost a part of myself.' Jane probably felt the same. Writing to the absent Cassandra, was she trying to capture every thought, share everything, to create across distance the joint being that the sisters shared, even when one sister was absent? Was Jane 'nervous' when separated from the other part of herself?

MARY WOLLSTONECRAFT

In the mid-eighteenth century, George Cheyne in *The English Malady* wrote that nervous disorders were a by-product of the nation's increasing luxuries and leisure. Towards the end of the century, medical theorists like William Cullen declared all disease a modification of nerves. At the beginning of the new century, Thomas Trotter linked 'the Nervous Temperament' to physical and mental lethargy. Blame fell now on idleness, now on indulgent consumption, now on a damaged gut, and now on simple self-obsession.

Throughout her adult life the conundrum of mind and body worried Mary Wollstonecraft. Once she'd held firm religious views, which placed emphasis on the suffering of mind and body as part of soul-making, a preparation on earth for the next world. But under life's afflictions and much reading in Enlightenment theory, her Christian faith faltered, and she moved to a more secular understanding, sensing that the individual mind, a sort of personalised brain, controlled the body.

In *A Vindication of the Rights of Woman* she claimed that rationality was the proper state for *all* human beings. The gendering of reason and sensibility as masculine and feminine did women immense disservice: it was a root cause of the wrongs of woman. Change habits, change the culture, change society and the individual, and those nervous ills women complain of would fade.

Wollstonecraft fulminated against men who wrote advice books aimed at *encouraging* girls to be emotional and weak. In his *A Father's Legacy to his Daughters*, Gregory wrote:

> We so naturally associate the idea of female softness and delicacy with a correspondent delicacy of constitution, that when a woman speaks of her great strength, her extraordinary appetite, her ability to bear excessive fatigue, we recoil at the description in a way she is little aware of.

Such emphasis horrified Mary Wollstonecraft.

The life delivered in her letters complicates the matter. At every stage, she wrestled with the problem of an excessive sensitivity she couldn't master and a body that proved recalcitrant to the mind's rational promptings.

Mind and body were interconnected, now one in the ascendant, now the other. 'Nerves' were sometimes mental, sometimes physical. 'My nerves daily grow worse and worse—yet I strive to occupy my mind,' she complained. This mind was harrassed owing to 'disordered nerves, that are injured beyond a *possibility* of receiving *any* aid from medicine'. Yet the reverse was also true. The mind preyed on the body, 'cankering' it. 'My harrassed mind will in time wear out my body.'

Throughout her short life – Wollstonecraft died at thirty-eight, even younger than Jane Austen – her views evolved. They changed and looped back to take in earlier notions. She attacked from different angles the insoluble problems. After a period of self-lacerating about a nervous mind she couldn't control, she'd swerve to lament the power and dominance of a demanding nervous body. Sometimes, in the manner of Cheyne in *The English Malady*, she comforted herself by ascribing her ailments to the unnatural sedentary life of middle-class women like herself.

Mental/physical, somatic/psychosomatic, it goes on being a problem. I had Chronic Fatigue Syndrome or ME in the 1990s.

It developed directly from a flu repeatedly attacked by stronger and stronger antibiotics – probably as destructive as the repeated bleeding Jane Austen's medical contemporaries imposed on patients. But it was also a difficult time in work and home life. A lot in Jane Austen and Mary Wollstonecraft resonates.

Does diagnosis depend on what you choose to think of yourself at any time? When a small child in a hot place, I was thrown by a family 'friend' into the water as a way of encouraging me to learn to swim. I spluttered, drank the salty sea, choked and dogpaddled like mad; I flopped back onto land furious. The event was nothing to that first night in boarding school to which I return and return, when nobody physically threw me anywhere.

(IN)DEPENDENCE

Wollstonecraft's obsession with the mind–body interaction leaps out of her correspondence from her early years in Ireland when she was employed by the aristocratic Kingsboroughs. She was serving as a most unwilling (and untameable) governess, and her letters make me think of those Jane Fairfax might have written. That is, if Mrs Elton had had her way in placing Jane as a governess in a family rich in money but poor in refinement. (I realise that Jane Austen's refusal to write a letter as if from Miss Darcy suggests that she mightn't have approved my speculation.)

But was the position of governess or hired teacher quite so distressing as real Mary Wollstonecraft and fictional Jane Fairfax make it seem? Was my boarding school as bad as I remember it?

In 'The Watsons', pretty refined Emma Watson returns to her poorer clerical family after a childhood with a wealthy aunt, holding ideas that, as her older pragmatic sister advises, are now above her middle-class station. Like Elizabeth Bennet and Charlotte Lucas in *Pride and Prejudice*, the sisters debate 'independence' versus marriage. Emma begins:

> 'To be so bent on marriage—to pursue a man merely for the sake of situation—is a sort of thing that shocks me; I cannot understand

it. Poverty is a great evil, but to a woman of education and feeling it ought not, it cannot be the greatest.—I would rather be teacher at a school (and I can think of nothing worse) than marry a man I did not like.—'

'I would rather do any thing than be teacher at a school—' said her sister. '*I* have been at school, Emma, and know what a life they lead; *you* never have.—I should not like marrying a disagreeable man any more than yourself,—but I do not think there *are* many very disagreeable men;—I think I could like any good-humoured man with a comfortable income.—I suppose my aunt brought you up to be rather refined.'

Emma thinks marriage unnecessary for an educated woman, while knowing nothing of the options outside. Incidentally, no heroine thinks of publishing, an ambition only allowed Frank Churchill in *Emma*. Knowing the reality, her sister dreads teaching and sees marriage as the only desirable outcome for a poor woman. Without experience, Jane Fairfax expresses similar horror of independence from family, the earning of a living by one's own work. Indeed, it never went well in fiction.

Yet many genteel women of the time *did* work comfortably outside the home: Mary Wollstonecraft's two sisters, Eliza and Everina, Elizabeth Inchbald, Hannah More and many others. Jane Austen's good friend Anne Sharp was a respected governess of the Knight girls at Godmersham. When she read the copy of *Emma* which Austen presented her, the response was: 'dissatisfied with Jane Fairfax'.

Did she think her friend had not given Jane Fairfax a sufficient inner life? Or did she find it unfortunate that this character is allowed to express such visceral horror of governessing and its nervous toll on mind and body? Miss Taylor, later Mrs Weston, the *actual* governess of *Emma*, escapes teaching through marriage. Jane Austen imagined such an escape for her friend Anne Sharp, who failed to respond to the fantasy. Perhaps she took a pride in her profession.

In her letters, Mary Wollstonecraft showed herself more in Jane Fairfax's mode than in Anne Sharp's. She loathed working as a subordinate within a family – she called the governess 'a kind of upper servant' – and expressed her loathing in nervous complaint. But there were ways out other than marriage. For a time, the Wollstonecraft sisters kept a quite successful school in Newington Green in London, and many other women also became entrepreneurs in education. Hannah More and her sisters had a thriving school in Bath, as did Miss Colborn, whose establishment Jane Austen much admired. After her friend's death, Anne Sharp started a school for girls in Liverpool. It kept her for many years. Perhaps it resembled Mrs Goddard's modest but worthy establishment for girls in *Emma* –and the free and easy Abbey School in Reading, which Jane and Cassandra attended from 1785 to 1786 under the elderly Madame Latournelle (probably, though not certainly, her real name was Sarah Hackitt). She had the distinction of a cork leg.

Mrs Elton thinks Jane Fairfax melodramatic when she believes she's comparing teaching with slavery. An inaccurate comparison of course, yet the analogy of (relatively) poor woman and slave hovers at the edge of Austen's novels; I touched on it in that interaction of Sir Thomas and his niece Fanny. No European woman's situation resembles that of enslaved Africans, sold by their compatriots, then dragged from Africa to America and the plantation islands, but wherever there's some involuntary 'transportation' there may be faint parallels.

Fanny Price is 'transported' only a short distance in southern and middle England but other genteel girls travelled farther: to India, there to be bought for a 'maintenance' by older men in the East India Company wanting English wives. In 'Catharine, or The Bower', the refined and ladylike Cecilia Wynne becomes an impoverished orphan. She's sent to 'Bengal or Barbadoes or

wherever' – in trivial Camilla's contemptuous words – on one of
the 'fishing fleets'. These took a girl from England to India to
look for a husband. Cecilia is as appalled at the transaction as Jane
Fairfax at the idea of becoming a governess:

> tho' infinitely against her inclinations [she] had been necessi-
> tated to embrace the only possibility that was offered to her, of a
> Maintenance; Yet it was *one*, so opposite to all her ideas of Pro-
> priety, so contrary to her Wishes, so repugnant to her feelings,
> that she would almost have preferred Servitude to it, had Choice
> been allowed her—.

Cecilia is duly married in Bengal to 'a Man of double her own age,
whose disposition was not amiable, and whose Manners were
unpleasing'. She's unhappy, with a 'hopelessness of sorrow'. It's a
bleak picture. She'd 'almost' have preferred 'Servitude' – being a
governess, presumably.

When Camilla says she's heard Cecilia called lucky to be
'equipped' (that is, rigged out for the journey) and to have found
a rich husband, the response is bitter:

> do you call it lucky, for a Girl of Genius and Feeling to be sent
> in quest of a Husband to Bengal, to be married there to a Man
> of whose Disposition she has no opportunity of judging till her
> Judgement is of no use to her, who may be a Tyrant, or a Fool
> or both for what she knows to the Contrary. Do you call *that*
> fortunate?

Jane Austen knew about this 'trade'. Her father's sister Philadelphia
had taken the passage to India. She found a husband and became
the mother of Jane's cousin Eliza de Feuillide. This flamboyant
and spirited young lady married a Frenchman who claimed to be a
count; he was guillotined in 1794. Eliza attracted both James and
Henry Austen while her vibrant personality, charm and French
culture much impressed young Jane. Later Eliza married Henry
and suffered much ill health before her early death in 1813.

LADY EAST

People of all ages and places who have enough time on their hands have worried about their volatile symptoms. In her self-preoccupation Mary Wollstonecraft resembles a multitude of other middle-class women who, by the end of the eighteenth and beginning of the nineteenth centuries, became uninhibited in physical and mental self-expression. They believed no self was *too* dull or bland to justify its owner's fascination.

As Austen biographers have tried to bring Jane Austen and Lord Byron together in Murray's drawing room or even on the doorstep of Albemarle Street, so in my biography of Mary Wollstonecraft I tried to find a connection between her and Jane Austen. I too failed, but I discovered a common acquaintance: Lady East of Field Place near Maidenhead.

It was like this: in 1796, following her suicide attempt after betrayal by her lover, Mary Wollstonecraft went to recuperate in Berkshire with her friend Mrs Cotton, a neighbour of Sir William and Lady East, who entertained them both. Lady East was on visiting terms with Jane Austen's wealthy aunt and uncle, the Leigh Perrots of Scarlets. In addition, Lady East's stepson, a frivolous youth called Gilbert, lodged with the Austens to be tutored for Oxford by the Rev George Austen, who was pleased to own a portrait of Sir William. Gilbert East met young Jane in the Steventon parsonage.

I bring in Lady East not primarily because of this tenuous connection but because, while rooting in the archives, I discovered her unpublished diary for the year 1791–2. It underlines my argument that, for some, the nervous *body* rules everything. Lady East is an extreme case but not unique.

Hers is a kind of empirical self-assertion which substitutes moods and bodily sensations for an inner life, religious or intellectual. The nearest she comes to any external moral framework is when, after one of her turns brought on by bingeing on a bun, she admits, 'I *deserve* it for my Gluttony.'

The diary is set against the elegant background of the Easts' grand modern house, Hall Place, in Burchetts Green, Hurley. Something like Mansfield Park, I fancy.

Lady East's diary is an extraordinary intimate and ridiculous document. Some little socialising with family and friends, yes, but mostly a minute account of Lady East's body. With no children and little interest in the philanthropic role of a gentry lady, she had much time for her obsession with her own health and Sir William's.

She records every ache and pain, every drop of blood from her nose. She numbers each dollop of phlegm and vomit from her husband's throat. Once she even berates herself for not listing *all* her symptoms and *all* the remedies tried. Anxiously she worries that she might have missed something.

For every ill there's a physical cause and she shrugs off any notion that the ill might be psychosomatic. She never suggests she should use willpower to control her mind or body. Shortness of breath is due to eating a baked apple, afternoon drowsiness to an imprudent 'very small Raspberry Puff'. She ate 'rhubarb & custard from a tart for supper & had the stomach ache'. She had heartburn, 'I fancy from eating a new bun'; so she takes magnesia and ginger. She damns all fish for causing lowness: 'I eat mackerel for my diner & was quite worn out & exhausted in the evening.' Irritability comes from milk.

Where in previous ages such people would have seen their afflictions in religious terms and used prayer for relief, the Easts have no notion of divine involvement. Instead of calling for a devotional work in his gouty extremity, Sir William sends to London for eight gold and silver fish to watch.

While reading this diary I wondered what exactly ailed Lady East? Was she ill? Possibly not, but she's within the culture of nerves and illness of her moment. She uses the terms we now find absurd, but which then had the currency we give to our own discoveries. When did we start hearing of the immune system, of being immunocompromised, COPD or borderline this or that? Or suffer from stress and anxiety? The medical and cultural are always intertwined, and nebulous complaints become organised and named differently at different times. Neurasthenia, hypochondriasis and hysteria have given way to clinical depression, ME, chronic fatigue and long Covid, all real, all physical, psychological and cultural miseries, but all shiftingly named.

THE POWER OF DEBILITY

'Nerves', Mr Bennet's old friend in *Pride and Prejudice*, are the refuge of his wife when matters don't go her way. She's a comic character, yet there may be hints of a backstory – involving sex, boredom and powerlessness – for she was once as spirited as her boisterous, man-mad daughter Lydia. Similarly with crabby Mary Musgrove in *Persuasion*. Her moaning about her special weakness suggests boredom, energy consuming itself through anger at being, well, marginal, left alone when men are out shooting and young girls are flirting: 'she had no resources for solitude'. Bitter perhaps that from childhood she was less pretty than her sisters, and not chosen first; the Musgrove girls wanted their brother to marry Anne, not Mary. She would have known that. Poor unmaternal Mary, no one likes her.

But these characters are peripheral. Something else is going on in the debility that afflicts the heroines in the later novels: Fanny Price and Anne Elliot, as well as Jane Fairfax, who glows smoulderingly from the margin of *Emma*.

First, Fanny Price lying prone on the sofa.

In Chapter 3, I mentioned the snobby fad of discriminating the lower-middle from the upper-middle class by the words they used. One of the key terms on the 'upper' list was the 'sofa'. Perhaps it had never been just a piece of furniture. It's the subject of a whole book in Cowper's *Task*: 'I sing the Sofa,' he begins, then goes on to describe it giving ease to the 'gouty limb' and suiting the old and nervous – and female. For Cowper it was a symbol of British pro-gress – 'the growth of what is excellent' – and of a refined present. When set down in foreign lands, however, it becomes decadent. In Byron's late poem *Don Juan* the sofa is a sensual 'low soft Ottoman' and, in reports of the scandalous doings of the Prince Regent's estranged wife, so entertaining to the British public, Princess Caroline is described lolling on a sofa in un-English heat.

In Jane Austen's fiction the sofa is usually lounged or lain upon by the powerful or demanding in their domestic world. After Lydia's elopement and before the arranged marriage, Mrs Bennet lies there disturbing the whole household. In *Emma* Mrs Churchill 'has not been able to leave the sopha for a week together' and in *Persuasion* Mary Musgrove reclines on one until rescued by her upright sister Anne. All are insufferable women.

Fanny Price is different. She's now in her late teens, not afflicted by any named disease, but so weakened by picking roses in the sun in the Park that she has to lie down on a sofa. (The only other character to be so afflicted by the sun is Mrs Elton in *Emma* after picking strawberries: she's more tranced into incoherence by the sun than debilitated.) The scene is played as a sort of trial between prosecutor Mrs Norris and defender Edmund. The contest is over the body of Fanny Price.

Edmund, looking around, said, 'But where is Fanny?—Is she gone to bed?'

'No, not that I know of,' replied Mrs. Norris; 'she was here a moment ago.'

Her own gentle voice speaking from the other end of the room, which was a very long one, told them that she was on the sofa. Mrs. Norris began scolding.

'That is a very foolish trick, Fanny, to be idling away all the evening upon a sofa. Why cannot you come and sit here, and employ yourself as *we* do? … it is a shocking trick for a young person to be always lolling upon a sofa. …'

'Fanny,' said Edmund, after looking at her attentively; 'I am sure you have the headach?'

She could not deny it, but said it was not very bad.

'I can hardly believe you,' he replied; 'I know your looks too well. How long have you had it?'

'Since a little before dinner. It is nothing but the heat.'

'Did you go out in the heat?'

'Go out! to be sure she did,' said Mrs. Norris; 'would you have her stay within such a fine day as this? Were not we *all* out? Even your mother was out to-day for above an hour.'

'Yes, indeed, Edmund,' added her ladyship, who had been thoroughly awakened by Mrs. Norris's sharp reprimand to Fanny; 'I was out above an hour. I sat three quarters of an hour in the flower garden, while Fanny cut the roses ...'

'Fanny has been cutting roses, has she?'

'Yes, and I am afraid they will be the last this year. Poor thing! *She* found it hot enough, but they were so full blown, that one could not wait.'

'There was no help for it certainly,' rejoined Mrs. Norris, in a rather softened voice; 'but I question whether her headach might not be caught *then*, sister. There is nothing so likely to give it as standing and stooping in a hot sun. But I dare say it will be well to-morrow. Suppose you let her have your aromatic vinegar; I always forget to have mine filled.'

'She has got it,' said Lady Bertram; 'she has had it ever since she came back from your house the second time.'

'What!' cried Edmund; 'has she been walking as well as cutting roses; walking across the hot park to your house, and doing it twice, ma'am?—No wonder her head aches.' ...

'... unluckily, Fanny forgot to lock the door of the room and bring away the key, so she was obliged to go again.'

Edmund got up and walked about the room, saying, '... it has been a very ill-managed business.'

...

'If Fanny would be more regular in her exercise, she would not be knocked up so soon. She has not been out on horseback now this long while, and I am persuaded, that when she does not ride, she ought to walk.'

Mrs Norris can't hide her irritation at seeing a lowly person like her niece 'idling away all the evening' on a sofa. It's 'a very foolish trick', she snaps. It's close to what her sister Lady Bertram does. Perhaps that lady's fashionable lethargy was one of the 'tricks', along with her beauty, that delivered her a rich husband. In which case, Mrs Norris is displacing her annoyance from her privileged sister onto her niece. She's quick to bring Lady Bertram into the argument, making the pair of sister and niece into two femininely delicate creatures. Then she goes further, forming herself and her sister into rivals to appeal to Edmund. Which aunt is to blame for Fanny's headache?

The battle is won, as it must be, by the supine lady of the house, 'the picture of health, wealth, ease, and tranquillity'. Lady Bertram candidly admits how the heat befuddled her, making again the link with delicate Fanny that Mrs Norris so much dreads.

The phrase 'picture of health', with an added adjective, is repeated in *Emma* where the heroine becomes the 'complete picture of grown-up health' in Mrs Weston's eyes. In Emma, adulthood includes the energy and spirits so lacking in healthy but almost vegetable Lady Bertram.

Mrs Norris has to accept Fanny's headache as real, though insisting that it's temporary. Deflecting Edmund's charge that she's persecuted her niece, she insists like Lady East that bodily pains have material causes; so she offers her niece a *physical* not a mental or social remedy: the stimulant of aromatic vinegar. Later, bested again in her effort to impose physical meaning on Fanny's debility, she proposes exercise.

Yes, the sun was hot, yes Fanny had a headache. But it's difficult for the reader not to see other factors at work. Fanny forgets to lock the spare room in the parsonage. We wouldn't expect her to be so careless. Was she headachy by then, feeling faint, sick from the sun or already letting jealousy infect her mind because Edmund was away with Mary Crawford?

It's left to Edmund to make the episode into a social sickness, an 'ill-managed business'. He's firmly on the side of feminine delicacy here. When Mrs Norris asserts her own activity, energy and robust health – three times a day in all weathers she takes the walk that's knocked out Fanny – Edmund makes the aunt's energy seem unfeminine.

At the close of the incident, Edmund offers Fanny 'a glass of Madeira'. The kindly action brings to her mind and the reader's that first kindness to the little girl on the stairs when Edmund began the process of becoming brother, father and finally best beloved of his cousin.

Fanny would rather not have drunk the wine – she wants no physical remedy – 'but the tears which a variety of feelings created, made it easier to swallow than to speak'. Those feminine 'tears', along with the headache, have worked on Edmund. The blame swirling round Fanny's debilitated body moving from Mrs Norris to Lady Bertram and back has landed finally on himself. The four days of flirting with Mary Crawford in the field made possible by his offering Mary Fanny's pony to ride are now seen as a betrayal of his cousin. Mary, a natural rider unlike any Austen heroine and certainly unlike frightened Fanny, has engrossed the horse and Edmund with it. He resolves to check Mary's (and his) 'pleasure' to help Fanny back to health.

To emphasise the confusion of physical pain and mental disarray, in pops the narrator to bring the clarity Fanny will not, even in her moments of introspection, quite let herself achieve:

> The state of her spirits had probably had its share in her indisposition; for she had been feeling neglected, and been struggling against discontent and envy for some days past. As she leant on the sofa, to which she had retreated that she might not be seen, the pain of her mind had been much beyond that in her head; and the sudden change which Edmund's kindness had then occasioned, made her hardly know how to support herself.

Picking roses, running errands and feeling surges of jealousy, it's an achy mix in which the mind's pain predominates over the head's. It's the period's problems caught in a nutshell. I'll return to female headaches in the next chapter. They demand a section to themselves.

Edmund offers Madeira to heal a breaking heart. In *Sense and Sensibility* Mrs Jennings suggests expensive Constantia wine (once used for her dead husband's 'cholicky gout') to soothe Marianne's lovesickness. A little foolish perhaps but, when Marianne has a respite during her severe self-inflicted illness,

Elinor administers 'cordials'. Both she and Mrs Jennings have George Cheyne's support: in his *Essay on Health and Long Life*, he wrote that for women of 'weak nerves … the only Remedy for them, is drinking *Bristol* Water and red Wine, with a *low* and *light Diet*'.

In *Mansfield Park* the Madeira is unimportant, the confusion of mind and body absurd: the giver is everything.

Similar delicate irony tinges another episode with Fanny, this time in hectic Portsmouth.

Mr Price is reading the newspaper when he comes across the notice of a 'matrimonial *fracas*', as the reporter terms it, concerning his niece, now Maria Rushworth. She has eloped from her husband's house with Henry Crawford, up to this point Fanny's declared suitor. His response is robust:

> by G— if she belonged to *me*, I'd give her the rope's end as long as
> I could stand over her. A little flogging for man and woman too,
> would be the best way of preventing such things.

Like most people living before our more compassionate times, Jane Austen approved corporal punishment, the changing of behaviour by paining the body. Once, noting little Charles Lefroy's 'want of Discipline', she hoped he'd get 'a wholesome thump, or two, whenever it is necessary'. Mr Price assumes that, had Maria been properly disciplined, she would have behaved better in society. Although he's not considering corporal punishment, the same thought on a higher plane strikes his brother-in-law Sir Thomas: in the upbringing of his girls, discipline of one sort or another has been wanting. There's a belief in coercion within the attitude of both men.

I came near to corporal punishment in a Welsh primary school. The teacher beat his little pupils with a cricket bat if we spelt a word wrong in the morning test. Offenders lined up, one or two whimpering, then bent over to offer their buttocks. I was not beaten because I quickly became good at spelling, a skill I failed to transfer to typewriting. I'd have chosen a beating over the jovial humiliation that was the alternative when I came back to the school from somewhere exotic and failed to explain where I'd been to the teacher and tittering class. Both were geographically challenged, I now realise, from having seen only the crude canvas map on the classroom wall presenting a world mostly coloured bright imperial red; I was frozen with fear as I saw the teacher confuse Burma with Bermuda. But 'choice' was not a word in 1950s education.

Fanny of course responds to the matrimonial '*fracas*' with all the force of her nature, letting the news of adultery overwhelm body and mind:

> the night was totally sleepless. She passed only from feelings of sickness to shudderings of horror; and from hot fits of fever to cold. The event was so shocking, that there were moments even when her heart revolted from it as impossible—when she thought it could not be. A woman married only six months ago, a man professing himself devoted, even *engaged*, to another—that other her near relation—the whole family, both families connected as they were by tie upon tie, all friends, all intimate together!—it was too horrible a confusion of guilt, too gross a complication of evil, for human nature, not in a state of utter barbarism, to be capable of!—

Assuming her own response universal, Fanny believes none of the family can survive the horror: it was

> scarcely possible for them to support life and reason under such disgrace; and it appeared to her, that as far as this world alone was concerned, the greatest blessing to every one of kindred with Mrs. Rushworth would be instant annihilation.

In *Sense and Sensibility* with Marianne – and in E*mma* with Jane Fairfax – these moments of 'hysterical' physical response to mental suffering, the nervous sick feelings and shuddering, are seen from the outside: Elinor is looking at Marianne, Mr Perry the apothecary is treating Jane. Here, the trauma is described from within, it's Fanny's sense of things we get, albeit delivered in that crafty free indirect speech.

Fanny's *moral* response is not mocked – Maria has done a terrible thing to herself and her family – but is that physical response just a little extreme? The use of the sentimental techniques for arousing pathos so ridiculed in Jane Austen's childhood writings – the dashes, underlining/italics, exclamation marks and run-on verbless phrases – suggests that the reaction might be over the top.

Mary Crawford downgrades adultery to 'folly' rather than, as Fanny sees it, a manifestation of 'guilt' and 'evil'. With her 'perversion of mind', Mary proposes to smooth over what Edmund calls 'the dreadful crime' and integrate Maria back into society with a series of 'good dinners, and large parties'. She's wickedly wrong of course, but the narrator's urbane comment that she hopes the cuckold will, if duped again, be duped with better humour and luck lets in a little air between the reader and poor, insomniac, shuddering Fanny.

Fanny's response to the adultery of Maria Rushworth and Henry Crawford goes far beyond her debility in the Mansfield drawing room. Her wan trembling lasts for days. Then Edmund comes to the rescue, this time with a magic letter rather than Madeira. He thinks he's delivering painful news but, for Fanny, his letter offers her all she desires. In a twinkling, she turns from abject misery and expectation of the annihilation of the whole Bertram family to the 'exquisite' happiness of a 'heart in a glow'.

It's pretty clear where Jane Austen thinks the power lies between body and mind – most of the time. Following her brother Henry's severe illness, she notes his 'self-persuasion of Improvement'.

Jane Fairfax has the combined bodily weakness and mental pain of Fanny Price. She arrives in Highbury already anxious over the secret engagement with Frank and suffering from a 'long-standing cold'. We see her in the claustrophobic Bates apartment where, like Emma in 'The Watsons', she's been deposited after a life of elegance – or like Fanny in Portsmouth after her years at

Mansfield. The psychosocial situation in which she finds herself is delicately delivered and yet, like Fanny's, the ailment itself and her almost tragic trajectory are again (comically) interrupted by amorous good luck.

In the free indirect speech of healthy Emma, she

> need no longer be unhappy about Jane, whose troubles and whose ill health having, of course, the same origin, must be equally under cure.—Her days of insignificance and evil were over.—She would soon be well, and happy, and prosperous.—

Of course.

Vigorous Emma Woodhouse knows the difference between the psychosomatic and the solely physical. When Mr Elton calls her visit to sick Harriet a 'cordial', Emma responds tartly:

> My visit was of use to the nervous part of her complaint, I hope; but not even I can charm away a sore throat.

Fever-ridden Marianne, ailing Fanny Price, fragile Jane Fairfax, don't they all perk up wonderfully when rescued into love and matrimony?

Finally, to *Persuasion*, which gives one of the most moving depictions of nervous depression in early literature. Yet, there's something incongruous about its context within a book which delivers so many *physical* diseases and mishaps.

Considering this is a work that lets in the naval war as no other, it's droll that people suffer damage on land more often than at sea. Only Captain Harville has actually been wounded in war (in *Mansfield Park* Fanny's father is 'disabled for active service' but we never hear why) and only the unappreciated Musgrove son has actually died. The energetic Crofts are in Bath because the

Admiral may have gout. Mrs Smith is there for her rheumatic fever. Little Charles Musgrove suffers a dislocated collar bone, and the concussion suffered by his young aunt Louisa after her impulsive leap off the Cobb reduces her to the nervous state of her moaning sister-in-law Mary. Even robust Mrs Croft manages to get a blister on her heel from too much walking the streets for the Admiral's benefit; he's told to walk to help his gout.

Physically unscathed, Anne Elliot escapes from nervous melancholy into mental health when her lover comes back to her.

Like Fanny Price, like Jane Fairfax.

A TOWN MADE FOR THE AILING BODY

The ailing characters in Austen's fiction, including the hypochondriacs and nervously self-indulgent, are prelude to a whole society of the sick and imagined sick in 'Sanditon' – written when Austen herself was gravely ill and (as we know, although she didn't) close to death. It's not quite an anti-medical satire in the manner of her predecessor, the medical novelist Tobias Smollett, but it does a fine job of mocking body-obsessives, patent-medicine quacks and the tribe of health entrepreneurs who congregated at the new seaside resorts.

In *Emma* Mr Woodhouse is a picture of nervous indulged debility. He exists on a diet of thin gruel and small eggs boiled very soft. How Mr Parker and Lady Denham would have rejoiced at the arrival of this rich exhausted man in their resort! That is, if he'd ever agreed to stir from Highbury and visit Sanditon instead of North-Sea Cromer, which his attentive apothecary holds 'to be the best of all the sea-bathing places'.

Instead, they host Tom Parker's sister, Diana. Before Charlotte Heywood settles into being the observer in the novel, Diana reveals her own, her sister Susan's, and her fat lazy brother Arthur's infirmities in a zesty letter to her credulous brother:

> We have entirely done with the whole medical tribe. We have consulted physician after physician in vain, till we are quite convinced that they can do nothing for us and that we must trust

to our own knowledge of our own wretched constitutions for any relief.—… my feelings tell me too plainly that in my present state, the sea air would probably be the death of me.—And neither of my dear companions will leave me, or I would promote their going down to you for a fortnight. But in truth, I doubt whether Susan's nerves would be equal to the effort. She has been suffering much from the headache and six leeches a day for ten days together relieved her so little that we thought it right to change our measures—and being convinced on examination that much of the evil lay in her gum, I persuaded her to attack the disorder there. She has accordingly had three teeth drawn, and is decidedly better, but her nerves are a good deal deranged. She can only speak in a whisper—and fainted away twice this morning on poor Arthur's trying to suppress a cough. He, I am happy to say, is tolerably well—though more languid than I like—and I fear for his liver.

When the eccentric trio arrive in Sanditon, they hole up in lodgings where they toast themselves in front of a fire and obsess about cocoa and butter. Mr Woodhouse believes cold air shouldn't touch heated bodies and he wants windows closed during the dance at the Crown Inn: the Parker siblings agree. They shut out a 'beautiful view of the sea' and a 'very fair English summer-day'.

It seems that none intends to dip into salt water.

Cold water bathing had been promoted for health from the early to mid-eighteenth century and by the time the Napoleonic Wars ended, England's south coast was a string of resorts to exploit the fashion. Jane Austen's imaginary Sanditon is the latest. Cowper looked askance at such places. Jumped-up and artificial, they ruined old ways and crafts through following an urban fashion for novelty. In them, visitors, sick and well, were prey to shoddy amusement, morbid restlessness and quacks, while locals were ruined for honest labour.

Contemplating the mushrooming resorts, the reforming journalist William Cobbett drily remarked that they had no commerce or agriculture, no purpose beyond catering for migrants' pleasure and nervous ailments, so were 'very pretty to behold; but dismal to think of' – all metaphorically built on shifting sand, all Sanditons.

More sustained ridicule came from Thomas Skinner Surr's *The Magic of Wealth*, which described the rich banker Flimflam creating 'Flimflam-town' to become 'a magnet of Fashion', with the help of sidekicks Puff and Rattle. The book mocks the 'trafficking spirit of the times' that has replaced the stationary gentry values of Mr Oldways. The resort project crumbles and Mr Flimflam goes bankrupt.

Perhaps this was the intended fate of Sanditon, built on speculation and with limited Mr Parker and greedy Lady Denham at its helm. Or perhaps it would in the end make money by catering to the 'little fever[s] & indisposition[s]' that had been the fashion in Lyme Regis, with the help of brisk Diana Parker and her imaginative proselytising.

There'll always be nerves to treat.

CHAPTER 6
The Unruly Body

Jane Austen's England was racked by epidemics. Typhus, typhoid, influenza, smallpox and cholera spread in the great unsanitary manufacturing towns that had expanded so dramatically through the North and Midlands. Within the countryside, too, disease flourished, with poor harvests, depressed wages and malnutrition.

In city and country alike, measles, mumps and scarlet fever killed babies and children, while puerperal fever and poor obstetrics destroyed their mothers. Partly through fear that epidemics would spread from lower to higher classes, 'houses of recovery' were founded in the 1790s. Beds were – as far as possible – disinfected after a corpse was removed.

Travel was limited and people often stayed their whole lives in one place. So a particular noxious strain of a fever could – unlike today – remain localised. But one large group of people was on the move throughout the nation. The country was at war during almost all Jane Austen's adult life and troops spread new infections caught in India, the Caribbean, France or Spain. An especially virulent epidemic occurred in 1815, when the Napoleonic Wars ended and weary troops returned from the Continent and farther afield.

Without experiencing anything like the recent Covid pandemic, Jane Austen saw much more illness and premature death than most of us will see in longer lifetimes. But contemporary responses to spreading disease were not far from ours: isolation and an anxious search for remedies. In *Sense and Sensibility* an infectious fever in their house causes the worthy but irritating Palmers to decamp in haste with their susceptible new-born son. At boarding school in the port city of Southampton, young Jane Austen nearly died in a typhus epidemic: she was saved when, hearing of the outbreak, her mother rushed from Steventon to snatch her away.

Might Jane Austen's severe childhood illness have contributed to her early death? Some diseases linger in the system and pounce when a person is weakest.

OBSERVING ILLNESS

In almost every letter Jane Austen mentions some kind of bodily ailment, hers or others', but there is little extensive lamenting. Perhaps she avoided the protracted complaining of Lady East and Mary Wollstonecraft because she was buoyed up by a stronger Christian faith or had a more robustly sceptical and equable temperament. Whatever the case, the letters record a succession of physical ailments, from colds to headaches, all of which she made light of:

> I caught a small cold in my way down & had some pain every eveng– not to last long, but rather severer than it had been lately. This has worn off however & I have scarcely felt anything for the last two days.

In 1807 she mentions having 'hooping cough' but simply as a topic of correspondence; whooping cough could be a dangerous disease for an adult, but we hear no more of it. She makes a joke of 'scarlet fever' (along with the superiority of aunts) in a letter to her niece Anna, now married to Ben Lefroy:

> I dare say Ben was in love with me once, & w^d never have thought of *You* if he had not supposed me dead of a Scarlet fever.

Outside the immediate family, Austen was reticent about symptoms; she confined most details to letters for Cassandra. Like sex, so overwritten in our time, so underwritten in hers, physical states were not for public airing. Illnesses are touched on and embedded in the humdrum, often comic, business of life. Austen rarely dwells long on the ailing body.

In this respect alone she was fortunate not to have grown old; for the aged, the body is preoccupation, fascination and constant cause for lament.

Austen tended to believe that brisk walks outdoors and a dose of rhubarb could do much. She describes nursing herself 'into as beautiful a state as I can'. By contrast, she castigated her brothers Charles and Henry for their habit of illness. Charles has 'a sad turn for being unwell' and 'Dearest Henry! What a turn he has for being ill'. Despite much poor health, Henry long outlived his sister.

Deploring the self-pity and petulance exhibited by the ailing and semi-ailing, Jane Austen can in her letters (and novels indeed) seem unsympathetic. A distant relative is

> the sort of woman who gives me the idea of being determined never to be well—& who likes her spasms & nervousness & the consequence they give her, better than anything else.

Another, wife of Edward Bridges (possibly once her own suitor), is called a 'poor honey', synonym here for the hypochondriac—although, ruefully, she'll use the same phrase for herself when she falls (fatally) ill.

Mostly she mentions colds, the plague of the English past and present in our damp patch of earth. Always someone seems to have one. Now Elizabeth Knight at Godmersham, now Mary Austen in the Steventon rectory (a heavy cold this time), now brother Henry in London, now a brace of children all with colds and sore throats. Jane's mother's colds of course linger longest.

Then there's gout. Often regarded as a disease of the wealthy and self-indulged, it's no surprise that her landowning brother Edward and her uncle James Leigh Perrot should suffer from it. Both were rich men.

As one might expect, gout became the speciality of the expensive urban physician. In practice in the spa town of Bath, Dr Caleb Parry concentrated on his rich gouty patients. The Bridges of Goodnestone Park were frequent clients. Fascinated, Jane Austen watched the interaction and treatment. Dr Parry seems

> to be half starving Mr Bridges; for he is restricted to much such a Diet as James's Bread, Water and Meat, & is never to eat so much of that as he wishes;–& he is to walk a great deal, walk till he drops, I believe, Gout or no Gout.

The Dowager Lady Bridges suffered from gout but there's no mention of her walking. Perhaps it wasn't necessary, for, as befitted a titled lady, hers was 'a good sort of Gout'. She was

> to spend the winter at Bath!—It was just decided on.—Dr Parry wished it,—not from thinking the Water necessary to Lady B.— but that he might be better able to judge how far his Treatment of her, which is totally different from anything she had been used to—is right; & I suppose he will not mind having a few more of her Ladyship's guineas.—His system is a Lowering one. He took twelve ounces of Blood from her when the Gout appeared, & forbids Wine, &c.

With so many well-off patients, Dr Parry could be calm about losing one: 'Dr Parry does not expect Mr E. to last much longer.'

Dr Parry's methods seem to have been a mix of externals, like taking the spa waters and exercising, and the more extreme bleeding and cupping. Other sufferers tried more eccentric remedies. Jane's brother Edward

> drinks at the Hetling Pump, is to bathe tomorrow, & try Electricity on Tuesday;—he proposed the latter himself to Dr Fellowes,

who made no objection to it, but I fancy we are all unanimous in expecting no advantage from it.

The 'Hetling Pump' room suited Edward. A pamphlet of 1820 described it as 'handsomely furnished and admirably suited for the invalid … the celebrated thermal springs of Bath issue from marble vases'. Electric shock treatment as a form of stimulation was sometimes prescribed although it was not common: relatives and friends regarded it as theatre and would assemble to watch the patient being jolted into health.

While Dr Parry dealt with rich fashionable clients in rich fashionable Bath, out in the shires there was only an apothecary or a surgeon to treat the sick. John Lyford, the surgeon of Basingstoke, often makes an appearance in Jane Austen's letters from the Steventon rectory.

A long, three-day journey thoroughly discomposed Mrs Austen:

my Mother began to suffer from the exercise & fatigue of travelling so far, & she was a good deal indisposed from that particular kind of evacuation which has generally preceded her Illnesses—. She had not a very good night at Staines, & felt a heat in her throat as we travelled yesterday morning, which seemed to foretell more Bile—.'

Too much information? Perhaps. But you can almost hear poor Mrs Austen, never a good traveller, telling her daughter how she suffered, and calling attention to her diarrhoea. Jane won't give her mother quite so much room for expression in her letters as the years go by.

After the ladies arrive back in Steventon, Mr Lyford prescribes drops of laudanum to Mrs Austen to help her sleep: they act 'as a Composer'. He will, he promises, call on her again, and perhaps add 'Dandelion Tea'. The nightly laudanum is measured out by Jane, who in the absence of Cassandra has temporarily taken over the caring.

Mr Lyford made his call while the family was at dinner and was invited to stay, for he was a gentlemanly man of good family (Jane danced with his son John and was friends with his daughter Susannah). Happily, unlike the sisters in 'The Watsons', disturbed at their frugal meal in a poorer rectory, Jane was unashamed of the 'elegant' fare they had to offer: 'some pease-soup, a sparerib, and a pudding'. After the meal, Mr Lyford much commended the Revd George Austen's mutton.

Details of the menu are followed by the alarming suggestion that Mr Lyford wanted his patient 'to look yellow and throw out a rash, but she will do neither'.

Jane Austen's letters ramble on mentioning physical ills and their remedies, bitters and leeches, teas and Steele's lavender water. The hartshorn (antler shavings mixed with ammonia), used in *Sense and Sensibility* to calm Marianne after Willoughby's brutal rejection at the party, is taken in life by Cassandra. She also took Huxham, a tincture of cinchona bark or quinine, and magnesia.

In her younger days Jane Austen records few visits to doctors, but she does note seeing Mr Lyford later when in the neighbourhood. The consultation was more for his sake than her own, at least so she claims. Her problem was earache:

> as I was determined that he sh^d not lose every pleasure I consult-
> ed him on my complaint. He recommended cotton, moistened
> with oil of sweet almonds, & it has done me good.

The remedy worked: 'Mr Lyford's prescription has entirely cured me'.

Through letters and novels Austen shows how much she admired those who make the best of things under severe pain, those who try 'mental Physick' rather than concocted potions.

The attitude is caught best in *Persuasion*'s Mrs Smith. Despite her 'cheerless situation', she lives mainly in the present and doesn't cling to a better past or hope too much for what may come. Impoverished, confined and in pain, she shows to her old schoolfriend Anne Elliot that elasticity of mind, that disposition to be comforted, that power of turning readily from evil to good, and of finding employment which carried her out of herself, which was from Nature alone. It was the choicest gift of Heaven.

NURSING

Austen was irreverent about the great business of women: childbearing. '[H]ow can she honestly be breeding again?' she exclaimed over a woman of thirty-three, now bearing her eighth child. Of her niece Anna, pregnant again after bearing two children, she wrote:

> Poor Animal, she will be worn out before she is thirty.—I am very sorry for her.—Mrs Clement too is in that way again. I am quite tired of so many Children.—Mrs Benn has a 13th—

For Mr and Mrs Deedes, who had just welcomed their eighteenth child into the world, she recommended 'the simple regimen of separate rooms'.

Lady Middleton is appalled when her mother refers openly to her younger sister's pregnancy, but even the spinster couldn't avoid the childbed. Unmarried sisters very often had to serve as unpaid nurses to their breeding in-laws.

In *Persuasion* Mrs Smith and Anne discuss the business of nursing. As so often, Anne shows herself an idealist. A lady visitor to the poor lodgings, she hasn't even seen the professional Nurse Rooke, who has let her into the chamber, yet she takes an heroic attitude towards nursing in general. Disabled Mrs Smith, who knows more of the reality, presumably through Rooke's gossip as well as her own experience, punctures this idealism.

Of the professional nurse, Anne comments:

> What instances must pass before them of ardent, disinterested, self-denying attachment, of heroism, fortitude, patience, resignation—of all the conflicts and all the sacrifices that ennoble us most. A sick chamber may often furnish the worth of volumes.

Mrs Smith is unconvinced:

> 'Yes,' said Mrs. Smith more doubtingly, 'sometimes it may, though
> I fear its lessons are not often in the elevated style you describe.
> Here and there, human nature may be great in times of trial, but
> generally speaking it is its weakness and not its strength that
> appears in a sick chamber; it is selfishness and impatience rather
> than generosity and fortitude, that one hears of.'

Anne is well aware at Kellynch of the family's duties to the lower
orders, but in Bath she doesn't notice the woman with Mrs Smith,
and her friend has to tell her that it is Nurse Rooke. Nursing outside the family was a lowly activity and there were many stories of
neglect, drunkenness and theft. Years later in *Martin Chuzzlewit*
Charles Dickens would immortalise the type in bibulous Sairey
Gamp, but the image was already current. One reason for the low
status was that, in respectable houses, nursing was mainly done
by a trusted servant in the family – or that spinster relative.

When Louisa Musgrove is concussed and thought dead, her
sister Henrietta faints and her sister-in-law has hysterics. Captain
Wentworth staggers against the wall in a fine show of male bewil-
derment in the face of collapsing femininity. (In *Sense and Sensibility*,
faced with his wife's loud and demanding hysterics, John Dashwood
is similarly incapable. According to down to earth Mrs Jennings,
'he walked about the room, and said he did not know what to do'.)
Anne Elliot or less genteel 'experienced' Mrs Harville could nurse
the wounded girl until a better carer is proposed. Charles Musgrove
goes to Uppercross to bring

> a far more useful person in the old nursery-maid of the family,
> one who having brought up all the children, and seen the last,
> the very last, the lingering and long-petted master Harry, sent to
> school after his brothers, was now living in her deserted nursery
> to mend stockings, and dress all the blains and bruises she could
> get near her.

In an earlier discussion on nursing, this time with her sister and brother-in-law in Uppercross, Anne is adamant that the nurse's role is female:

> Nursing does not belong to a man, it is not his province. A sick child is always the mother's property, her own feelings generally make it so.

In this case they don't, for the mother is Mary Musgrove, always eager to escape her uncontrollable children.

Thomas Gisborne, a self-appointed authority on women, wrote in *Duties of the Female Sex* that nursing and caring were feminine roles. They are the 'unassuming and virtuous activity' peculiar to the female character, he declared, which is to contribute

> daily and hourly to the comfort of husbands, of parents, of brothers and sisters, and of other relations, connections and friends, in the intercourse of domestic life, under every vicissitude of sickness and health, of joy and affliction.

Although she was away working as a companion, when her mother fell seriously ill Mary Wollstonecraft as the oldest girl of the family was summoned home to nurse. It was simply what was expected, whatever the girl's talents and whatever activities were interrupted.

When the Parkers are overturned in their coach on the wrong rocky road, ironically looking for a surgeon to lure to Sanditon, they're obliged to stay with the hospitable Heywoods. Again, the nursing duties are carried out by the eldest daughter still at home. Charlotte tends Mr Parker and his ankle. Her reward is a visit to the seaside to watch and judge a whole cast of supposedly ill characters. In *Emma* despite her enjoyment of elegant Hartfield, when sickening for a fever and in need of nursing, young Harriet Smith is eager to get back to school where she can be nursed by her substitute mother, Mrs Goddard.

Observing the various trips of the Austen sisters recorded in the letters, you can see they were dispatched here and there to be of use to brothers, their wives and numerous children. But it doesn't seem that Jane gloried in the role, unlike her character Anne Elliot, or indeed much wanted it for herself any more than she wanted much to do with housekeeping. She did her duty, however, and there she was – though more often there Cassandra was – at the many afflictions and physical dramas of the sprawling family: the confinements, the fevers and chronic complaints, the expected deaths. Off each spinster sister went, even when 'dog-tired'.

Family care was the norm when I was young, before the NHS established the notion of care by an institution outside the home – or in someone else's home. Just about every family had an elderly or disabled person with them cared for by women, the spinster daughter if one were available. Those without money and suitable relations were deposited in an 'asylum' or 'hospital', and, even when good provision was provided, the association of institutional care with pauperism lingered. In mid-Wales there was a huge psychiatric establishment at Talgarth that served the mentally disabled and elderly lacking money or supportive family. The place was designed to be self-sufficient, with workshops and its own farm, but it cast a grim shadow over the minds of anyone who feared to be 'sent away'. 'Don't send me to Talgarth.' I heard that often. The place closed in 1999 and is now derelict. Apparently, the slates on its sprawling roofs were its most valuable asset.

Some years ago I visited Talgarth, the name stigmatised even in my mind. I was hugely pleased to be talking at the jolly and very big Hay Festival and I found accommodation nearby in Talgarth. The B&B was good and the town attractive even in drizzle, but, there we go, names are imprinted on minds and aren't easily dislodged.

In the Austen family, the mentally disabled brother George was sent away to live with another family for the remainder of his life, not placed in an institution. In *Jane Eyre*, the madwoman was at home in the attic.

ILLNESS IN FICTION

After riding through the rain to Netherfield Park, shivery Jane Bennet in *Pride and Prejudice* has to be accommodated in one of Mr Bingley's spare bedrooms, with consequences that Mrs Bennet has foreseen. This has the added advantage of bringing her bright-eyed sister to Netherfield and into the constant presence of rich Mr Darcy.

Though Mrs Bennet dismisses the danger, it was a risk. Even slight symptoms could lead to lingering death. Medically trained, the poet John Keats understood at once what a sore throat meant, what that first drop of blood from the nose might foretell.

Something of this inflects the inset story within *Sense and Sensibility*, related in very different tone to the dramatised part of the novel. It describes Colonel Brandon's beloved cousin suffering a life of misery and degradation from an initial fall into 'vice', then contracting consumption (modern tuberculosis), then dying. When (in rather unnerving echo) young Marianne grows ill after what starts as a chill from sitting in wet stockings, some of the earlier anxiety touches this later sickness: she ends with a dangerous 'putrid fever'.

Her illness becomes a rite of passage to reform:

> My illness … had been entirely brought on by myself … Had I died,—it would have been self-destruction … I wonder at my recovery,—wonder that the very eagerness of my desire to live, to have time for atonement to my God, and to you all, did not kill me at once.

Marianne changes within a Christian framework. So too does Tom Bertram in *Mansfield Park*: 'He was the better for ever for his illness. … He became what he ought to be.' Although there's no mention of God in the passage, his complete reformation occurs in a novel tilting just a little towards evangelical Christianity. Sudden conversion is rare in Austen and most peripheral characters are like Lydia in *Pride and Prejudice* following her brush with disaster: 'Lydia was Lydia still'. Marianne's near-death experience teaches right thinking and directs her to a more sensible, if less dashing, choice of life partner. But her good resolutions are, unlike Tom Bertram's, characteristically extreme.

Jane Austen will not be so melodramatic again and perhaps there's a mocking self-reference to this earlier novel in *Emma*. Always on the lookout for threats to the body, finicky Mr Woodhouse is troubled about wet stockings. He fusses over Jane Fairfax and her rainy walks to the post office: 'My dear, did you change your stockings?' he enquires.

When I arrived at this point in my book, I had a mind to investigate every ailment of the body mentioned by Jane Austen, to rummage in the fiction and letters, and even follow the family in their private diaries. I thought to pursue 'the spasm', beginning with Marianne Dashwood's 'spasm in her throat' when, following her sister's plea for restraint, she represses any exclamation on hearing Mrs Jennings praise Edward's affections for Lucy Steele instead of Elinor. Then proceed to the 'cough', not always nervous, not always irritating like Mary Bennet's. And so on. But – and there's always a useful quotation to be had from Austen – if I'd gone down this rabbit hole, I'd not have 'time on paper for half that I want to say'.

She also wrote, 'I need not enter into the particulars'. Quite. I'll follow only two complaints; the larger project was the wild dream of an ex-encyclopaedia-maker. Just headache and toothache; but, first, I can't resist a short detour on skin.

THE MODEST SKIN

Charlotte Brontë dismissed Jane Austen as a writer of the surface, not the inner self:

> Her business is not half so much with the human heart as with the human eyes, mouth, hands and feet; what sees deeply, speaks aptly, moves flexibly, it suits her to study, but what throbs fast and full, though hidden, what the blood rushes through, what is the unseen seat of Life and the sentient target of death – this Miss Austen ignores.

Brontë makes of Austen a sort of literary Sir Walter Elliot, never seeing beneath the skin. It feels a little like jealousy, as do so many comments by Virginia Woolf on Jane Austen, whom for the most part she admired. For both great authors, Brontë and Woolf, their predecessor was used to berate them for some skill they themselves were supposed to lack – impersonality in the one, character-creation in the other. It must have been irritating when they were trying to do something quite different.

But Brontë is right about Austen's concern for 'eyes, mouth, hands and feet'. Teeth and skin too.

Sir Walter Elliot, the great connoisseur of skin, his own and other people's, believes himself ageless – does he have tinted mirrors in his dressing-room? He watches for physical signs of decay outside himself. He sees skin degrading all round him: 'Anne haggard, Mary coarse, every face in the neighbourhood worsting'.

Wrinkled Admiral Baldwin looks to Sir Walter like a man in his sixties when he's a mere forty. Thinking on this unfortunate sailor, he imagines Admiral Croft, a man who's seen action at the battle of Trafalgar and travelled to the East Indies, will have a face 'as orange as the cuffs and cape of my livery'. We don't know if his expectation was fulfilled, but Mrs Croft has a 'weather-beaten complexion'.

Likely of similar age to Sir Walter, Lady Russell has developed 'crow's foot' wrinkles at the corners of her eyes; she should, thinks Sir Walter, use rouge. Perhaps if she raised any amorous interest, Sir Walter would cease noticing these wrinkles, as he stops seeing freckles on his steward's charming daughter, Mrs Clay.

To stay fixated on skin is a sign of shallowness in Sir Walter. Similarly in Frank Churchill, who never quite understands the moral worth of his clever, sensitive fiancée. Rather distastefully he enthuses about her skin:

Did you ever see such a skin?—such smoothness! such delicacy!—and yet without being actually fair.— ... a most distinguishing complexion!—So peculiarly the lady in it.—Just colour enough for beauty.

Jane's skin must have been striking, though, for on first meeting after many years Emma also responds to it:

> but the skin, which she had been used to cavil at, as wanting col-
> our, had a clearness and delicacy which really needed no fuller
> bloom.

This skin becomes the source of a little flirtatious banter between Emma and Frank, about which Emma coyly reminds him once all is revealed.

Skin is the location of that most complicated of facial responses, so beloved by novelists: the blush. Samuel Richardson assumed that women hardened in vice couldn't blush; Mrs Norris *reddens* in anger rather than blushes. For Fanny Price, blushing becomes the sign of her modesty, or it might also express the reverse, repressed anger at any offending of this modesty.

In the posthumous biographical notice with which he prefaced *Northanger Abbey* and *Persuasion*, Henry Austen described his sister's complexion as 'of the finest texture'. He drew on lines of the seventeenth-century poet John Donne:

> Her pure, and eloquent blood
> Spoke in her cheekes, and so distinctly wrought,
> That one might almost say, her body thought.

In Henry's version this becomes: 'her eloquent blood spoke through her modest cheek' – his addition being the adjective 'modest'. He's describing his sister as if she were herself a literary creation.

THE HEADACHE: JANE CAVE AND ANNE SHARP

In more romantic fiction than Austen's, a headache may let a lady escape seductive danger. The popular Gothic novelist Regina Maria Roche used the strategy in *Clermont, A Tale*: 'Madeline ... excused herself by pleading a head-ache. Clermont sighed, as he thought that a heart-ache was what she should have said.' *Clermont* was one of the 'horrid' novels recommended by Isabella Thorpe to

2334344444

Catherine Morland in *Northanger Abbey*. Jane Austen's fictional headaches are more realistic, less delicate.

Woolf thought the English language had no words for headache and shivers, but the constant appearance of 'headache' in the list of ailments to be cured by patent medicines suggests how widespread was the malaise affecting temples, skull and neck, however inclusive its labelling. Frequently joined with 'nervous' as we now join it with 'stress' and anxiety, headaches denoted physical and psychological pain. They could be suffered modestly, agonisingly or strategically, as is the case with Roche's Madeline.

Among the modest sufferers is Emma's sister Isabella Knightley. She complains of 'those little nervous head-aches and palpitations which I am never entirely free from any where'. Fanny Price's headache after picking roses is again more akin to a nervous complaint, despite the use of the article 'the headache' suggesting she may be a frequent sufferer. The only agonising headaches afflict Jane Fairfax who, after breaking up with Frank – as we later learn – is declared by the apothecary Mr Perry to be 'suffering under severe headachs, and a nervous fever ... her health seemed for the moment completely deranged'.

A female writer whom Jane Austen might have read was the poet Jane Cave. Both women vacationed at Teignmouth on the Devon coast, though without overlapping, but since Jane Cave used Teignmouth in the title of a poem, it's likely she was featured in the local circulating library or shop, where Jane Austen may have come across her name.

Although Cave was rather below the Austens in social status, her first collection, *Poems on Various Subjects*, had many highly placed subscribers from the Church and Oxford Colleges, with both of which the Austens were connected. No Austens or Leigh Perrots, but there's a Knight and a Papillon, a family connection of the Knights well known to Jane Austen and among the earliest readers of her novels. .

Jane Cave probably suffered from severe migraines. Three poems deal directly with her misery. The first, 'The Head-ach, or, An Ode to Health', was published in a Bristol newspaper and its acceptance of a poem of such length suggests the subject struck a chord in its readers.

> Through ev'ry particle the torture flies,
> But centers in the *temples*, *brain*, and *eyes*;
> The efforts of the hands and feet are vain,
> While bows the head with agonizing pain …

Poor Jane Cave tried any remedy suggested to her; she ran through snuff, patent medicines, blisters, boluses, 'the lancet, leech, and cupping', but still her headaches persisted. The poem ends with a request for help from readers who might know of yet another cure. In 'The Castaway', his startling poem of Calvinist damnation, Cowper notes that 'misery still delights to trace / Its semblance in another's case'. This was so with poor Jane Cave. She was seeking fellow-sufferers.

'The Head-ach, or, An Ode to Health' has the subtitle, 'Written the first morning of the Author's bathing at Teignmouth for the Head-ach'. It was inspired by a second try at a salt-water cure. On the first occasion she approached the cold sea with the kind of trepidation Diana Parker noted in Miss Lambe, brought to Sanditon for curative bathing but presumably used to a rather warmer climate and sea.

Tears coursed down Jane Cave's cheeks and she was fearful that actually plunging into the cold water would unsettle her 'weak afflicted brain', so much so that she'd die from the pain. She surmounted her fears and ducked into the water twice. The submersion was so stimulating that she went on and on. She was experiencing the 'exquisite pain and pleasure' which Mary Wollstonecraft ascribed to those with 'finely fashioned nerves'.

Painful delight was short-lived. The final poem in her collection, the sad 'Invocation to Death', suggests that Jane Cave wanted to die rather than go on suffering. Doctors had become mere predators on the sick: they'd made her waste money on a vain pursuit of health.

In the first headache poem she'd reached out to the newspaper readers for help; here, in despair, she asks that, after her death, her corpse may be dissected so the cause of her suffering can be understood and others might escape her pain.

As I said, Jane Austen may or may not have heard of Jane Cave or read her work – we Janeites do a lot of speculating – but she was certainly a close friend of another migraine-sufferer: the Godmersham governess, Anne Sharp.

In September 1805 Jane, her family and the governess were together at Worthing in Sussex. Whereas the Austens would have been 'dipping' for pleasure and health, like Jane Cave at Teignmouth Anne Sharp would have been looking for some relief from her afflicting headaches. According to Austen's niece Fanny, while aunt Cassandra went into the warmer indoor bath, 'I went with Gmama in the morning to buy fish on the Beach & afterwards with Mama and Miss Sharpe to Bathe where I had a most delicious dip ...' Young Fanny enjoyed it—but what of her governess?

Anne Sharp's severe migraines and the eye problems they brought on meant that she was always in search of remedies and new healers just as Jane Cave had been. She tried such cures as a painful suture in the nape of her neck, electrodes to her head and the cutting off of all her hair. Perhaps Diana Parker's activities in 'Sanditon' aren't so wildly improbable as they first appear.

Possibly Miss Sharp persisted with the quacks and painful remedies because she knew that continued ill health would put paid to her modest prospects. She didn't share her friend's kind fantasy that she might marry a relative of her rich employer and so escape from governessing, like fictional Miss Taylor. She was a teacher and needed to teach for a living.

When out of sorts herself, Jane Austen could be irritated by Anne Sharp's debility, her constant headaches, and her naïve hopes for healers and cures. She ridiculed those who rushed to doctors at every twinge or believed in their nostrums with almost religious fervour. Anne Sharp would 'praise to the heavens the last medical authority consulted, only to be swiftly disillusioned':

> she has been again obliged to exert herself more than ever—
> in a more distressing, more harrassed state—& has met with

another excellent old Physician & his Wife, with every virtue under Heaven who takes to her & cures her from pure Love & Benevolence.

Does this spurt of impatience suggest she's thinking rather of her mother than of her suffering friend, displacing some of her exasperation?

Mrs Austen often complained of her 'complication of disorders' and desire for remedies. 'She seldom gets through the 24 hours without some pain in her head,' wrote Jane and, more tartly, 'Tho' Sunday, my Mother begins it without any ailment.' Nerves, fatigue, always something. On one occasion Jane calls her mother's head-ache 'oppression in *her head*', a variation to which a similarly aged friend responded: this sort of thing was

> frequent at her age & mine. Last year I had for some time the Sensation of a Peck Loaf on my head, & they talked of cupping me, but I came off with a dose or two of calomel & and have never heard of it since.

'Calomel': mercurious chloride, an extreme and unpredictable remedy, very popular at the time and for centuries before. It was used to treat a huge array of ailments from smallpox to cataracts and venereal diseases – and headaches. Powerful, clearly, for here it removes the sensation of a 17-pound loaf of bread from an elderly lady's head.

Although quite different, composed of zinc and ferric oxides, 'cal-amine lotion' invariably swims into my mind. In my hot childhood years, there was no rubbing sunscreen or olive oil on pale vulnerable backs and I regularly burnt. I took joy in peeling off the dead skin where I could reach it; it felt like peeling a ripe mango with the added frisson of a little pain when the flesh came away too. When raw and angry looking, it was doused with calamine lotion which left a covering like pinkish white dust. It gave a penitential look.

Sutures, electrodes, calomel and mercury worry me as a mod-ern reader. Yet what will the future say of our remedies, even our calamine lotion? Some years back, I had early morning sessions with a radiation machine to interrupt a cancer. Such nuclear weapons halt the nasty cells (if you're lucky) but at the price of burning bits that once worked (reasonably) well. A century hence I imagine this treatment will seem as barbaric as calomel, electrodes and mercury. I visualise the great machine propped against a white wall in a future museum displaying the quaint life and dangerous remedies of our period. People will gaze a moment in disbelief, especially if, as seems likely, they'll have survived a nuclear war – like looking at barbed medieval arrows and learning they were shot into people to cure their dysentery or at the triangular boring instruments for trepanning heads.

Time travel goes in both directions. I think I hear Jane Austen giggle at the way we hang on every new drug and cure, how, by adopting new exercise routines and strange exotic food from half-way round the world, we intend to live on and on. I do wonder what she'd have thought of our belief that there must be something that can interrupt the body when once it moves towards its inevitable end. Perhaps the rhubarb and electrodes are no more risible than the nostrums we prefer. The hope's the same.

Anne Sharp quickly regained Jane Austen's sympathy and Jane wrote her last letter from Chawton to her 'dearest Anne', sending affectionate farewell. She described with 'all the Egotism of an Invalid' her own appalling symptoms. She now understood her poor friend all too well.

THE HEADACHE: MARIA BECKFORD
AND JANE AUSTEN

Like most women sewing and reading and writing in poor light, Jane Austen suffered from headaches, but she avoided the horrors experienced by Anne Sharp and Jane Cave. Her own two headache poems are far lighter than Cave's, but she echoes her fellow poet in scepticism about apothecaries' medicines and treatments.

The first poem is about the headache of her friend Maria Beckford. Maria was living at Chawton House, rented from Jane's brother Edward Knight, where she acted as housekeeper for her widowed brother. She was often sickly. 'Poor Miss B. has been suffering again from her old complaint, & looks thinner than ever,' Jane wrote. One day the two ladies, Jane and Maria, walked from Chawton into nearby Alton for Maria to consult the apothecary Mr Newnham. He prescribed calomel.

Relishing the comedy of names throughout her life, Austen has fun with this combination of friend and chemist:

> I've a pain in my head
>   Said the suffering Beckford
> To her Doctor so dread.
>   Oh! what shall I take for't?
>
> Said this Doctor so dread,
>   Whose name it was Newnham.
> For this pain in your head,
>   Ah! what can you do Ma'am?
>
> Said Miss Beckford, Suppose
>   If you think there's no risk,
> I take a good Dose
>   Of calomel, brisk.—
>
> What a praise-worthy notion.
>   Replied Mr. Newnham,
> You shall have such a potion,
>   And so will I too Ma'am.—

Calomel again, the 'brisk' sort.

Headaches were less comical when suffered by Jane Austen herself. She still managed lightness of tone with her quirky rhymes and thudding metre. (I can't rid my mind of W. S. Gilbert's patter song in *Iolanthe*: 'When you're lying awake / With a dismal headache …')

> When stretch'd on one's bed
> With a fierce-throbbing head

Which precludes alike Thought or Repose,
How little one cares
For the grandest affairs
That may busy the world as it goes! —
....
How little the Bells,
Ring they Peels, toll they Knells
Can attract our attention or Ears!—
The Bride may be married,
The Corse may be carried,
And touch nor our hopes nor our fears.

Our own bodily pains
Ev'ry faculty chains;
We can feel on no subject beside.
'Tis in health & in Ease
We the Power must seize
For our friends & our Souls to provide.

Exactly. Jane Austen was a realist as well as a moralist.

TEETH

I've spent the last two years with dental miseries. Knowing well
what Cowper knew:

As life declines, speeds rapidly away,
And not a year but pilfers as he goes
Some youthful grace that age would gladly keep,
A tooth ...

I looked to Jane Austen for help as I held warm pads against an
aching jaw. Here's what I found.

In 'Catharine, or the Bower', the heroine, variously called
Catharine, Catherine or Kitty, cannot go to a ball because she
has a sudden horrid toothache. Her 'friend' Camilla torments her
with irksome pity:

'I wish there were no such things as Teeth in the World; they are nothing but plagues to one, and I dare say that People might easily invent something to eat with instead of them; Poor Thing! what pain you are in! I declare it is quite Shocking to look at you. But you w'ont have it out, will you? For Heaven's sake do'nt; for there is nothing I dread so much. I declare I had rather undergo the greatest Tortures in the World than have a tooth drawn. Well! how patiently you do bear it! how can you be so quiet ? Lord, if I were in your place I should make such a fuss, there would be no bearing me. I should torment you to Death.'

'So you do, as it is,' thought Kitty.

Teeth and toothache don't much feature in the published novels, but in *Emma* Harriet Smith has a 'bad tooth' and needs a dentist. That the tooth requires attention just after Emma has understood that she, rather than Harriet, is the object of Mr Knightley's love provides a convenient excuse for Emma to get the girl she's so befuddled out of Highbury.

Invited by Emma's sister Isabella, Harriet goes off to London in the Woodhouse carriage; how else would she be able to consult a practising dentist instead of a rural tooth-drawer or apothecary? There, in due course the Knightley brothers do their own more successful bit of matchmaking. Faithful love-sick Robert Martin and not-so-foolish Harriet meet as arranged at Astley's Amphitheatre. After the show, Robert Martin can outdo the gallantry of Frank Churchill with the gypsies and Mr Knightley with his invitation to dance by saving 'uneasy' Harriet from the London crowds. Later, under the same roof in Brunswick Square, all is concluded.

As for 'the business', the visit to the dentist, it's resolved early in her stay, but what happened there and what became of the painful tooth we hear nothing.

Jane Austen was seventeen when she wrote 'Catharine, or the Bower', but the same horror she expressed as a teenager recurs in her final fragment written at forty-one. In 'Sanditon' Susan Parker has *three* teeth pulled on a whim. She faints from the extractions but survives to tell the tale. Charlotte Heywood is amazed when she hears of this through Diana's letter to her brother:

> I am astonished at the cheerful style of the Letter, consider-ing the state in which both Sisters appear to be.—Three Teeth drawn at once!—frightful! Your Sister Diana seems almost as ill as possible, but those three Teeth of your Sister Susan's are more distressing than all the rest.—

Susan lives on to self-medicate and talk a great deal, and Diana to bustle around Sanditon taking lodgings for phantom visitors.

Teeth make one starring appearance in Jane Austen's letters. It's unmissable for anyone thinking of consulting a dentist. When staying with her brother Henry in London in September 1813, she accompanied her young nieces Fanny, Marianne and Lizzy Knight to a dentist called Spence.

From the beginning it was a 'sad Business & cost us many tears'. The girls had to suffer a second consultation before the dentist could do anything beyond checking the teeth. Their father came too, perhaps to keep an eye on them and perhaps on the fees as well. They had to return the next day: the dentist was not finished with Lizzy.

> There have been no Teeth taken out however, nor will be I believe, but he finds *hers* in a very bad state, & seems to think particularly ill of their Durableness.—They have been all cleaned, *hers* filed, and are to be filed again. There's a very bad hole between two of her front Teeth.

Still the dentist was not done with 'the poor Girls & their Teeth!'
Worse was to follow in a most 'disagreable hour' (no mention of analgesics). Here's Jane Austen's reaction as spectator (and auditor):

> we were a whole hour at Spence's, & Lizzy's [teeth] were filed & lamented over again & poor Marianne had two taken out after all,

the two just beyond the Eye teeth ... When her doom was fixed, Fanny Lizzy & I walked into the next room, where we heard each of the two sharp hasty Screams.—

Fanny escaped with having her teeth cleaned and gold inserted, but the dentist talked 'gravely' about seeing all the girls again and soon. Lizzie and Marianne should return in the next couple of months. Indeed, he pressed for them 'all coming to him'.

Jane Austen was sceptical:

The little girls teeth I can suppose in a critical state, but he must be a Lover of Teeth & Money & Mischeif to parade about Fannys.—I would not have him look at mine for a shilling a tooth & double it.

So, if you want advice about teeth from Jane Austen, there it is: stay away from dentists.

CHAPTER 7
Into Nature

Jane Austen's novels evoke an elegant, pre-industrial world of snug parsonages, prosperous farms and country mansions. Her genteel characters stroll through a landscape of untroubled husbandry and tamed nature. They sit in shrubberies surrounded by cultivated parks and gardens, by planned 'wildernesses' and picturesquely nurtured woodland. Austenland is England before steam power, before technological modernity, before consumer demands forced wholesale extraction from the earth, and communities were fragmented by mechanisation and fast travel. Along with their cinematic spinoffs and their nostalgic tinted landscapes, the novels have become a refuge from powerlessness and unease in the real overcrowded, over-trafficked environment most of us inhabit. They soothe us dwellers in the post-industrial Anthropocene.

Of course Austen's land was never so simple; it was already man-made. But, since her day, we've killed off plants and insects and dug up an awful lot of earth.

WEATHER

Henry James accused Austen of a 'want of consciousness of nature'. He has a point, if he excludes the weather. But you can't exclude weather, and Jane Austen's fiction and letters are full of clouds and sun, mud and puddles. Scarcely a novel or private letter fails to remark the rain making treacherous roads for carriages and filthy paths for improperly shod walkers, or keeping people moping indoors.

In countryside and villages, weather takes on attributes of an old acquaintance, never to be entirely ignored, however irritating.

Unpredictable weather is typical of England. It's a constant topic of trivial conversation. Then as now, it eases the awkward or unfamiliar social moment. You can comment on the weather in the bus shelter, in the post office queue, in the train compartment facing a long journey, on the woodland path if anxious about a large figure approaching you in the twilight. 'Lovely evening,' you say, and the bearded youth with a small whippet gives you back a strange, but not unfriendly look. In *Sense and Sensibility* Lady Middleton times her remarks on rain to interrupt what's socially unpalatable to her and painful to Elinor. Weather is always acceptable as a topic, always available when talk or silence becomes oppressive.

Weather differs in town and country. Writing to Cassandra from London Jane pauses in her relation of her brother's illness and the 'plague' of visitors to remark: 'A change of weather at last!—Wind & Rain.' A month later she rejoiced:

> It was a fine sunshiney day *here*—(in the Country perhaps you might have Clouds & fogs—Dare I say so?—I shall not deceive *you*, if I do, as to my estimation of the Climate of London)

'[E]exquisite' London weather becomes physical bliss:

> I enjoy it all over me, from top to toe, from right to left, Longitudinally, Perpendicularly, Diagonally;—& I cannot but selfishly hope we are to have it last till Christmas;—nice, unwholesome, Unseasonable, relaxing, close, muggy weather!—

July is the wet month. In one especially miserable year in Chawton, it's 'much worse than anybody *can* bear, & I begin to think it will never be fine again'. Then Jane adds the saving hope:

> This is a finesse of mine, for I have often observed that if one writes about the Weather, it is generally completely changed before the Letter is read.

Email, WhatsApp and TikTok are too quick to allow such optimism.

Weather enters almost every letter Jane Austen wrote. 'What weather, and what news! We have enough to do to admire them both,' she exclaimed from Godmersham, the two – social and meteorological – equally significant.

On Mr Woodhouse in *Emma* all weather impinges, though he scarcely leaves his fireside. Summer heat unnerves him; he can be kept tolerably comfortable only by ceaseless attention from his daughter. Snow is even more distressing.

Belittled by Mr Knightley and feared by Mr Woodhouse, the Christmas snow invades all the characters. It drives Emma into her comfortable carriage with tipsy Mr Elton to vie with him in snobbishness. Then it provides a welcome excuse for her to be stationary after the disastrous encounter:

> The ground covered with snow, and the atmosphere in that unsettled state between frost and thaw, which is of all others the most unfriendly for exercise, every morning beginning in rain or snow, and every evening setting in to freeze, she was for many days a most honourable prisoner.

Occasionally, as in poetry, weather heightens or complements mood. When Emma learns of Jane and Frank's relationship, she chides herself for inflicting pain on the one woman she should have chosen for a friend:

> The evening of this day was very long, and melancholy, at Hart-field. The weather added what it could of gloom. A cold stormy

rain set in, and nothing of July appeared but in the trees and
shrubs, which the wind was despoiling, and the length of the day,
which only made such cruel sights the longer visible.

Weather then cooperates at the denouement. It's still July – so, of
course, wet. Gloomy Emma is stuck indoors. Until, there comes
the sun:

> The weather continued much the same all the following morn-
> ing; and the same loneliness, and the same melancholy, seemed
> to reign at Hartfield—but in the afternoon it cleared; the wind
> changed into a softer quarter; the clouds were carried off; the sun
> appeared; it was summer again. With all the eagerness which
> such a transition gives, Emma resolved to be out of doors as soon
> as possible. Never had the exquisite sight, smell, sensation of
> nature, tranquil, warm, and brilliant after a storm, been more
> attractive to her. She longed for the serenity they might gradual-
> ly introduce … she lost no time in hurrying into the shrubbery.—
> There, with spirits freshened, and thoughts a little relieved, she
> had taken a few turns, when …

Mr Knightley strides in.
'I think everybody feels a north-east wind,' remarks Mrs Weston,
solicitous of Emma usually so bonny but wilting a little under the
love she realises she feels for her brother-in-law before knowing it
requited. Not even the east wind can do damage once he's spoken.

Emma was written in 1815, *Persuasion* the following year. 1816 was the
terrible year without a summer. In far off Indonesia Mount Tambora
erupted, making Europe's air dark grey and its earth dank and cold
even in the height of summer. In letters Austen mentions the 'coldness
of the weather', the 'rain' and 'more rain', 'Floods' and 'Damps'.

All over England crops failed: Jane Austen in Hampshire heard
from a farmer about the ruined wheat and corn, while a friend
reported that France was devastated by weather as well as war – it

was 'general Poverty & Misery'. Away on Lake Geneva the dismal summer produced the famous night of inspiration when the competition to write a ghost story would, given time, produce Mary Shelley's *Frankenstein* and Polidori's Byron-inspired 'The Vampyre'. Nothing so sensational came from Austen's pen, but perhaps the rain and wind that afflict Anne Elliot were a faint response.

In almost all the novels rain accelerates plots. It pitches romantic Marianne into the arms of her dashing (though sadly fickle) 'preserver'. It gives useful illness to Jane Bennet, keeping her close to the man that both she and her mother desire for her. A downpour confines Fanny Price to the rectory in unwanted intimacy with her rival Mary Crawford. Young Harriet Smith, however, dashes out when rain is likely, then stops, wavers and shilly-shallies in dizzying echo of her flighty affections for one man, then another.

Unaware of giving pain, John Knightley remarks that Jane Fairfax must want very much to go to the post if she sets off when rain is promised. The rainy walk opens the poor young woman to comments from Mr Woodhouse and Mrs Elton. Even Mr Weston chimes in, more properly since he knows Jane has suffered from severe colds in the past. Against the impudent interference of Mrs Elton – and against common sense – Jane Fairfax has to insist that going to the post is a pleasure, rain or shine. Only later do we learn she goes with the hope of finding letters from Frank. In 'The Watsons', the sisters splash along the dirty lanes behind their old mare after it's been raining. They don't enjoy it.

UMBRELLAS

In *Emma*, snug and unwelcome in the comfortable Woodhouse coach, Mr Elton remarks that here 'one is so ... guarded from the weather, that ... [w]eather becomes absolutely of no consequence'. He's wrong: weather is always of 'consequence'.

No one riding in a close carriage has use for umbrellas, but there's a challenging world outside. In the childhood 'Collection of Letters', young Jane makes a titled lady snub an inferior by telling her that, if it rains, she may use an umbrella, for she'll have no carriage to transport her and her finery to a party.

The snub assumes a *woman* holding an umbrella; it's quite different when borne aloft by gentlemen. In cartoons and illustrations from the time, umbrellas look flimsy, almost see-through. This is misleading, since umbrellas of the Regency were formed of thick waxed or oiled cotton (unlike our light synthetic materials). They'd have been heavy to hold aloft.

In *Emma* umbrellas act like theatrical props for men, amorous tools to be proffered with gallantry. Mr Elton dashes out with umbrellas for Harriet and Emma as they pass down the lane near his vicarage. His swift act echoes the romance of Miss Taylor and Mr Weston. This began in 'mizzle', with the demand for the attentiveness of umbrellas. In Broadway Lane, spying Emma and her governess, Mr Weston 'darted away with so much gallantry, and borrowed two umbrellas for us from Farmer Mitchell's'. Emma misjudges Mr Elton's act when he goes on a similar errand, translating it into pursuit of Harriet, not her rich self.

There's more. The farmer Robert Martin is busy with an umbrella while his beloved Harriet quakes at seeing her rejected lover. Frank Churchill uses umbrellas to get close to Jane Fairfax under cover of defending her aunt Miss Bates against the rain; the Eltons were supposed to have taken the ladies in their carriage to the party at the Crown Inn but had forgotten. Even lazy Dr Grant must do a polite umbrella-manoeuvre when poor Fanny Price is glimpsed dripping wet outside the Mansfield parsonage.

For themselves, without women to please, worthy men seem uninterested in umbrellas. Forgoing such aid, Mr Knightley dashes through rain from Donwell Abbey to Hartfield to court Emma after he learns she might be affected by Frank Churchill's delinquency. In *Persuasion* vain Sir Walter uses umbrellas at Kellynch to minister to his state, placing them where they demand the maximum service from attendants.

If umbrellas are mostly male accessories used for gallantry – or just against rain – dainty light parasols of silk or taffeta are female. They shielded a fashionably pale complexion against the sun, like screens placed against a fire. They could be modestly employed by the girl not yet quite 'out' or, as in 'Sanditon', a small version could be a toy for a female child. The Parkers propose to buy a parasol for their daughter from the local trinket store; by contrast, her brothers can run about and get berry-brown. The sea wind that her uncle Arthur avoids would probably blow it out of the girl's hand on its first excursion. Frequently, parasols could, like the adroitly wielded umbrella, aid flirtation: they might be interposed between lovers or coquettishly twisted and twirled in an elegantly gloved hand.

All of which makes it strange that the only *heroine* with a parasol is Elizabeth Bennet, who runs back into the house for hers when Lady Catherine makes her momentous visit to Longbourn. Not to keep off the sun, surely, for she hadn't been worried about sunburn when tripping across fields and stiles to Netherfield or on the Midlands tour when she arrived at Pemberley quite 'tanned', to Caroline Bingley's disgust. Perhaps it was required for verbal duelling with the great lady, equivalent of the flirtatious sparring with the great man on the dance floor. Or maybe she needed a shield against Lady Catherine's assault.

CREATED LANDSCAPE

Nature had been written about in general and detail, made sympathetic to a viewer and fashioned into a work of art for many centuries before Jane Austen. However, her time was especially clamorous with voices discussing the owned natural world, its purpose and meaning. They argued about how land, flora and fauna should be exploited and prized to please their owners; how much cruelty and coercion were appropriate for a human aesthetic to flourish. Occupying vast swathes of the country, the wealthier classes used them for their own profit and pleasure: they insisted that the land they viewed from their mansions and approached in their carriages become an artefact, a picture. Compensation perhaps for what Oscar Wilde's Vivian in the essay 'The Decay of Lying' called 'Nature's lack of design'.

In *The Task*, his great poem of ecological anxiety, William Cowper termed 'improvement' 'the idol of the age'. He condemned the over modified and tamed nature associated with the radical landscape gardener, Lancelot 'Capability' Brown. He called him 'the omnipotent magician', a fearful adjective for pious Cowper to use. Brown moved immense acres of virgin land to form his aesthetic vistas, seeming to parody creation itself. Cowper saw the result as an impious, ostentatious yet sadly uniform landscape which could only be viewed panoptically from the drawing room window. It would never be experienced as original created nature.

By Jane Austen's time, the Brown parkland was old-fashioned. In Chapter 2, I contrasted the grounds of Sir Charles Grandison with those of Mr Darcy. The professional gardener in vogue was now Humphry Repton, who, as a real person, makes a surprising appearance by name in *Mansfield Park*, distinguished by the enthusiasm of Henry Crawford so eager to improve other people's grounds. Repton modified the Brown aesthetic and, though still an earth-mover and water-controller, was less keen to shift villagers' cottages to improve a view or raze entire woods. He wouldn't have suited *Northanger Abbey*'s General Tilney, who enjoyed the notion of removing a cottage with a gesture.

What did Jane Austen herself think? She admired what she saw in her wealthy relatives' lovely gardens in Adlestrop, the arranged walks and vistas contrived by Repton, but, as so often, there's distance between opinions in letters and those suggested in her fiction. In her novels her narrators and heroines express the discomfort of the traditionalist.

Of course, what they and other nostalgic writers regretted was often the plantings of a past age and taste, rather than original wildness. Very little of this remained in the midland and southern counties of England: years of human managing and exploitation had seen to that.

In *The Task* Cowper bemoaned the destruction of an avenue of limes described as a 'monument of ancient taste'. He approved it because it was old and because 'Our fathers knew the value of a screen / From sultry suns', which he calls – rather comically – 'the obsolete prolixity of shade'. In *Mansfield Park* Fanny Price echoes Cowper and anticipates Gerard Manley Hopkins in his distress over felled Binsey poplars:

O if we but knew what we do
When we delve or hew —
Hack and rack the growing green!

Fanny laments the notion of Sotherton's long oak avenue being uprooted to serve new fashion. Her cousin Edmund feels less of this backward yearning. When he considers his new parsonage, he's prepared to remove the farmyard to have a better view, but baulks at the ideas of Henry Crawford who pronounces as a man of wealth and unconcern for those beneath him. He proposes to Edmund:

> 'The farm-yard must be cleared away entirely, and planted up to shut out the blacksmith's shop. The house must be turned to front the east instead of the north—the entrance and principal rooms, I mean, must be on that side, where the view is really very pretty; I am sure it may be done. And *there* must be your approach—through what is at present the garden ... The meadows beyond what *will be* the garden ... must be all laid together of course; very pretty meadows they are, finely sprinkled with timber. They belong to the living, I suppose. If not, you must purchase them. Then the stream—something must be done with the stream ...'

Edmund demurs. He wants no professional help, no wholesale improvement.

> 'I have two or three ideas also,' said Edmund, 'and one of them is that very little of your plan for Thornton Lacey will ever be put in practice ... I think the house and premises may be made comfortable, and given the air of a gentleman's residence without any very heavy expense, and that must suffice me; and I hope may suffice all who care about me.'

Despite his worthy notions of clerical duties, Edmund is not enough integrated into ordinary parish life to think that as a farmer of glebe land he might look on an actual farmyard from his house, but he rejects the wholesale conversion of a rectory into a small mansion – or 'a *place*' as Henry Crawford terms it – 'the residence of a man of education, taste, modern manners, good connections' rather than of a clergyman. But class will out. The son of Sir Thomas Bertram of Mansfield Park must have a house that has 'the air of a gentleman's residence'.

IN NATURE WITH GILPIN

The earth-moving and river-damming 'improvements' that made owned landscape into high art were available only to the rich or aristocratic. But everyone had eyes. The cultural prism through which the middle classes looked was formed by the many books of William Gilpin.

I know. He keeps popping onto my pages like the intrusive King Charles's head that interferes with the autobiography of fragile Mr Dick in *David Copperfield*. He was fully formed in Chapter 1 and I bring him back in the next chapter too. I feel justified. Henry Austen wrote that his sister was 'at a very early age ... enamoured of Gilpin on the Picturesque'. He also claimed, 'she seldom changed her opinions either on books or men'. On the evidence of her writings, Gilpin as much as any writer seems to have inhabited Jane Austen's mind.

Is this too much to assert? Maybe the habitation is in my head as much as hers, for I spent many hours in the chilly rare book room in the Cambridge University Library reading – and enjoying – his many tours. I appreciated what he was suggesting, that 'scenery' – a word once the preserve of the dramatic stage – is prettier as a kind of picture to be looked at than it is when you step into it. If 'pretty' is what you want. Even truer now that everyone has become a tourist, not just Mrs Elton who enjoyed 'a delightful exploring party from Maple Grove to Kings Weston'.

Gilpin is a man of the eighteenth not the nineteenth century, and I feel that Jane Austen mentally lived there too when it came to describing nature (most of the time). I can understand this. I live in the twenty-first century, but have not quite left the twentieth.

Gilpin became so popular in his age that he was said to have formed the national taste. Naturally he inspired mockery, not only from young Jane's unpublished 'Tour through Wales'! The most famous skit was William Combe's *The Tour of Dr Syntax in Search of the Picturesque*, with comic sketches by the great cartoonist, Thomas Rowlandson. (I have two of them framed on my sitting-room wall. I bought them at an auction in the Lake District during a Wordsworth conference.)

Pictured with the long chin that amused Jane Austen, Dr Syntax was a modern-day Don Quixote riding out on Grizzle. His aim was to force nature into picturesque tableaux. Faced with a farmyard of 'Cows, asses, sheep, and ducks and geese', he fails dismally:

> The sheep all baa'd, the asses bray'd,
> The moo-cows low'd, and Grizzle neigh'd!
> 'Stop, brutes,' he cried, 'your noisy glee;
> I do not want to hear – but see;
> Though by the picturesquish laws,
> You're better too with open jaws.'

Dr Syntax travels and writes primarily for money. If partly true of Gilpin, I doubt Jane Austen would have minded. She was interested in '*pewter*' and promoted the sale of her books through her wide circle of acquaintances (though never as energetically as Burney, who put a notice of *Camilla* in *The Morning Chronicle*). The wealthy owned the land, why shouldn't others exploit it a little? 'I'll ride and *write*, and *sketch* and *print*, / And thus create a real mint,' says Combe's anti-hero.

The central joke of the satire is that, while pursuing his lucrative scheme, Dr Syntax is insensitive to real nature:

> The morning lark ascends on high,
> And with its music greets the sky ...
> While ev'ry hedge and ev'ry tree
> Resound with vocal minstrelsy.
> But Syntax, wrapt in thought profound,

Is deaf to each enliv'ning sound:
Revolving many a golden scheme.

The underlying point is serious: that writing about nature is not necessarily appreciating it, that words can stand between the thing and the perceiver as surely as an umbrella against rain.

Despite admiration, Austen herself mocks the celebrity of Gilpin in *Northanger Abbey* with Henry Tilney, the charming mansplainer of the Austen canon. He leads young Catherine up Beechen Cliff near Bath, then 'talked of fore-grounds, distances, and second distances—side-screens and perspectives—lights and shades' so that the impressionable girl, in deference to this desirable man's views, comes to reject blue skies and the whole city of Bath as part of a landscape. The interaction makes fools of teacher as well as eager pupil.

In *Sense and Sensibility* Marianne, eager and passionate about nature and picturesque looking, is overwhelmed by the popularity of the Gilpin method and its language. She laments:

> Every body pretends to feel and tries to describe with the taste and elegance of him who first defined what picturesque beauty was.

Words used to express admiration have become 'worn and hackneyed out of all sense and meaning'. Could they be recuperated? Marianne tries but is trounced by the mimicry of Willoughby who, we later learn, has been feeding back to her both her language and opinions to win her heart.

IN NATURE WITH THE POETS

Jane Austen's narrative descriptions of the natural world are surprisingly abstract and general, like her descriptions of human physical appearance. She portrays the world as it's seen by her sensitive, bookish young heroines. Well understanding the affective power of place, she describes the construction of human subjectivity through engagement with what's outside, so landscapes are mediated, expressive of mind. Why need particulars?

From Barton Cottage in *Sense and Sensibility* the Dashwood ladies see a country not primarily made up of fine woods and useful pastures. They do not notice any specific tree, shrub or animal: instead what they see is a landscape that offers them 'beautiful walks'. The high downs of Devon invite them through the window to come up the hill to experience the 'exquisite enjoyment of air'. More than what's seen, the looking/gazing eye is Austen's subject.

Although revised later, *Sense and Sensibility* is in essence an early novel, one of the three drafted in Austen's childhood home of Steventon. In the works begun in her final years in the cottage at Chawton, there is a similar sense of place as visually perceived, but an added stress on the mediation of words, as well as on the nature which human emotional experience overlays.

As Elizabeth Bennet has Gilpin in mind when she visits Pemberley, so the more introspective Fanny Price and Anne Elliot stray out of doors with the poets, especially Cowper. Both accept his emphasis on local happiness; both notice not just the general beauty of a landscape but details of local fields, even of cottages and roads. Here's Fanny Price on the way to Sotherton in Cowper mode. (Does she ever think about nature without the erotic patina of Edmund? Perhaps she's justified here, for he's been her teacher, and this surprising utilitarian looking may have come from books lent by him.)

> Their road was through a pleasant country; and Fanny, whose rides had never been extensive, was soon beyond her knowledge, and was very happy in observing all that was new, and admiring all that was pretty. ... in observing the appearance of the country, the bearings of the roads, the difference of soil, the state of the harvest, the cottages, the cattle, the children, she found entertainment that could only have been heightened by having Edmund to speak to of what she felt.

Fair enough, for Maria is marrying for money and the land is money; they're all being transported to Sotherton to see the worth of what she's getting in exchange for herself.

The intense scrutiny of soil, harvest and cottage helps to quell the jealousy Fanny feels when contemplating Edmund who, she now fears, loves someone else. Usually her view of nature is dreamy, and, well, a bit prissy. Here, sitting under the trees in the garden of the Mansfield parsonage, she addresses her rival Mary Crawford (as Marianne Dashwood supposed, it's indeed difficult to express feelings for nature in unhackneyed words):

> 'Here's harmony!' said she, 'Here's repose! Here's what may leave all painting and all music behind, and what poetry only can attempt to describe. Here's what may tranquillise every care, and lift the heart to rapture! When I look out on such a night as this, I feel as if there could be neither wickedness nor sorrow in the world; and there certainly would be less of both if the sublimity of Nature were more attended to, and people were carried more out of themselves by contemplating such a scene.'

The passage resembles long sections of Radcliffe, when the author pauses her Gothic tale of villainy and high adventure to tell us through the admirable Emily or Ellena of the proper moral and aesthetic response to sublime nature of mountains and mists. Fanny's speech is comically naïve, for she proposes to *attend* to sublimity rather than being struck by it like the Radcliffe heroine, as if sublimity were a schoolmistress you must pay attention to. And instead of being in the high Alps or Apennines (however imaginary), Fanny is in a commonplace rural garden. Mary Crawford answers her 'rambling fancy' by declaring, 'I see no wonder in this shrubbery equal to seeing myself in it.' A naughty (and funny) response that gives a good deal of shade to Fanny's odd little rapture.

For Fanny, nature offers refuge from the nagging and demands in the great house, the more precious because so often her moments of 'rapture' are interrupted or snatched from her. When she tries to be alone, she's often invaded; when she wants to be out on a horse, better riders take it; when she wants to stroll round Sotherton grounds, she accepts her fatigue and is quickly abandoned, forced to spectate.

'God made the country, and man made the town' is Cowper's most quoted line and in his poetry all cities are damned, especially London which displays 'rank abundance', sloth, 'riot and incontinence'. In London fashion becomes truth. Despite Austen's obvious enjoyment of London during her visits to Henry, her character Fanny Price stays firmly with Cowper in his attitude to cities.

When miserable, Fanny and Anne Elliot in *Persuasion* both recoil from the 'white glare' of stone and stucco in the urban environment, beloved by more worldly acquaintances like Mary Crawford and Lady Russell. When unhappy in love or loss, when they suffer from irrepressible envy or feel excluded among a crowd, they don't turn to society and entertainment to dull their pain but instead walk out into nature. For these young women, the natural world is more intrusive, more pressing and above all more literary than for the earlier heroines, even enthusiastic Marianne Dashwood.

Although aware of picturesque looking, they don't rush to frame and distance in the Gilpin manner: rather, they look at scenes of nature with the help of their favourite poets – Cowper of course, but also James Beattie and Charlotte Smith in Anne Elliot's case. Solitary, they respond to weather and atmosphere, so that the poetry mingles with sight, sound and touch to form an almost synaesthetic appreciation. Nonetheless, for the most part, their response remains a method of *using* nature.

Inevitably so, for Jane Austen's genre is social comedy. The worthy characters are moving towards romantic conclusion, and any lonely contemplation is only a stage on the way to the true sociability of the well-matched couple. This is true even for the introspective heroines with their heightened receptivity.

In her pensive walk to Winthrop, Anne Elliot yearns to take the arm of Wentworth, the handsome lover of her youth, seemingly lost through her timidity, and, like Fanny Price with her detailing of soil and harvest while feeling the loss of beloved Edmund, she consciously tries for solace both through careful looking and through a literature that might momentarily help her transcend her immediate emotions.

Austen's reporting on nature in her letters is mainly down to earth, minimal even, or just occasionally mock poetic: 'The shades of evening are descending', or, quoting the poet James Beattie, ''Tis Night & the Landscape is lovely no more'. She gives Anne Elliot this habit, sometimes making her comment tritely, more often with beautiful appropriateness as she struggles to influence or just soften her mood. The poetic words for nature act like mnemonics or mantras; her quotations have been Anne's standby in times of melancholy:

> Her *pleasure* in the walk must arise from the exercise and the day, from the view of the last smiles of the year upon the tawny leaves and withered hedges, and from repeating to herself some few of the thousand poetical descriptions extant of autumn, that season of peculiar and inexhaustible influence on the mind of taste and tenderness, that season which has drawn from every poet, worthy of being read, some attempt at description, or some lines of feeling.

'Tawny leaves' and 'withered hedges'. Like Shakespeare's last yellow leaves on the tree of life, they conjure up aloneness and the fear of growing old.

The seasons in their glory exist properly only in the country, and yet it's in towns that these late heroines begin their recovery. Anne Elliot gets her 'second spring' in Bath, a place she hated both as a motherless child and as a tormented adult. The same with Fanny Price. Exiled from her second, more beloved home of Mansfield, she's in urban Portsmouth, smelly and overcrowded like all big towns, when she receives the reviving letter from Edmund.

Before it arrived, she'd lost 'all the pleasures of spring'; she'd missed the 'animation both of body and mind' that she'd known at Mansfield when she'd witnessed 'increasing beauties, from the earliest flowers, in the warmest divisions of her aunt's garden, to the opening of leaves of her uncle's plantations, and the glory of his woods'. There's a possessiveness here, a stress on the *ownership* of these country beauties.

Spring is more beautiful in the country, yet one of the loveliest nature passages in *Mansfield Park* occurs on the edge of smelly noisy Portsmouth. Staying with Frank and his wife in Southampton, Jane Austen took long walks by the sea and out into the country; she may have called on those memories for this enchanting urban seascape:

> The day was uncommonly lovely. It was really March; but it was April in its mild air, brisk soft wind, and bright sun, occasionally clouded for a minute; and every thing looked so beautiful under the influence of such a sky, the effects of the shadows pursuing each other, on the ships at Spithead and the island beyond, with the ever-varying hues of the sea now at high water, dancing in its glee and dashing against the ramparts with so fine a sound.

Fanny Price and Anne Elliot understand the rhythm of the natural world. They find it simultaneously healing and melancholy, depending on their mood. Anne Elliot is brought back to bloom and Fanny grows bright and bonny in the Mansfield summer. Yet one-directional time always remains an undertow for the conscious human being, separating her from the annual renewal of nature. Anne Elliot is allowed a second chance at love, but no human being is really renewed like nature, and that melancholy truth is always just out of the frame.

Which brings me to a conjunction. Seasons are natural but they're also incorporated in the Anglican cyclical year, which is progressive and meaningfully structured. Jane Austen was a child of the rectory, the daughter and sister of parsons, so she was as thoroughly attuned to the ritual and calendar of the Church of England as to distinct English seasons. She and her family felt the need to attend services whenever they could, often braving rain to do so. It was a moral and social obligation, like observing sabbath customs: Anne Elliot finds her cousin William Walter Elliot morally wanting because he travelled on a Sunday, the day of rest. Dramatised in the novels, the Church of England becomes a matter of sermons and parsonages, ordination and tithes, but in the letters, underneath the worldly concerns, the Church emerges as a way of life, of experiencing life, like noting when Spring arrives, Autumn fades or Christmas approaches. It's a very 'moderate' seasonal English way of being religious.

WALKING IN TOWN AND COUNTRY

Fanny Price sits still to rhapsodise on nature, but to appreciate, to come where you can properly see, you must be on foot. Walking is the essence of experience in Austenian nature.

In a different context, Mary Wollstonecraft, an astute political economist, praises walking as almost a human right and a natural necessity in a labouring job. In her *Historical and Moral View of the French Revolution*, she took issue with the philosopher of capitalism, Adam Smith, who in *The Wealth of Nations* argued for division of labour as a method of increasing productivity of goods. He mocked the 'country workman' for wasting time by 'sauntering' from one part of his job to another while making a single item. A passionate anti-capitalist, Wollstonecraft argued that the time which is 'sauntered away', in going from one part of an employment to another is the very time that preserves the man from degenerating into a brute'. Walking, moving legs and feet on his own volition, makes the country worker human.

Although Catherine Morland 'was come to be happy' in Bath, she's at her most contented when walking out of it with true friends. Within the city she's confined to vapid Isabella, who walks to display herself or pursue young men, or to inane Mrs Allen, who thinks only of clothes as she struggles through the Pump Room. In her melancholy phase Anne Elliot too is a country-lover, but human love trumps enjoyment of nature, and her passion is renewed in the city. In both, she walks.

At first she's overwhelmed by the sensory bombardment of Bath while Lady Russell's 'spirits rose' with urban noise. Sensations change when Anne walks on pavements with the right company: she passes in joy from Camden-place to Westgate-buildings when she thinks of Wentworth's returning love, and the final romantic stroll of the lovers, where past and present are blessedly fused, remains resolutely urban. Even the noisy inhabitants who distressed Anne on her first arrival in Bath can be occluded by love: she and Wentworth see 'neither sauntering politicians, bustling house-keepers, flirting girls, nor nursery-maids and children'. There's no return to the country here.

Walking indoors is the most constraining of activities, a movement without progress. The funniest example is supplied in *Pride and Prejudice*. The party is assembled at Netherfield. Trying to attract Mr Darcy, Caroline Bingley proposes to Elizabeth that they take 'a turn about the room'. She invites Darcy but he declines, assuming they walk together because intimate or because they wish to display their figures. There follows the semi-flirtatious, serious conversation about character traits between Elizabeth and Darcy, so not a lot of walking is done. Caroline Bingley gets bored and suggests they wake supine Mr Hurst and have some music.

I'm reminded of a wildly disparate anecdote from my time of existentialist enthusiasm. Kierkegaard, the daddy of the movement, describes a situation (I assume his own) where, when he was a young boy, his father wouldn't let him leave the house but instead walked up and down the room with him portraying the world so minutely and vividly that the boy came to see what was described. When older he joined in and, walking together, it was as though they were looking at the world anew. They made a drama of combined words and walking: inside but imagining outside.

Walking really should be done outdoors and within nature, despite Anne Elliot's finding bliss in Bath. Some Austen characters walk out to reflect or muse, listening perhaps to the thud of boots or pattens on the ground as well as to the sound of birds and swaying trees. For a few, walking outside offers escape from a claustrophobic home. Elizabeth Bennet makes a bid for independence in that unfeminine striding across the fields to Netherfield, forgetful of dress and decorum. A joyful peace falls over her alone and out of doors.

No other heroine escapes her flawed family as joyfully as Elizabeth but each finds some freedom in walking out and away – if only to a shrubbery. 'I am fatigued; but it is not the sort of fatigue – quick walking will refresh me,' gasps Jane Fairfax desperate to escape over-solicitous society and process her misery. In *Persuasion* before breakfasting, Anne Elliot and Henrietta Musgrove walk by the sea in Lyme Regis and share a moment of exquisite pleasure:

> They went to the sands, to watch the flowing of the tide, which a fine south-easterly breeze was bringing in with all the grandeur which so flat a shore admitted. They praised the morning; gloried in the sea; sympathized in the delight of the fresh-feeling breeze—and were silent.

Then self intrudes, and Henrietta begins thinking how her suitor Charles Hayter might be found a Church living.

According to her letters, Jane Austen walked and walked. There's a story designed to show her devotion to Cassandra, but which also reveals her childish zeal. When she was only six, she dragged her three-year-old 'particular little brother' Charles with her to walk the six miles to meet the chaise returning with her beloved sister Cassandra in it.

When the sisters were in Chawton, they walked together, again and again along the same paths and lanes, sometimes slower, sometimes faster, seeing something different or absorbing, as you do each time you go out. They walked from necessity – to go somewhere – and for pleasure. They walked when suffering aching backs or dripping colds.

When apart, Jane describes her walking to Cassandra. From Goodnestone Park in Kent, the childhood home of her sister-in-law Elizabeth Knight, she relates:

> We have walked to Rowling on each of the two last days after dinner, and very great was my pleasure in going over the house and

grounds. We have also found time to visit all the principal walks of this place, except the walk round the top of the park, which we shall accomplish probably to-day.

From Goodnestone to Rowling was only a mile.

There's not a lot about footwear for walking. Emma performs an elaborate charade with her half-boot to keep Harriet and Mr Elton talking. But she stays indoors when the ground is wet or dirty.

Cowper would agree with her. In poor weather, ladies should be indoors:

> Fearless of humid air and gathering rains
> Forth steps the man, an emblem of myself,
> More delicate his tim'rous mate retires.
> When Winter soaks the fields, and female feet
> Too weak to struggle with tenacious clay,
> Or ford the rivulets, are best at home ...

Advice which Marianne Dashwood failed to follow at Cleveland, so contracting her self-inflicted fever.

Cowper seems not to be thinking of determined walkers like the Austen sisters. They walked in rain or shine. Caroline Austen remembers her aunts clip-clopping down the lanes in pattens.

When Jane was a little out of sorts, she often walked herself into health or enough mental well-being to think herself in health. So it becomes especially poignant that the stages of her final illness can be measured by her inability to try this remedy. Unless the weather were particularly treacherous, she was used to walking every day but, as her disease progressed, mobility declined. The letters make almost unbearable reading as we experience her slowing down, taking fewer and fewer steps.

By the end of 1816 Jane Austen was unable to go the less than two miles to her niece Anna's house Wyards just outside Chawton. At the close of January the following year, she felt a little better and could *imagine* walking this distance. By mid-March she'd relapsed though declaring herself 'quite equal to walking about & enjoying the Air'. She did not say how far she walked: that thermometer of well-being was discarded. She was just 'walking about'.

She made plans to ride the donkey that usually pulled their little family cart. The donkey is sad proof that Jane Austen, the great walker and promoter of walking, had stopped walking.

JANE AUSTEN IN MY FICTIONAL GARDEN

In *Jane Austen and Shelley in the Garden* I dared to make a character of Jane Austen. I set her in a Norfolk garden when my protagonist Fran was about to sell her country cottage:

> Jane Austen is muttering about fruit. Mrs Jennings stuffing on mulberries, Mrs Norris's apricot no tastier than Dr Grant's potato, General Tilney boasting of pineapples, Mrs Elton gorging on Donwell's gourmet strawberries.
>
> Why this displacing of vulgarity onto fruit? smiles Fran …
>
> She hums as she pulls up nettles and dead plants, murmuring Sweet place, all nature has a feeling, landscape listens. Despite her poetizing earthy pull, she knows the cottage and garden have demanded too much maintenance: her trees are overbearing, her flowers too needy.

Later she sees Jane Austen strolling by the bare apple tree quoting lines from Cowper's *Task*:

> The sloping land recedes into the clouds;
> Displaying on its varied side the grace
> Of hedgerow beauties numberless.

> It's winter, thinks Fran, but no matter. Words and things don't necessarily coalesce in Austen or in life.
>
> She ambles over to meet her Author. You haven't always made my life better here, she says, with your caution, civility and repression, your maddening romantic endings.
>
> As ever, you misinterpret me, replies Jane Austen serenely.

Fran anticipates her move into a large house with two friends – in homage (I now see, though I didn't when I wrote the book) to that cottage community of Jane, Cassandra and their friend Martha Lloyd. As an only child, I always noticed the sisterly bond of Jane and Cassandra – and, as I mentioned earlier, made much of it in *Women's Friendship in Literature*. But the relationship with Martha, that intimate friendship between women, because so little delivered to us in the letters compared with the Jane–Cassandra tie, I now see as close and tender, and easier for me to understand. I will always see the tie of siblings imaginatively from the outside, but I can bring my own experience to bear on close female friendship in fiction – in life perhaps as important as the marriage tie.

> Fran packs up her editions of the sacred works in their different formats: reprinted paperbacks in new covers with bonneted girls looking through saucy modern eyes; annotated hardbacks with Hugh Thomson illustrations; comic cartoon versions of *Pride and Prejudice*.
>
> You'll look well out there by the hollyhocks, she remarks to Jane Austen. You can serve expensive teas on rosy plates when the sky's blue. Celebrity has responsibilities, and pretty gardens need upkeep.
>
> I am no enthusiast of hollyhocks, replies Jane Austen, a Victorian taste. I will need pinks, sweet Williams, columbines, cornflowers, Cowper's ivory-pure syringa, his laburnum rich in streaming gold. Fruits and flowers, she murmurs again, flowers and fruits.

I intended in my novel to set Jane Austen in a nature that she'd enhance, but, from this little excerpt, I see I've made her bossy. I'll introduce her in pedagogic mode in the next chapter.

CHAPTER 8
Giving and Taking Advice

ADVICE FROM BOOKS: IMPROVING EXTRACTS

Jane Austen mocked the girlish habit, encouraged by compilers of extracts and anthologies, of writing out or memorising exemplary snippets of wisdom. Perhaps there was some self-mockery here, for as a child she owned a copy of Vicesimus Knox's *Elegant Extracts*. When her family left the Steventon rectory for Bath, she passed it on to her niece Anna. She must have thought the volume useful.

Nonetheless, when she presents Catherine Morland between the ages of fifteen and seventeen memorising extracts, Austen is having fun with her:

> From Pope, she learnt to censure those who
> > 'bear about the mockery of woe.'
> From Gray, that
> > 'Many a flower is born to blush unseen,
> > And waste its fragrance on the desert air.'
> From Thompson, that
> > ———'It is a delightful task
> > To teach the young idea how to shoot.'

And from Shakespeare she gained a great store of information—amongst the rest, that

     ————'Trifles light as air,
    Are, to the jealous, confirmation strong,
    As proofs of Holy Writ.'

That

    'The poor beetle, which we tread upon,
    In corporal sufferance feels a pang as great
    As when a giant dies.'

And that a young woman in love always looks

    ————'like Patience on a monument
    Smiling at Grief.'

The poets Alexander Pope, Thomas Gray and James Thomson
along with Shakespeare are not bad literary authorities, however
comically excerpted, and, used well, could indeed be 'so serviceable
and so soothing' in the inevitable trials of life, even one lived in
nothing more Gothic than a quiet English parsonage.

I recognise myself as the butt of this mockery for I too was an
inveterate extractor of moral exempla. I was more in the Mary
Bennet than the Catherine Morland line and would have been
laughed out of the house by Elizabeth and her father had I been
dropped into Longbourn.

I used sometimes to memorise these grave and useful snippets
of wisdom, which I also wrote down in a five-year diary with a
gold-coloured clasp. It came with a small key that wouldn't turn.
Why a clasp? Privacy I assume. What wonderful hope it implied:
that someone would wish to pry into the jottings of an earnest
schoolgirl in plaits. The volume was compiled in preparation for
my serious adult years, much in the manner of jollier Catherine
Morland.

'Existence is prior to essence,' I wrote. Character is made by
unconstrained choices. I didn't get this saying direct from Sartre or
Kierkegaard but from that popular promoter of existentialist ideas

and extracts for the un-philosophically trained, Colin Wilson in *The Outsider*. I adored that book. I suspect it prepared me to flirt with 'French Theory' in the 1970s; if so, it was a leaky preparation. I excerpted great chunks, as I did from another semi-anthology, Bertrand Russell's *History of Western Philosophy*.

Recently I came across the notion of existentialism where I least expected it. I was in the Accademia art gallery in Venice when I paused in front of an arresting painting of an old woman, said to be Giorgione's mother. She glances out sideways at the spectator through sad eyes, slack mouth revealing crooked bottom teeth. Gesturing to herself, she holds a paper which reads 'col tempo': with time.

In the past, galleries used to label paintings with the name of the artist and date of composition; now they tell us what to think. Perhaps the writer of the accompanying label doubted or didn't like the obvious interpretation: the label suggests that the portrait might be 'a celebration of a season of emancipation from earthly pleasures and of spiritual elevation towards the love of God'; in which case it becomes 'the representation of an existential condition'.

Nice try! But the painting is so striking because it delivers unvarnished the dejection and gloominess of old age.

With different material but similar habits to mine, my father and grandfather were excerpters. My father could never spy newly opened daffodils without reciting four lines from Wordsworth or pass the first blossoming cherry tree in an urban garden without falling into the beginning of A. E. Housman's 'Loveliest of trees'; he had a little book of sayings of Marcus Aurelius, his favourite being: 'You have power over your own mind—not over outside events.' He also memorised that irritatingly true 'serenity' prayer of Reinhold Niebuhr: 'God grant me the serenity to accept the things I cannot change; courage to change the things I can; and the wisdom to know the difference.' He quoted it a lot and I think tried to live by it; I can't say the same for my pretentious aphorisms.

When my father died, I found among his few possessions his own father's book of rather different extracts: sentimental passages concerning gentle love and English flowers, which my grandfather had carried with him to the Boer War at Ladysmith and to the Afghan Wars in the Khyber Pass. It must have returned with him from Flanders when he was dispatched home to die from gas inhaled in the trenches of Ypres.

All three generations would, I fear, be laughed at by Jane Austen. But she had her odd habits too. She collected and wrote down riddles and charades. She gives this habit to Emma and young Harriet in place of the serious reading Emma once purposed. It's delivered in a wonderfully sardonic passage leading up to the main use of the collecting, catching Mr Elton as suitor for Harriet:

> the only literary pursuit which engaged Harriet at present, the only mental provision she was making for the evening of life, was the collecting and transcribing all the riddles of every sort that she could meet with, into a thin quarto of hot-pressed paper, made up by her friend, and ornamented with cyphers and trophies.
>
> In this age of literature, such collections on a very grand scale are not uncommon. Miss Nash, head-teacher at Mrs. Goddard's, had written out at least three hundred; and Harriet, who had taken the first hint of it from her, hoped, with Miss Woodhouse's help, to get a great many more. Emma assisted with her invention, memory and taste; and as Harriet wrote a very pretty hand, it was likely to be an arrangement of the first order, in form as well as quantity.
>
> Mr. Woodhouse was almost as much interested in the business as the girls, and tried very often to recollect something worth their putting in. 'So many clever riddles as there used to be when he was young—he wondered he could not remember them! but he hoped he should in time.' And it always ended in 'Kitty, a fair but frozen maid.'
>
> His good friend Perry too, whom he had spoken to on the subject, did not at present recollect any thing of the riddle kind; but he had desired Perry to be upon the watch, and as he went about so much, something, he thought, might come from that quarter.
>
> It was by no means his daughter's wish that the intellects of Highbury in general should be put under requisition. Mr. Elton was the only one whose assistance she asked.

The riddles, though not immediately understood by Harriet, had answers. By contrast, the excerpts I made were sometimes thrillingly unintelligible. I concluded later that this was due to a childhood of religion rather than philosophy. Later still, I found the problem was sometimes in the translation: the results were incomprehensible because the translators were poor. I think the same went for a good deal of French Theory when read in English.

Did I then avoid Jane Austen, in part because I thought she didn't write 'well enough to be unintelligible'? That sounds like my pushy, bewildered self.

I'm unsure what spiritual or moral use I made of this reading and copying. I might have discovered the ordinary, sensible advice (contrary to what I'd gained from nightmarish *Pilgrim's Progress*) to stop looking somewhere else, for, without an afterlife, this is all there is. And, if you miss it through restless searching into past or future, you'll lose the experience of existing now, lose life I suppose. For people like me who assume they have to strive, do more, never stop doing, surpassing, competing, and not ever asking 'what for?' this advice was about as easy to follow as instructions for assembling an IKEA wardrobe from diagrams.

In any case, I could have got this 'presentism' from my father's Marcus Aurelius excerpts. Now in simpler language and with more sentimental wrapping, the advice is everywhere, with no demand for abstruse reading. It even comes from the government via the NHS. Along with all that bombarding counsel on eating fibre and losing body fat, we're told to be 'mindful', breathe slowly, and live in the present.

My speculation for Jane Austen is that, however she mocked anthologies and excerpting in *Northanger Abbey* and *Emma*, she'd done a fair bit of it herself, along with that collecting of riddles. Perhaps those repeated literary allusions in her novels come from extracts memorised years earlier in her youth.

ADVICE IN LOVE: THE MIXED MESSAGE
OF *PERSUASION*

The aim of vain Sir Walter Elliot is to stay the same age for ever. He notes ageing in others but none when, in his daily reading, he contemplates his static image in the *Baronetage*. Even more than his reflection in his many looking glasses, this is his magic mirror. Having a sense of urgency in her quest for a suitable offer of marriage, Elizabeth Elliot is less petrified than her father but, as years pass by and she remains unattached, she achieves something of her father's stasis, repeating in each season the same social duties.

Anne, the second daughter, is far from her limited relatives in intellectual and emotional understanding, yet there's something of the Elliot fixedness there. She's let one romantic summer keep her static. She resembles Miss Havisham, who's allowed an instant of the past to dominate present and future. Like Sir Walter, Anne has tried to stop time. When she and her beloved Wentworth meet again, he finds her miserably changed, she sees him unaltered.

In earlier heroines, moments of profound experience are clear, Anne Elliot's are presented as fading and blurred. Austen catches the way Anne feels and simultaneously how the world appears to her under tumultuous emotions. Blocking out the external, the rush of passion makes her dizzy, her surroundings hazy.

The first sight of Wentworth overwhelms her:

> a bow, a curtsey passed; she heard his voice—he talked to Mary, said all that was right; said something to the Miss Musgroves, enough to mark an easy footing: the room seemed full—full of persons and voices—

A similar moment of oxymoronic stillness and rush happens at the White Hart, the coaching inn in Bath: 'For a few minutes she saw nothing before her.' All was confusion, a cacophony of sounds, 'the almost ceaseless slam of the door, and ceaseless buzz of persons walking through'.

When Fanny Price responded so harshly to the adultery of Maria Bertram and Henry Crawford, I argued that, despite sympathy, the narrator through direct comment let in some air, so that the reader could judge as well as empathise. Fanny is just slightly destabilised by the reader's sense that she's being presented in free indirect speech rather than in dramatic monologue – though we remain enclosed in the character.

When Anne is first introduced, it's as a member of her chilly family:

> Anne, with an elegance of mind and sweetness of character, which must have placed her high with any people of real understanding, was nobody with either father or sister: her word had no weight; her convenience was always to give way;—she was only Anne.

'[O]nly Anne': the phrase tugs at the reader, demanding unconditional sympathy. The same demand will come when Anne makes her famous declaration of female constancy in the White Hart Inn.

The early part of *Persuasion* presents a profound picture of estrangement, of mental crippling brought on by a mind colluding with circumstance in a way psychologists now describe as a depressive condition. Sometimes Anne's inner life is so demanding she appears ill. While the loss of a beloved mother and the selfish contempt of father and sister are enough to dampen the spirits of any young girl, the root cause of Anne's melancholy, the novel insists, is lost love. She should have accepted Wentworth and become engaged, despite feeling she should also have obeyed her cautious surrogate mother, Lady Russell. In the context of Austen's letters and other fictions, this is a strange predicament.

Obsessive love is not given full rein in any of the other novels, not even *Mansfield Park*. The narrator tells us that, had Edmund married Mary Crawford and Henry continued his pursuit, Fanny would have married him. And been unhappy to be sure, but comedies end in weddings – they don't look further into the future. However, in this final novel of many wounds, Austen allows a single 'ardent' love to be rewarded.

With a cynicism belied by the plot, the narrator remarks that a second attachment would have been the best antidote to lost hopeless love. But there's no such possibility for Anne Elliot, no good earthly future without this particular man, despite the fact that he began his second movement towards her like Darcy in *Pride and Prejudice* by criticising her body. Elizabeth Bennet had not been beautiful enough to tempt Mr Darcy; faded, haggard Anne is not sufficiently blooming to tempt a returning warrior. There's another comparison with Darcy. Both write powerful letters: on the contents of Wentworth's letter 'depended all which this world could do for her!' Mr Darcy's letter was potent, Wentworth's is omnipotent.

In her childhood tales, Jane Austen mocked the romantic idea of a woman giving up her life to one, often escaping, man. In 'Jack and Alice', Alice desires only Charles Adams, whose heart is 'cold and indifferent'. Losing him leaves her but one option: to get drunk.

The novels support the point. In *Sense and Sensibility*, when Elinor consoles Marianne for the loss of Willoughby, she notes: 'Had you married, you must have been always poor', though for one exhausted moment after she herself has felt Willoughby's seduction, she fantasises Marianne united with her first love through the death of his wife. In *Mansfield Park* the youngest Ward sister follows only her heart and weds Lieutenant Price of the marines with no consideration of income; she's reduced to relative poverty. Captain Wentworth is far from Mr Price, but the future life of Mrs Price remains a cautionary tale. In *Emma*, Jane Fairfax enters an engagement without the certainly that she and her fiancé can soon marry; she falls ill under the strain.

Austen advised her niece Fanny Knight not to marry a man she didn't love, even if it disappointed him: 'it is no creed of mine … that such sort of Disappointments kill anybody'. She contemplated 'a lady who has married and now lives in the most private way possible in Portsmouth with no servant at all'. She remarked: 'What a prodigious innate love of virtue she must have, to marry under such circumstances.'

In *Persuasion* Anne comes close to being killed emotionally by letting remembered love grow burdensome, allowing memory to crowd out the present in exactly the way sprightly Elizabeth Bennet advises Darcy not to do. It's what Mary Wollstonecraft did in her obsession with Imlay I described in Chapter 2. As a result of this mental fixation Anne grows dead inside, unserved and solitary, while continuing to serve her selfish relations. Inwardly mocking her father and sister for their vanity and snobbery, she rarely shows distaste. She observes Wentworth and the Musgrove girls making emotional errors and longs 'for the power of representing to them all what they [are] about', but she stays silent.

Anne's intense feelings allow the novel to investigate the closeness of pleasure and pain. Seeing Wentworth in Bath, she feels confusion, then 'agitation, pain, pleasure, a something between delight and misery'. Everything is compressed, and she can catch 'the happiness of such misery, or the misery of such happiness'. Her melancholy is diminished by change and bustle, however dreaded, and the body, so often mentioned in this novel, is shaken into greater life, invigorated by wind and weather and new acquaintances. At the end, 'when pain is over, the remembrance of it often becomes a pleasure'.

There's something beyond painful pleasure and pleasurable pain in the climactic scene at the White Hart Inn. Here Anne's speech reaches out from the book. It's like an operatic aria of passion, demanding attention and reducing the reader to a single response. It's also a statement of feminine emotional masochism.

In the first version of the climactic scene Anne and Wentworth are brought together by Admiral Croft. This version lets in a subtle irony as it picks up on the use of 'nobody' at the beginning of the book. It also continues *Persuasion*'s theme of wordless emotions, expressed through the body. The reunion happens silently with 'a hand taken and pressed'.

The second version sets the resolution in the White Hart Inn. Captain Harville claims that active men have stronger feelings than women. Anne argues that claustrophobic female lives breed intensity:

> We cannot help ourselves. We live at home, quiet, confined, and
> our feelings prey upon us … All the privilege I claim for my own
> sex (it is not a very enviable one, you need not covet it) is that of
> loving longest, when existence or when hope is gone.

Eloquence does its work and Wentworth proposes. Anne has 'all
which this world could do for her'.

The second version of the denouement is certainly more emotional than the first. Something made Austen break a lifetime
of restraint to let passion flare out in such powerful expression
with no ironic reservation. The words lead to a walk and talk that
become a 'blessing' in the present and future.

Austen is usually sceptical of the myth that grants only one true
passion in a life; yet here she allows it. Earlier, the narrator appears
uneasy, worrying about what might just be seen as sentimental in
Anne's fidelity; or why add this when Anne begins to be convinced
of Wentworth's returning love?

> Prettier musings of high-wrought love and eternal constancy,
> could never have passed along the streets of Bath, than Anne was
> sporting with from Camden-place to Westgate-buildings. It was
> almost enough to spread purification and perfume all the way.

It feels like a smirk from the narrator.

Perhaps I make too much of Anne Elliot's different treatment, and
the advice her story seems to offer. In their various fashions, all
Austen's heroines achieve some way of controlling the mind and
its contents, a realistic accommodation with memory. The strength
of Austen's sceptical vision (most of the time) is that it's anchored
in this life, wherever it happens to be, so that the commonplace, the
ordinary can be suddenly and magically revealed as transcendent.
But (still) there's something curious going on here.

Anne is described as 'forced into prudence in her youth' and
learning 'romance as she grew older'. Beside these words Cassandra

wrote: 'Dear, dear Jane! This deserves to be written in letters of gold.' When she wrote this, Cassandra was alone, grieving for a beloved sister. Would her sister, mistress of slippery words, have wanted any of hers made so static?

Jane Austen found Anne Elliot 'almost too good'. Perhaps her response was to smile if not laugh at her a little more than we often allow ourselves to do. In the interchange of Anne with Mrs Smith on nursing (see Chapter 6), the narrator shows she doesn't entirely share her heroine's tendency to idealise.

Throughout the last part of the novel Anne has become more controlling: she seeks out Wentworth, watches for him and intercepts him. So here at the end in the White Hart Inn – it's a mischievous thought – might she not perceive that her talk with Captain Harville is overheard by its subject, might she not know very well what she's about?

I don't want to overdo this. *Persuasion* is intensely moving, but, in the context of Jane Austen as advice-giver, I find its message on love confusing.

Best fall back on my own experience: in life the same man rarely returns and, having invested so much in mourning him, would you want him to?

COERCIVE TRAVELLING WITH JANE AUSTEN

Like Anne Elliot's speech on eternal love, Fanny Price's on harmony in nature extrudes from her novel. I could make it into an elegant extract were I continuing my teenage habits. Like my extracts, this one has the ring of the teacherly, though its internal listener, Mary Crawford, comically punctures the impression. We can heed or not heed her at will.

But in *Persuasion*, when she takes her characters to Lyme Regis, Jane Austen in narrative voice is a great deal more forceful: she strides out in strict guidebook mode.

This descriptive way of writing became pervasive in the early nineteenth century, especially following the end of the Napoleonic Wars when travel increased. Guidebooks proliferated and Austen's publisher John Murray printed a goodly number; few tourists set off without one to tell them what to see and what to ignore. Staring at details of foreign churches too long, Lord Byron said he felt his brain had become a guidebook.

Partly in the interest of research for an edition of 'Sanditon', I visited Lyme for a few days of walking in the bracing November of 2021. (This was the month when Anne Elliot was there, and when Jane Austen herself first visited the town in 1803 and witnessed a great fire burning.) I found accommodation 'cramped but welcoming', though not as 'unexpensive' as Captain Harville who chose the town for the cheapness of its lodgings. Things have changed much in popular Lyme in the last 200 years.

I didn't enter that cold grey sea. Without bathing machines and bullying bathing attendants or an acquaintance like Diana Parker, who urges along timid Miss Lambe, it's a challenging enterprise. Instead, I watched from a glassed-in terrace as a dozen or so courageous women hurried over the sand, paused at the water's edge, paused again when the water lapped their waists, then dived in and swam. They came out sharpish but elated, laughing and chatting, their voices ringing through the cold air as they wrapped towels round themselves and each other, then headed for the bacon butties. It was a most heartening sight.

Turning back to the novel, I found Austen in uncharacteristically wordy manner, full of advice. There's no way to illustrate long-windedness except by long quotation. The characters have, to quote Mrs Elton, 'explored' to Lyme:

> as there is nothing to admire in the buildings themselves, the remarkable situation of the town, the principal street almost hurrying into the water, the walk to the Cobb, skirting round the pleasant little bay, which in the season is animated with bathing machines and company, the Cobb itself, its old wonders and new improvements, with the very beautiful line of cliffs stretching out to the east of the town, are what the stranger's eye will seek; and a very strange stranger it must be, who does not see charms in the immediate environs of Lyme, to make him wish to know

it better. The scenes in its neighbourhood, Charmouth, with its
high grounds and extensive sweeps of country, and still more its
sweet retired bay, backed by dark cliffs, where fragments of low
rock among the sands make it the happiest spot for watching
the flow of the tide, for sitting in unwearied contemplation;—the
woody varieties of the cheerful village of Up Lyme, and, above all,
Pinny, with its green chasms between romantic rocks, where the
scattered forest trees and orchards of luxuriant growth declare
that many a generation must have passed away since the first
partial falling of the cliff prepared the ground for such a state,
where a scene so wonderful and so lovely is exhibited, as may
more than equal any of the resembling scenes of the far-famed
Isle of Wight: these places must be visited, and visited again, to
make the worth of Lyme understood.

The party from Uppercross passing down by the now deserted
and melancholy looking rooms, and still descending, soon found
themselves on the sea shore, and lingering only, as all must linger
and gaze on a first return to the sea, who ever deserve to look on
it at all, proceeded toward the Cobb ...

This is guidebook writing. Yet it pulls in Gilpin with that stress
on the *way* of looking and with the 'far-famed Isle of Wight'.

The Isle of Wight was part of Fanny Price's view from the
ramparts in Portsmouth and the reference reminded readers of
how, as a child just deposited at Mansfield, she amused her cousins
by referring to it as '*the Island*'. But the Isle of Wight is far from
Lyme and is brought together with it only through Gilpin's tours.
Austen simply can't let Gilpin go.

Who owns the demanding, coercing voice, the one that tells
us not to be a 'a very strange stranger'? Jane Austen, her narrator, Anne Elliot or Captain Wentworth, whose enthusiasm has
brought about the expedition? Does this long paragraph work for
you within a novel? Does the author falter here? Do we dare pass
a negative judgement on the Mistress of the Novel?

It may be that, like all great writers from Homer onwards, Austen
sometimes nods. Had she lived to revise further, this guidebook

passage might have been assimilated into the consciousness of her heroine – and perhaps achieved some revisionary irony – or it might have been cut or completely removed.

Or it might have stayed to tell us readers just to look carefully. Then it would become a prolix postcard to a future which lacks a proper attention span.

I suspect that Jane Austen is here flirting with the didactic (teaching, not preaching) mode which mostly we now deny her, though once she was routinely offered to schoolgirls and colonials to train and edify their minds. Maybe we should listen, be less self-absorbed, relinquish personality, be goaded by descriptive prose to catch peripheral vision as well as the self-saturated frontal.

Maybe we need telling. Perhaps that's the purpose.

HOW TO WRITE.

In *A Room of One's Own* Virginia Woolf declared, 'a woman must have money and a room of her own if she is to write fiction' – or in fact, to write anything, do anything creative. Taking the room as real rather than metaphorical, did Austen have what a woman required to write and was it required?

There's a story told in the *Memoir of Jane Austen*:

> she had no separate study to retire to, and most of the work must have been done in the general sitting-room, subject to all kinds of casual interruptions. She was careful that her occupation should not be suspected by servants, or visitors, or any persons beyond her own family party. She wrote upon small sheets of paper which could easily be put away, or covered with a piece of blotting paper. There was, between the front door and the offices, a swing door which creaked when it was opened; but she objected to having this little inconvenience remedied, because it gave her notice when anyone was coming.

Presumably the interruption of the creaking door never killed inspiration in the way 'the person from Porlock' killed Coleridge's opium-inspired 'Kubla Khan' before he'd finished writing it down.

The poet Stevie Smith doubted the Romantic anecdote: why did Coleridge 'hurry to let him in? / He could have hid in the house'. She suspected that the famous Romantic poet was simply stuck.

Like Stevie Smith with the 'person from Porlock', I suspect a little the authenticity of the creaking-door story. It seems to me that Austen needed more peace than this implies. Certainly she was let off much housekeeping, for she makes a point that on one occasion: 'I carry about the keys of the Wine & Closet; & twice … have had orders to give in the Kitchen.' Not her usual role, then.

It's likely she was given time for her writing in Steventon and Chawton while other women largely ran the house. Space of a sort too. She knew her privilege and years later she wrote to Cassandra, referring to one of her least-favourite novelists, prolific Jane West:

> I often wonder how *you* can find time for what you do, in addition to the care of the House;—And how good Mrs West c^d have written such Books & collected so many hard words, with all her family cares, is still more a matter of astonishment! Composition seems to me Impossible, with a head full of Joints of Mutton & doses of rhubarb.

Wherever she was and wherever she had her first inspiration, all manuscript evidence points to much tinkering, much dogged revision after the first impression. Austen doesn't set up as a Romantic. She didn't need opium or claim such wild and delicate inspiration.

So, if you intend to write anything, best not follow Virginia Woolf and wait for your own room and money and certainly not depend on inspiration, but do avoid much housekeeping.

In her last years living in Chawton Jane Austen enjoyed reading the manuscript novels of her young relatives. She praised where she could and snuck in a little general advice:

> Do not give 'false representations' and express the sense 'in fewer words'.

CHAPTER 9

Being in the Moment

Every age has its apocalypse. Nuclear annihilation felt round the corner in my early teens. I assumed an early explosive death very probable. I knew people who built bunkers in their gardens and stocked them with tins of Campbell's soups, sardines and baked beans.

Long before I was aware of that particular Armageddon, I expected more individual destruction in the manner described by Bunyan in *The Pilgrim's Progress*, with which I began this book. But Bunyan, though never completely superseded – his visions of guilt and shame in the trek to the Celestial City were too vigorous – diminished during my teen years. His severe monotheism was giving place to a (pubescent?) pagan enthusiasm for green leaves and fields. I chose as my form prize at boarding school (which couldn't have been all bad) *The Collected Poems of Dylan Thomas*.

The poem which produced goose pimples in me was 'A Refusal to Mourn the Death, by Fire, of a Child in London'. It described 'the last light breaking' – like the bomb going off – the attractive moment of death when

> the still hour
> Is come of the sea tumbling in harness

And I must enter again the round
Zion of the water bead
And the synagogue of the ear of corn.

I rejoiced in the quiet pantheism, which gave the dead 'stars at elbow and foot'. At fourteen or fifteen, death is surprisingly appealing, its grisly leadup unimaginable. Better than being stuck in a bunker for years eating sardines or having your feet mired in the Slough of Despond.

Now environmental catastrophe is upon us. Everywhere. Touching even those places Jane Austen thought almost too distant for belief: Kamchatka (mentioned in 'Plan of a Novel') and Timbuktu (in 'Sanditon').

Austen's period was equally tumultuous: a time of war and accelerated social change. The country was pioneering the Industrial Revolution, laying the foundations for the threats and wonders of the modern world with its enormous population, unbridled consumption and exploitation of the Earth.

While many in Austen's time accepted the pains such transformation implied – especially if felt by those distant or beneath them – others withdrew from the materialistic present. 'The world is too much with us,' wrote Wordsworth, 'Getting and spending, we lay waste our powers'. He found a refuge in remote Grasmere in the Lake District, where he lived in his happy valley protected from the ills of urban consumerist modernity.

MARY WOLLSTONECRAFT

In *The Prelude* Wordsworth noted:

There are in our existence spots of time,
That with distinct pre-eminence retain
A renovating virtue.

Wordsworth's notion of 'spots of time' could yoke the imaginary to the political as well as to the personal. Burke paused his passionate argument against the French Revolution to make a timeless image of aesthetic feudal stasis as he contemplated that symbol of luxury and failed politics, the French queen Marie Antoinette (coupled for me now and forever with Mrs Elton and her strawberry picnic). Momentarily Burke saw an ordinary woman made visionary and gorgeous by 'an age of chivalry', 'glittering like the morning star full of life and splendour and joy'.

This was far from Mary Wollstonecraft's mode when, in her rationalist phase, she welcomed the French Revolution as a universal virtuous event. Always vehement in her opposition to Burke, both for his content and for his rhetorical tricks, she reduced Marie Antoinette to a vacuous doll, a kind of half-being created by the libertine male imagination. Yet, as she moved in her thinking to accommodate more and more of the emotionality she once deplored, she herself edged towards an understanding of the value and power of the precious, arresting, moment.

I try to avoid thinking that Wollstonecraft was softened by betrayal and misery into something mellower because I admire so much the spiky, angry feminist. But, in her sad journey with her baby through Scandinavia following betrayal by her lover, she took time – I almost wrote 'time out' – to record the fleeting, imaginatively realised moment, in rhetorical language not so very far from Burke's.

Such moments are caught in the book of travels she compiled on her return to England, *Letters written in Sweden, Norway and Denmark*. They have a fullness that allows time to be layered in past, present and future. For that instant, the self dissolves:

> The cow's bell has ceased to tinkle the herd to rest; they have all paced across the heath. Is not this the witching time of night? The waters murmur, and fall with more than mortal music … Eternity is in these moments. Worldly cares melt into the airy stuff that dreams are made of, and reveries, mild and enchanting as the first hopes of love or the recollection of lost enjoyment, carry the hapless wight into futurity, who in bustling life has vainly strove to throw off the grief which lies heavy at the heart … A crescent hangs out in the vault before, which woos me to stray abroad. It is not a silvery reflection of the sun, but glows with all

its golden splendour. Who fears the fallen dew? It only makes the mown grass smell more fragrant.

This is close to Romantic poetry, but a little embarrassed in its effort to enact spontaneity, in its archaic vocabulary, Shakespearean echoes and rhetorical questioning. And, unlike the poetry of Wordsworth, it refuses to move from the particular emotion into a new awareness. Later, Wollstonecraft exclaims, 'Phantoms of bliss! ideal forms of excellence! again enclose me in your magic circle.' Magic, illusory.

So she reins herself in and returns to 'the straight road of observation', moving back into concrete detail and more standard punctuation. But she has recorded that dreamy, intense moment and given it reality.

Later, more sceptical Jane Austen would not, could not have written like this. Yet, there are moments where she lets something almost inexpressible take over her protagonists. In the Chawton novels I find times when, through her watching or waiting women, she allows the headlong rush of life to halt or linger and something to happen that isn't quite disclosed.

JANE AUSTEN'S STILL MOMENTS

Austen's climactic moments crystallise thought and make the character understand something beyond the ordinary, not necessarily final and not quite about the self; not the kind of understanding that makes Elizabeth Bennet suddenly believe she 'knows herself' on her walk at Rosings, but an understanding of what might be called being within the world. Of course, since they're created by Austen and not Wollstonecraft, the 'mindful' moments may be tinged not with embarrassment but with irony, which it's up to us readers to value or ignore.

Emma's moments of profound experience come in stillness away from home, for in Hartfield, mistress though she may be, she's at the beck and call of her needy father. To be quiet and open, and neither imposing herself on another nor being imposed upon, she must step out.

This is the scene when Emma waits for Harriet at the door of Ford's shop in Highbury:

Emma went to the door for amusement.—Much could not be hoped from the traffic of even the busiest part of Highbury;— Mr. Perry walking hastily by, Mr. William Cox letting himself in at the office door, Mr. Cole's carriage horses returning from exercise, or a stray letter-boy on an obstinate mule, were the liveliest objects she could presume to expect; and when her eyes fell only on the butcher with his tray, a tidy old woman travelling homewards from shop with her full basket, two curs quarrelling over a dirty bone, and a string of dawdling children round the baker's little bow-window eyeing the gingerbread, she knew she had no reason to complain, and was amused enough; quite enough still to stand at the door. A mind lively and at ease, can do with seeing nothing, and can see nothing that does not answer.

This busy serenity is not far from the calm attitude of the maid described in Book 12 of Wordsworth's *Prelude*:

She welcomed what was given, and craved no more;
Whate'er the scene presented to her view
That was the best, to that she was attuned
By her benign simplicity of life ...

It may be too extravagant to associate Emma with 'benign simplicity of life' and a solitary, ingenuous inhabitant of the Lake District, but, momentarily, she achieves a similar serenity. The village of Highbury near London has businessmen, an apothecary, children and old people: all present in Emma's vision. Poverty is a little occluded; no sign of paupers like John Abdy or the family with its 'wants and sufferings' living down Vicarage Lane, only 'two curs', those paupers of the canine world. The rural society of southern England differs from Scotland and Ireland portrayed in the novels of Scott and Edgeworth, where ranks are more separated and the social message more distinct. It also differs from

the description of Bath in *Persuasion*, a town developed to separate rich from poor, areas of elegant wide streets from crowded
unsanitary parts.

Unlike Pemberley in *Pride and Prejudice*, the estate of Donwell
Abbey and the mansion of Hartfield are not feudally connected with
the lower orders; although stratified, there's an interdependence.
The circulation of goods and services – the hind quarters of pork
and baskets of apples and potions, the offer of coach and driver – is
sometimes patronising, but also uniting.

I see Emma at Ford's looking aesthetically and, semi-consciously,
integrating the elements of her ordinary village, but I don't want
to make too much of the social aspect. Most of the time, she gazes
through eyes trained by her privileged life and, while what she
sees here expresses change within stasis, when she thinks consciously of her village she tries to retain earlier, more hierarchical
ways of seeing. Then she appreciates little of the fluctuating social
composition of Highbury and has difficulty including the rising
mercantile and medical families in her own world.

Yet, however socially limited she shows herself elsewhere,
this vision from Ford's remains a beautiful passage, which I find
extraordinarily calming; it occurs while young Harriet dithers over
what to buy. It's part of Jane Austen's genius that, with her subtle
techniques of free indirect speech, her shifting closeness to and
ironic distance from the heroine, she allows the reader to appreciate both the seductiveness of Emma's vision and its limitation.

When I had to preside at weekly formal dinners in my old college,
I used to regale (or bore) the students with useful passages from
literature before the grace. Most students were studying science
and I thought my quoting – 'extracts' again – would be useful. I
tried this passage on them: I think many were bemused.

Another moment for Emma of reflection or meditation occurs at
Donwell Abbey, the inherited and ancient home of Mr Knightley.

It happens during the strawberry party Mrs Elton had failed to turn into a modern 'event'. Emma strolls off, not quite alone but mainly with her thoughts.

She looks with pride at the estate to which she's bound through her sister Isabella's marriage. She sees unimproved, unexploited grounds that connect the generations of gentlemanly owners:

> she viewed the respectable size and style of the building, its suitable, becoming characteristic situation, low and sheltered— its ample gardens stretching down to meadows washed by a stream, of which the Abbey, with all the old neglect of prospect, had scarcely a sight—and its abundance of timber in rows and avenues, which neither fashion nor extravagance had rooted up. The house ... was just what it ought to be, and it looked what it was.

She strays further and arrives at

> the delicious shade of a broad short avenue of limes, which stretching beyond the garden at an equal distance from the river, seemed the finish of the pleasure grounds.—It led to nothing; nothing but a view at the end over a low stone wall with high pillars, which seemed intended, in their erection, to give the appearance of an approach to the house, which never had been there.

Emma looks over the view and sees woods and slopes and 'Abbey-Mill Farm, with meadows in front, and the river making a close and handsome curve around it':

> It was a sweet view—sweet to the eye and the mind. English verdure, English culture, English comfort, seen under a sun bright, without being oppressive.

Although everyone and everyone's thought processes are fallible in this most equivocal of Austen's novels – in which only the very attentive reader can get anywhere near security – it's possible that this specific view of land is closest to a 'spot of time', a moment where conflict is contained.

In discussing Pemberley, I argued about the plenitude of the 'something' Elizabeth saw in the prospect of becoming mistress of the estate, of proxy ownership, of fantasy. Here in place of 'something', 'nothing' dominates, as it did in the description of the view from Ford's. The *nothing* is redolent of moderation, ease and balance – a pragmatism.

The pleasure grounds Emma contemplates are not formal, not answering to any abstraction, not planned in the way of improvers of land, people or states. Donwell has unstraightened paths and lacks contrived views. The long avenue of old trees 'led to nothing'. In *Mansfield Park*, Mary Crawford thinks 'a clergyman is nothing'. Lovestruck Edmund replies that the guardian of religion and morals is not 'nothing'. The word 'nothing' carries a lot of weight in these Chawton novels.

The 'nothing' of the view in Donwell and from Ford's suggests no transcendental meaning. Nor is there anxiety. The moment I quoted from *Letters from Sweden* leaves something negative behind – in the book Wollstonecraft worries about death as non-being and as corporeal decay. The timelessness caught for an instant emphasises time. Jane Austen doesn't echo Wollstonecraft's anxiety.

The great eighteenth-century philosopher and historian David Hume, whose temperament I find close to what I discern of Jane Austen's in her novels, comprehended both attitudes when he summed up his return from the rational philosophical emptiness he'd been investigating. After speculation and metaphysical worrying, he goes off to dine, play backgammon and be merry with friends, concluding, 'Here then I find myself absolutely and necessarily determin'd to live, and talk, and act like other people in the common affairs of life.'

Donwell is as meaningful as the view of desultory life from Ford's door. In neither case are the descriptive words quite Emma's conscious ones, though they are her thoughts. They're delivered almost in the complete sentences of ordered self-investigation and are unlike the rushed, disordered, elliptical monologues – still in free indirect speech – of Miss Bates or Mrs Elton. The narrator is quietly present.

I want to connect *Emma*'s 'nothing' with the nothing expressed so loudly in the letters: unexpectedly, I'm finding a theme of emptiness, of vacuity running through both public and private work. It's a theme that may suggest some perturbation, but mostly to me it signifies a sort of intellectual freedom in understanding, a refusal of ultimate conforming, a side-stepping from ideologies of any sort.

A DEGREE OF PATRIOTISM

That triple repetition of 'English' in the 'sweet view' at Donwell – you can't avoid noticing it – under a moderate sun.

I doubt there's an imperialist point here, that England's moderate climate is superior to that of more southern lands now under British rule, but there might well be something anti-French. The sun of England is bright or open, but not oppressive like the sun shining on French lands given to creating emperors and tyrants. However, compared with other contemporary writers, it's a quiet antagonism. Maria Edgeworth's frenchified Olivia in *Leonora* complains about the 'nationality' of a young Englishwoman: 'All her ideas are exclusively English: she has what is called English good sense, and English humour, and English prejudices of all sorts.'

English 'patriotism' is a challenging subject now. We're in the orbit of the United States rather than of Europe, with the colossal empire gone but not quite the sense of exceptionalism that went along with it. With a huge new immigrant population from different cultures, we've come to be embarrassed about any sign of English 'patriotism'. For us the word now requires those quotation marks. Readers and critics who want to allow Austen more conventionally progressive politics than I can now discover in her, must find irony in the words, or posit a narrator (and author) quite separate from her heroine here. But my reading of the letters has drawn me to a rather different view from the one I earlier held, when I strove to bring Mary Wollstonecraft and Jane Austen closer together in liberal, internationalist views.

English patriotism is out of fashion in the twenty-first century, compared with that of the other components of the not-so-united United Kingdom: Wales, Scotland and Northern Ireland, all far more prone to expressing a proud sense of nationhood. Nowadays when declared, English patriotism seems grotesquely out of kilter with the position England holds in the world. It's far from the almost abstract love of country and countryside that I was encouraged to feel in my childhood – for *England*, the dominant bit of the United Kingdom that, since I'm Welsh, wasn't strictly mine.

In the 1940s and '50s a patriotic Englishness was still strong, served by heroic imperial visions of the never-setting sun and memories of a recently fought and won world war. Despite my school with its songs in euphonious Welsh, I read and learnt by heart Robert Browning's 'Nobly, nobly Cape Saint Vincent' and demanded how I could 'help England' in the fervent way he did. I also learnt Browning's 'Oh to be in England' with its insistence that the buttercup was superior to the 'gaudy melon-flower', and Rupert Brooke's First World War soldier lying in some foreign field which is 'for ever England', as if the mud of Grantchester Meadows was transcendentally rich and always under a heaven itself turned 'English'. 'England' became something supranational, a way of thinking, I don't quite know what, but I felt it strongly in Wales, Sri Lanka, Bermuda, Ghana and Puerto Rico, whatever pleasant better-climated place I happened to be living in.

I still love the fields, hedgerows and slow rivers of England, but feel none of that weird nostalgia for what it once seemed to mean to me and so many others, the patriotism that justified all sorts of sad activities in other people's lands over the centuries since Jane Austen wrote her novels. But can we not allow her to feel something just a little like what was so prevalent in the 1940s and '50s? Would it be so odd? Her country had suffered two decades of war and, although *Emma* was written in the false peace before Napoleon returned to renew the conflict, for the previous two decades the lives of her brothers Frank and Charles had been in constant danger. To the Austens, French Napoleon had been as much a bogeyman as Hitler to my generation.

The letters catch the attitude. When Frank was away on his ship fighting in the Baltic, Jane wrote:

> It must be real enjoyment to you, since you are obliged to leave England, to be where you are, seeing something of a new Country … I have a great respect for former Sweden. So zealous as it was for Protestan[t]ism!—And I have always fancied it more like England than many Countries;—& according to the Map, many of the names have a strong resemblance to the English.

To her friend Alethea Bigg, she wrote:

> I hope your letters from abroad are satisfactory. They would not be satisfactory to me, I confess, unless they breathed a strong spirit of regret for not being in England.

And:

> We have got the 2^d vol. of Espriella's Letters, & I read it aloud by candlelight. The Man describes well, but is horribly anti-english. He deserves to be the foreigner he assumes.

The author of this work with its Spanish narrator was the poet laureate Robert Southey; later Austen would read 'with much approbation' his long patriotic *Poet's Pilgrimage to Waterloo* which glorified Britain's victory, declaring 'parts of it suit me better than much that he has written before'.

In *Emma*, a discussion between Frank Churchill and Emma directly touches on love of one's country – and, again, that common Francophobic (wartime) theme. Frank declares, 'I am sick of England—and would leave it tomorrow, if I could.'

Emma replies, 'You are sick of prosperity and indulgence.'

This weariness with his native land underlines Frank's shallowness, while Emma's response judges spoilt Frank (Francis, France), and associates England with 'prosperity'.

I don't find Jane Austen loudly patriotic – she makes no ideology of patriotism and prejudice in the manner of Burke – but, unlike Mary Wollstonecraft, she never questions the morality of her country's political system or its imperial adventuring, what Anna Laetitia Barbauld saw as the worm in the core of the body politic. The letters are clear in their love of England, though not always of its government; Austen deplored the Prince Regent and a short-lived Whig-dominated Ministry that, though it abolished the slave trade, achieved little else: she called it 'pitiful, angry, mean'.

In the Introduction I mentioned her equanimity about profi-teering during the long wars. She's equally accepting of the war itself. Unlike the generation that welcomed the fall of the Bastille as the beginning of a new progressive era for all, hers was doubtful about any notion of perfectible human systems, the inspiration of French and English radicals. The heroic fighting men in her family are *justly* fighting Napoleonic France, but there's no need to make a parade of it.

Wentworth's heroic war stories are told to entertain and impress – true even of his near-death experience on the *Asp*. Likewise, William Price in *Mansfield Park*, though he mentions the horror as well as the adventure of war, impresses his hearers with his energetic telling. Other women writers created very different returning warriors, frequently contrasting their stirring stories with their broken bodies, 'bent and feeble, helpless and forlorn', as the poet and dramatist Joanna Baillie expressed it.

Anna Laetitia Barbauld, Mary Robinson and Charlotte Smith raged at the awful human cost of the almost global conflict, the absurdity of fighting to settle political disputes. Barbauld made conflict vivid for her readers with individual sketches of returning wounded men finding themselves homeless and reduced to beg-ging on the streets, as well as of grieving mothers of dead boys: 'No son returns ... / Her fallen blossoms strew a foreign strand.' Jane Cave, the sufferer of those dreadful headaches, saw no heroes but only battlefields 'drench'd with human blood'. Many detected

God's hand in the vicissitudes of war, a country's sins punished by military catastrophe.

Jane Austen doesn't personalise war in this political way, nor, like Cave and Barbauld, set it in a religious context. In one letter, however, she comes close when she comments on the death of Sir John Moore at the British retreat at Corunna (La Coruña) in Spain in 1809.

Sir John's last words were widely reported in the British press as: 'I hope my country will do me justice!' Jane Austen added, 'I wish Sir John had united something of the Christian with the Hero in his death.' Although she called the disastrous military action 'grievous news', she went on to remark, 'Thank Heaven! We have had no one to care for particularly among the Troops'. She presents it as a sentimental affectation to become too upset for those one did not know, to be truly moved by mass slaughter.

In her last year, with war over, Jane Austen felt how precarious was the 'prosperity' of England. The affluence that brother Henry had enjoyed while fighting persisted proved paper-thin when it stopped. Southey noted the national disappointment with peace. The significance of battles once so triumphantly applauded diminished. In 'Sanditon' they're reduced to names for seaside villas. Nelson's Trafalgar, which meant so much to the sailor brothers, lost cultural, even decorative, cachet, to be replaced by more recent Waterloo, the bubble of whose fame would likely be popped long before the paint on the house-signs had flaked.

Near where I live, streets record Britain's painful imperial struggle with the Boers: Kimberley and Pretoria. Some day soon people will want to swap them for more fashionable names. The Council Offices are already in Mandela House.

The fear of invasion of the south coast worried England from the 1780s until 1815. Now with the threat vanquished, 'Sanditon' could comically rework the trope, with multiplying seaside resorts invading the land. The sea that once kept England free from foreign armies exists for pleasure and ease. The old romance of fighting on and against the sea has given way to seaside frolics, as Emma's pretty English vision of unimproved parkland and tenanted meadows has been replaced by a windy clifftop 'view'. The stable land that produced food for victory against anarchic France no longer defines the nation. The entrepreneur Tom Parker has left his ancestral home and now must buy his produce; he declares that he couldn't stand seeing a cabbage bed in winter. It's hard to imagine Mr Knightley turning his back on English 'culture' (agriculture) for the sake of avoiding a view of cabbage stalks.

MEDITATION APART

In the finished novels there are moments when the heroines step aside. They stop the treadmill of polite conversation and obligatory social interchange on which they spend most of their lives. Or rather they step off it for a while to think, to be mindful perhaps, or, as we might now say, to 'process'. The moments are not self-centred but they may centre on the self and sometimes suggest a communion with something beyond.

Without being overtly religious, these moments, prayerful and cloistered, resemble a stoical Christian meditative state in which the mind becomes stilled. Perhaps the woman is simply 'reasoning with herself', perhaps trying to gain composure to cope with a disruptive emotion or endeavouring to arrange feelings so they can be investigated later – or just accepting emptiness. Often there's a physical movement away, a withdrawing.

Cowper described how he set aside moments for creative reflection and latency outside the bustle and demand of everyday life. He sat still by the fireside entering into a liminal place. With the 'mind contemplative', he half created what he saw. This was less fancy than a willing 'vacuity of thought' that allowed repose before he returned to his rational mind refreshed. 'How calm is my recess,' he exclaimed.

In *Sense and Sensibility*, where Marianne in love is 'unquiet', 'restless and dissatisfied', her sister Elinor controls herself physically in the face of sudden sadness. When alone, having confronted something even worse than losing Edward – the death of her sister – she has a moment apart. Quiet and understated, it hangs there between the drama of Marianne's near fatal illness and the melodrama of Willoughby's arrival. It's a true moment of reflective calm:

> Elinor could not be cheerful. Her joy was of a different kind, and led to anything rather than to gaiety. Marianne restored to life, health, friends, and to her doating mother, was an idea to fill her heart with sensations of exquisite comfort, and expand it in fervent gratitude;—but it led to no outward demonstrations of joy, no words, no smiles. All within Elinor's breast was satisfaction, silent and strong.

What Emma saw in Donwell Abbey grounds was delivered in negatives; so too here Elinor's apartness, her undemonstrative satisfaction, is expressed in what it is not: no gaiety, no smiles, no words. Instead, in this beautifully restrained passage, she feels 'exquisite comfort' and 'gratitude' – presumably to God, though he's unnamed. Her joy is emotional, intellectual and spiritual.

In the Introduction I wrote about memory, its value, cunning and power over the present, keeping the self in thrall to what it made of the past. In *Mansfield Park*, the description of the vacated East Room that Fanny Price takes for her own catches her past as crystallised moments.

The narrator delivers it with a little gently sardonic humour. The room holds the images of beloved William and Edmund and does duty for home and family, or rather it fuses Mansfield and Portsmouth. In this separated space, Fanny brings together external items that articulate a sentimental yearning self kept under wraps elsewhere.

Though it has a 'good aspect', Fanny's room is cold, its coldness suiting her quietness and need for modest bodily suffering. It's her creation, her solace, and her memory:

> She could go there after any thing unpleasant below, and find immediate consolation in some pursuit, or some train of thought

at hand. … she could scarcely see an object in that room which had not an interesting remembrance connected with it.—Every thing was a friend, or bore her thoughts to a friend; and though there had been sometimes much of suffering to her—though her motives had been often misunderstood, her feelings disregarded, and her comprehension undervalued; though she had known the pains of tyranny, of ridicule, and neglect, yet almost every recurrence of either had led to something consolatory … the whole was now so blended together, so harmonized by distance, that every former affliction had its charm. The room was most dear to her, and she would not have changed its furniture for the handsomest in the house.

Here time is halted. The private room becomes a kind of embodied, concrete memory.

So it becomes momentous when the space is invaded by Edmund and Mary, the couple that Fanny hates to see anywhere, most of all here where they interrupt past, present and future. When she's alone in the room, Edmund is hers. When he stands before her, he's no longer so. In the flesh he damages the calm profile that had been her image of him and her possession.

COMFORTABLE MOMENTS WITH GOOD FOOD

It may seem eccentric to relate spiritual moments of calm with eating – but need it be? Both are delivered in Austen's words, which can hold off time where they will.

Byron said the word 'comfort' couldn't be applied to anything outside England. It implied warmth and cosiness, ample food and drink: Mr Weston's good wine and Mrs Weston's wedding cake.

Even during that hard autumn of 1815 when she was shut up in London with her sick brother Henry, Jane enjoyed moments of comfort with delicious food: 'Good apple-pies are a considerable part of our domestic happiness,' she wrote. Presents of 'Hare & 4 Rabbits' came from Edward's Godmersham and a 'brace of

Pheasants' from her friends, the Fowles. Probably she smiled at the appropriateness of the gift.

Good food combined with warmth demanded money and Austen experienced both at Godmersham. Like Cowper, she relished moments of such comfortable unison. Her delight in the gustatory side of her visits echoes earlier contentment shared with her mother when together they visited Mrs Austen's cousin at grand Stoneleigh Abbey. Mrs Austen wrote of the occasion:

> Eating Fish, venison and all manner of good things, at a late hour, in a Noble large Parlour hung round with family Pictures—every thing is very Grand and very fine and very Large

The breakfast table held 'Plumb Cake, Pound Cake, Hot Rolls, Cold Rolls', chocolate, coffee and tea.

Now, staying at Godmersham, Jane too lauded the comfort of food in letters to Cassandra, eating more frugally in the Chawton cottage:

> I am happy to hear of the Honey.—I was thinking of it the other day.—Let me know when you begin the new Tea—& the new White Wine.—My present Elegancies have not yet made me indifferent to such Matters. I am still a Cat if I see a Mouse. ...
>
> I have no occasion to think of the price of Bread or of Meat where I am now—let me shake off vulgar cares & conform to the happy Indifference of East Kent wealth

And the expensive warmth: a fire every evening. Jane is 'very, snug, in my own room, lovely morning, excellent fire—fancy me'.

The rub was that such *bodily* comfort as Godmersham offered rarely coexisted with intellectual stimulus. The luxurious moments were paid for in boredom.

> A Whist Table for the Gentlemen, a grown-up musical young Lady to play Backgammon with Fanny, & engravings of the Colleges at Cambridge for me.

Oh dear, those Cambridge colleges.

There is nobody Brilliant nowadays.

Of one Godmersham visitor, she wrote:

> He seems a very harmless sort of young Man—nothing to like
> or dislike in him;— goes out shooting or hunting with the two
> others all the morng.—and plays at whist & makes queer faces
> in the eveng.

Grand Godmersham was not about the 'company of clever, well-informed people, who have a great deal of conversation' (the 'best' company according to Mr Elliot in *Persuasion*) but about the body's comfort: food and warmth, not talk.

THE COMFORT OF TOAST

At home where the company could be 'brilliant', comfort could be had more cheaply with an ordinary piece of toast. With complementing butter – 'butter, costlier still', as Cowper described it. Contrary as so often, Mrs Austen preferred 'dry toast'.

English toast existed because the nation had come to prefer quickly staling white over Continental rye bread, and to favour open fires over closed stoves. It became a sign of national well-being and comfort, requiring informality – on which, too, the English prided themselves.

In Victorian novels, toasting bread is often a metonym for the cosy home. In modern television costume drama too. In the 2007 film of *Northanger Abbey*, wanting more domestic romance than Austen's book allowed, Andrew Davies created a momentary scene of toasting in the grand Abbey.

In his satiric poem *Don Juan*, Byron, long absent from England, said no one sings of toast. It became for English expatriates a sort of equivalent before the event of Proust's memory-laden madeleine (Proust's manuscript reveals that his famous madeleine was originally a piece of honey-soaked *toast*).

When he arrived at an English country house, P. G. Wodehouse said he liked 'the cup of tea, the crackling logs and buttered toast; the general atmosphere of leisured cosiness'. For imprisoned Toad in *The Wind in the Willows*, buttered toast is the ultimate comfort food: its smell

> talked of warm kitchens, of breakfasts on bright frosty mornings, of cosy parlour firesides on winter evenings, when one's ramble was over and slippered feet were propped on the fender.

In wireless talks on the BBC's Home Service in the 1950s, the poet John Betjeman made buttered toast a symbol of the nation's common culture.

Within Jane Austen's work, toast makes its gala appearance in 'Sanditon'. In the resort touting sunshine and freshness, the Parker siblings sit inside by a roaring fire in their Terrace lodgings. Arthur, the most robust of the invalids (delicious parody of the equally coddled but elderly and weakly Mr Woodhouse of *Emma*) summons the family energy for toasting. A tussle ensues over the amount of butter allowed. Soon he's engrossed

> toasting some slices of bread, brought up ready-prepared in the toast rack—and till it was all done, [Charlotte] heard nothing of his voice but the murmuring of a few broken sentences of self-approbation and success.

The farcical Parker tea party with toast swims out of the novel to become a parody of sentimental English domesticity, of English bodily comfort. Or its cynosure. An English equivalent of foreign champagne and caviar.

Or – and this can only be my personal conjoining – equivalent of the gargantuan Russian feast of Dmitri and Grushenka in *The Brothers Karamazov*, which so thrilled and shocked my thrifty adolescent self with its reckless indulgence.

When we lived so happily in Sri Lanka – though admittedly too stiflingly hot – my mother once said out of the blue, 'I should so like to be in England eating some hot buttered toast with marmalade by an open window.' I remember it because it was so strange a thing.

When we finally met after my boarding-school years and sat in a B&B with the rain meandering down the window pane, I forgot to ask her whether the toast of England tasted as she'd hoped.

CHAPTER 10
How to Die

Sleepe after toyle, port after stormie seas,
Ease after warre, death after life does greatly please.

Death in Austen's fiction is pushed to the peripheries. There's the strange interpolated tale of the two Elizas in *Sense and Sensibility*, the first of whom dies of consumption. Not a realised death, it's there more to give the grave Colonel sentimental bulk. Mrs Tilney of *Northanger Abbey* again dies outside the frame.

The rest are quasi-absurd, comical. Despotic Mrs Churchill, appreciated only when she proved she was not a demanding malingerer, is redeemed by death for the Highbury folk, then given the adjective 'poor'. Gluttonous Dr Grant in *Mansfield Park*, killed by 'three great institutionary dinners in one week' so that the worthy Edmund Bertrams can move into the rich Mansfield rectory. Fat Mrs Musgrove's unsatisfactory son Dick dying largely unlamented even by the family that sent him as a child to sea.

Speculative deaths are more common. In that naughty way she had with her characters, Jane Austen revealed that Mr Woodhouse of *Emma*, for whose convenience the master of Donwell Abbey gave up his proper place, would not keep his son-in-law from home for many years. Like Mrs Churchill, he was not in good health after all. In *Mansfield Park*, Mary Crawford fantasises the death of Tom Bertram so that the man she loves, the more nobly named Edmund, might inherit house and baronetcy. Mrs Bennet fixates on the death of Mr Bennet, which threatens the loss not so much of a husband as of a house. It results in one of those little chats between the senior Bennets that are the delight of the book.

Mrs Bennet has learnt that the heir of Longbourn, Mr Collins, is to marry Charlotte Lucas:

> 'Indeed, Mr. Bennet,' said she, 'it is very hard to think that Charlotte Lucas should ever be mistress of this house, that *I* should be forced to make way for *her*, and live to see her take my place in it!'
>
> 'My dear, do not give way to such gloomy thoughts. Let us hope for better things. Let us flatter ourselves that *I* may be the survivor.'
>
> This was not very consoling to Mrs. Bennet.

Death is apprehended in the strange ending of *Persuasion* with its mention of 'the tax of quick alarm' paid by the families of those serving in the navy. For all his prize money, Captain Wentworth is still a sailor, still may die at sea.

In which case – and I'm indulging again in speculation – Anne, so long a spinster, would become a widow, to live perhaps – is this going too far? – with the widowed Mrs Smith, now glowing with spirits: Mrs Smith who shares the last paragraph of the novel with Anne. At the close of *Mansfield Park*, the sisters Mary Crawford and Mrs Grant go to live together, one without the lover that Tom Bertram wickedly imagined her wanting, the other, after forfeiting Edmund's love, 'in need of the true kindness of her sister's heart, and the rational tranquillity of her ways'. Something like this, if it came to that wartime worst, might be a pleasant future for the two old schoolfriends of *Persuasion*.

I'm back again at Chawton cottage: Martha and the Austen sisters.

DEATH IN LETTERS

Austen's letters are casual about deaths. Often, as in the novels, they hover on the edge of comedy.

In Basingstoke a haberdasher dies; mourning is interrupted by the hope that the next one will sell her goods more cheaply.

> Sir Tho: Miller is dead. I treat you with a dead Baronet in almost every Letter.

> Mr Waller is dead, I see;—I cannot greive about it, nor perhaps can his Widow very much.

> [T]here is no reason to suppose that Miss Morgan is dead after all.

Then the unseemly joke that so appalled E. M. Forster:

> Mrs Hall of Sherbourn was brought to bed yesterday of a dead child, some weeks before she expected, oweing to a fright.—I suppose she happened unawares to look at her husband.–There has been a great deal of rain here…

So unsentimentally juxtaposed with that rain, this glimpse of a marriage is tasteless but undeniably funny.

I've argued that Jane Austen was always ambivalent over childbearing, pitying those 'poor animals' she saw all round her relentlessly breeding. Every lying-in endangered the mother. Sometimes, as with her sisters-in-law, Elizabeth, Edward's wife, and Fanny, Charles's wife, it was fatal, leaving the bereaved husband with eleven motherless children in one case, four in the other.

Other deaths were appropriate. When Elizabeth Leigh, a relative of her mother's, died aged eighty, Jane wrote:

> the death of a person at her advanced age, so fit to die, & by her own feelings so *ready* to die, is not to be regretted.—

The Misses Hulberts of Speen Hill, both in 'indifferent' health, 'really are breaking now. Not so stout as the old Jackass.' Stouter than Jane Austen, for both survived her, one dying at ninety-six.

Jane Austen admired the satirical poet George Crabbe and fantasied being Mrs Crabbe. (A good joke when every other woman in England was dreaming of being Lady Byron!) Once Jane and Crabbe were in London at the same time –along with the real Mrs Crabbe. Jane went to the theatre hoping for a sight.

> I was particularly disappointed at seeing nothing of Mr Crabbe. I felt sure of him when I saw that the boxes were fitted with Crimson velvet.

Presumably an allusion to one of Crabbe's poems. I looked but found nothing quite right.

Then Mrs Crabbe was rumoured to be dead. Jane wrote cheerily:

> No; I have never seen the death of Mrs Crabbe. I have only just been making out from one of his prefaces that he probably was married. It is almost ridiculous. Poor woman! I will comfort *him* as well as I can, but I do not undertake to be good to her children. She had better not leave any.

'*Her*', not their children.

Mrs Crabbe wasn't dead but she died a few days later.

In my late teens I nourished a similar fantasy of being Mrs Aldous Huxley. I was enthralled by Huxley's sophisticated novels, set in a world so utterly different from my own that they might as well have been on Mars. I imagined leading the purblind genius through the palm fronds of mythical California. If I'd known he had a wife, I'd have probably fantasised a touching death for her.

SIGNIFICANT DEATHS

On Jane Austen's twenty-ninth birthday, 16 December 1804, one of her dearest friends died. Anne Lefroy (sometimes called Madam) was the cultured wife of the rector of Ashe, a parish about two miles from Jane's home in Steventon. She became a mentor and close friend of young Jane. By the time she died, the Austens were living in Bath, and Jane's eldest brother James had taken over the Steventon rectory.

Anne Lefroy had gone shopping with her manservant to the nearby town of Overton. There she met James, chatted with him, and complained about the stupidity and sluggishness of her horse. She couldn't persuade it to canter.

On the way home Mrs Lefroy and her manservant reached Overton Hill. There Mrs Lefroy's horse, either scared or suddenly skittish, sped off. The servant rode up to try to catch the bridle rein; he failed, making the horse bolt. What happened next is obscure; perhaps in her fright Mrs Lefroy tried to jump off or perhaps she was thrown. She fell onto hard ground and died a few hours later.

The dreadful news soon reached Jane and her family. The Revd James Austen conducted Anne Lefroy's funeral service.

No surviving letter describes Jane's emotions at the loss of this dear friend, but there's a poem written four years later, on her own thirty-third birthday. The only truly serious poem among the extant verses and riddles, it serves as elegy to Anne Lefroy. Perhaps it was in part that coincidence of her own birthday and her friend's death day that was the inspiration. These things matter.

Since I began to live with Mary Wollstonecraft, I've always been aware that she died on my birthday and, try as I might not to think of her when the day comes round, I always do. The tenth of September is also World Suicide Prevention Day.

Jane Austen loved Mrs Lefroy. She learnt much from this cultivated older lady and always spoke of her with admiration. Biographers assume Mrs Lefroy separated her nephew Tom from young almost penniless Jane after she observed the now famous flirtation between them. Had there been love? Who knows? If there had been, perhaps Jane stayed resentful, then resented her resentment and felt contrite. If so, nothing of this creeps into the poem.

Probably the most famous elegy in English is Milton's 'Lycidas', as much about the living writer as about the dead man. Here in Jane's modest elegy, the coincidence of death and birth echoes

'Lycidas' in linking the two women: 'The day returns again, my natal day'. The second stanza continues the link:

> The day, commemorative of my birth
> Bestowing Life & Light & Hope on me,
> Brings back the hour which was thy last on Earth.
> Oh! bitter pang of torturing Memory!—

The poem is warm, well-meaning, but also rather trite in expression.

> Angelic Woman! past my power to praise
> In Language meet, thy Talents, Temper, Mind,
> Thy solid Worth, thy captivating Grace!—
> Thou friend & ornament of Humankind!—

What follows is curious. The speaker, who must be Jane herself, for her birthday is so emphasised, imagines the dead woman reanimated, moving and speaking. She creates an almost passionate conjunction of herself and her older friend, one living, one dead:

> Come then fond Fancy, thou indulgent Power,—
> —Hope is desponding, chill, severe to thee!—
> Bless thou, this little portion of an hour,
> Let me behold her as she used to be.
>
> I see her here, with all her smiles benign,
> Her looks of eager Love, her accents sweet.
> That voice & Countenance almost divine!—
> Expression, Harmony, alike complete.—
>
> I listen—'tis not sound alone—'tis sense,
> 'Tis Genius, Taste, & Tenderness of soul.
> 'Tis genuine warmth of heart without pretence
> And purity of Mind that crowns the whole.
>
> She speaks; 'tis Eloquence—that grace of Tongue

Then, it's as though the speaker feels she asks too much, is presumptuous in wanting to bring back this wonderful woman for her own benefit:

> the Vision disappears

> 'Tis past & gone—We meet no more below.
> Short is the Cheat of Fancy o'er the Tomb.
> Oh! might I hope to equal Bliss to go!
> To meet thee Angel! in thy future home!—

The 'Cheat of Fancy' recalls John Keats's 'Ode to a Nightingale', published two years after Jane Austen's death, in which the poet, after rapturous contemplation of the invisible bird and 'easeful death', realises that 'the fancy cannot cheat so well / As she is fam'd to do'. In both cases, Keats and Austen try irrationally to identify beyond themselves with what they describe and to hold the union through imagination. Both fail and return to their own bodies.

Austen's poem is full of the clichés she'd never have allowed into her novels. But this is not fiction and there's no irony puncturing the conventional diction. Perhaps she felt that, faced with a significant death and thinking on the afterlife, only this 'poetic' and biblical language was suitable.

(Austen at her devotions is inevitably hidden from us. Long after her death three prayers were ascribed to her, but to me they seem more likely to be the work of one of her clerical brothers – she's known to have copied out a sermon for James – especially since they echo in simplified, extemporised form the collects of the *Book of Common Prayer*, and appear to be written for collective rather than personal worship. Much concerned to stress his sister's piety, Henry Austen made no mention of these prayers when he wrote his biographical sketch.)

In terms of its effect on her life and so on her writings, the most momentous death in Jane's young adult years is that of her father, Rev. George Austen, six weeks after Mrs Lefroy's, on 21 January 1805.

George Austen had been one of the first to admire the literary talent of his second daughter. He'd instructed her, given her a writing slope and notebooks in which to copy her creative work, and in 1797 he offered her first completed novel to the publisher Thomas Cadell in London. The work was, he wrote, about the length of Frances Burney's *Evelina*.

It's commonly assumed that the proposed novel was the original of *Pride and Prejudice*. I think it more likely to have been the original of *Sense and Sensibility*, which became the first work Austen herself chose to publish; she might have been fiddling with it ever since her father's kindly offer. Also, to me, it fits better in length and subject matter with his mention of *Evelina*. Whichever it was, Cadell never saw it: the letter was returned unread.

For all the family, George Austen's sudden death was an immense emotional loss but, for his wife and daughters who depended on him, it was social and economic as well. James had become curate in Steventon, and the incumbent rector's income from tithes was still going to his father. With George's death, this income could no longer benefit his wife and daughters. Livings in the Church of England tied to those elegant parsonages, so very desirable as spacious residences now, seem from the outside to deliver a most pleasant way of life. However, for the clergyman's dependent womenfolk, existence was as precarious as Mrs Bennet felt hers to be at entailed Longbourn. The Austen ladies had some personal money but insufficient for a genteel life if lodging needed to be paid from it; henceforward, they'd have to look to the brothers for extra support and live in reduced circumstances.

Having contemplated her income and expenses, Jane wrote briskly to Cassandra from Godmersham, 'prepare ... for the sight of a sister sunk in poverty, that it may not overcome your Spirits.' Later, she memorably observed, 'Single Women have a dreadful propensity for being poor.'

It fell to Jane to inform brother Frank, whose ship was in Portsmouth, of their father's death and the circumstances of his dying. For this formal letter she used conventional language, as she'd done in the elegy on Madam Lefroy. In fact, she always wrote more formally to this energetic but serious man than to her other close relatives. Their father

> was mercifully spared from knowing that he was about to quit the Objects so beloved, so fondly cherished as his wife & Children ever were.

In a sentence that sounds strange to twenty-first-century ears, as it wouldn't have done at the time, she notes the moment when her father's death is not his but his family's, when the living man becomes a corpse: 'The Serenity of the Corpse is most delightful!' Years later, Mrs Austen would die aged eighty-seven and her granddaughter would note that, on the corpse, 'the very wrinkles seemed smoothed out of her face' and 'the beauty of youth [was] restored to it'.

Given the bond between father and daughter, it's curious that in Jane Austen's novels the most realised paternal characters are feeble or inadequate: Mr Bennet is irresponsible, Mr Price is coarse and drunken, Mr Woodhouse is a foolish cypher and Sir Walter Elliot is ridiculous. All these characters are created in a period which specialised in sentimental pictures of father/guardian–daughter relationships. A fine example is the novel George Austen mentioned in his letter to Cadell, Frances Burney's phenomenally popular *Evelina*.

A SLOW DECLINE

In her adult life Jane Austen seems to have suffered few illnesses beyond whooping cough and the usual colds, headaches and feelings of fatigue. Her last year, however, was dominated by the disease that would prove fatal, and the letters of 1816–17 make painful reading.

She'd noticed that Henry's illness, suffered through the Autumn of 1815, had begun with a cold; after many weeks confined in the London house caring for him, she herself reported that she'd caught cold. Was she ever really quite well again? I shouldn't impose our knowledge on her, making it her foreknowledge, but there's some evidence that, from time to time, she now sensed a physical decline. In *Persuasion* Mrs Smith becomes a 'pitiable' invalid following a cold and is in constant pain.

Always weather impinged. Jane Austen had enjoyed the muggy warm weather of London in late 1815, though it can't have been good for her, pent up in the house. Then back in Chawton she suffered 'sad weather', with an overflowing pond and damp cottage walls. So began 1816, that gloomy year without a summer, terrible for the nation but rather good for literature, as we know. Jane Austen finished the first draft of *Persuasion* in July.

Rain beat against the Chawton cottage windows – of course: it was July. Jane went out in the donkey cart and got wet.

There are many diagnoses offered for what killed her. Addison's disease, Hodgkin's Lymphoma, a variant of tuberculosis, poisoning caused by one of the noxious substances people of the time regularly used on themselves or their houses, like lead, arsenic and mercury. Or murder by a rival author suspecting Jane Austen's gigantic future fame and wishing to dampen it at least in the present – it has been suggested.

She was given to diagnosing herself as symptoms emerged and disappeared, only to recur. One constant suspicion is of the 'bile' her mother complained of back in their Steventon days; it seemed to mark the lingeringly ill and the malingering alike.

There's something genteel about a 'cold'; it's acceptable to mention it in polite company. 'Biliousness' may be less so – like drawing attention to one's urinary tract infection or bleeding bowels now – not quite appropriate, though very common. 'Bilious' is everywhere in Austen's letters.

Mr Buller, a former pupil of Jane's father, is 'bilious' and so far compromised that the waters in Bath are ineffective. He's in 'a confirmed Decline', able to do only 'a good deal of quiet walking'.

'Bilious' intrudes into fiction. Mrs Tilney, whom Catherine Morland imagined victim of a brutal murdering husband, died according to her son of a 'bilious fever'. In *Emma* Mr Perry, the apothecary is thought to be 'bilious'. He's taken insufficient care of himself, the implication being that he's giving too much to his patients. Perhaps he should buy a carriage after all. (The idea crept into one of those secret letters between Frank and Jane Fairfax, nearly exposing them to the eagle-eyed Highbury community.) Whether or not Mr Perry is actually 'bilious', he diagnoses the condition in his patient Mr Cole.

No one is bilious in sunny *Pride and Prejudice.* Healthy Elizabeth bids adieu to disappointment and 'spleen', something of a crossover organ of physical distress and mental dissatisfaction. The Bennets, taken together, do not strike one as 'bilious'.

To me the word 'bilious' is irretrievably funny. In the 1940s my aunt said her neighbour Gertie was 'bilious' and that was why she never left the house. I pictured this unseen woman shaking and prowling round her curtained home in a sort of Gothic whirl.

RELATIONS

The year 1816 was not a good one for the Austens. Charles, who'd lost his wife after childbirth, had been sent to capture pirates near Smyrna. His ship struck rocks and was wrecked off the Turkish coast. No fatalities, but he was blamed for the shipwreck and court-martialled. In the end he was acquitted and censure fell on local pilots, but Charles didn't receive another command for many years.

The ladies at Chawton probably heard this news about the time they learnt of a calamity touching them even more nearly.

Henry had benefited from the long French and Napoleonic Wars. He'd first joined the local militia, soon becoming paymaster and agent. Then he resigned his commission and set up as a banker in London, partnering local banks in Kent and Hampshire. He rode high; the wartime economy demanded huge defence spending, and import restrictions kept agricultural prices buoyant. It was safe to lend money to prosperous clients, especially landed aristocrats.

For example, Lord Moira, Anglo-Irish politician and soldier, a man who'd helped Charles Austen to his first naval command. He was a friend of the Prince Regent's: 'Moira and I,' the Prince would say, 'are like two brothers, when one wants money he puts his hand in the other's pocket'. Part of the Moira pocket had been filled by Henry Austen.

The name of Moira suggests how tiny a world Jane Austen exists in compared with our own: small population and smaller elite. This same politically ambitious, unscrupulous and extravagant Lord Moira features prominently in my biography of Mary Wollstonecraft's aristocratic pupils in Ireland, *Rebel Daughters.* For Henry Austen, Moira would become one of the entitled people surrounding the Prince Regent who saw no reason to pay those beneath them.

War ended. Huge financial and social adjustment followed, along with national depression. Henry's banks collapsed in a welter of debts in March 1816. 'I lost everything,' he wrote: home, possessions and livelihood. He was declared bankrupt. He accused Lord Moira of defrauding him of £6,000.

As ever, the immediate family laid little blame on charming Henry despite being implicated in his failure. His brothers all lost money, but Edward and their uncle Thomas Leigh Perrot as sureties lost most.

Soon resilient Henry was writing 'chearfully'; he arrived to visit his brother James 'in unbroken spirits'. He would join the Church.

Meanwhile, Jane must have felt unease, some sense that her body was not right, for in spring 1816 she went to Cheltenham for a fortnight to take the spa waters, supposedly good for those bilious complaints. She gained little benefit.

Circumspect in how she communicated her suffering to others, she tried whenever possible for that humour that so often erupts from the letters. It was only to Cassandra that she complained of symptoms that simply couldn't be ignored. She wouldn't foist her pain on distant friends or on her young nieces and nephews: Fanny Knight, and James's children Anna, Caroline and James Edward. The young should be, and were, concerned primarily with their own affairs.

By now James's three children were busy writing fiction in emulation of their clever aunt, sending their efforts to be read and critiqued at the Chawton cottage. Like Jane's own work, these writings were read aloud and the characters discussed for plausibility and interest. The letters Jane wrote to these aspiring novelists form a lively contrapuntal melody above the sad bass notes in her description of herself to those nearer her in age.

> [James] Edward is writing a Novel—we have all heard what he has written—it is extremely clever, written with great ease & spirit.

The young man was about to proceed from school at Winchester to college in Oxford and Aunt Jane wrote him a lively jokey letter full of *his* life and, like Emma with young Harriet, foisting suitable emotions onto him: glee at leaving school and having at last the liberty to tell what it was truly like – or to invent anecdotes of scandalous behaviour.

Then she turned to his fiction, humorously reminding him of his uncle Henry now writing 'superior Sermons' for his new role as parson. Perhaps she and James Edward could use one of these as a 'fine help to a volume; & we could make our Heroine read it aloud of a Sunday Evening'. This sounds like a reference to the playful letter she'd written so many years before about her light and sparkling *Pride and Prejudice*: it wanted 'shade' that might be provided by some 'solemn specious nonsense, about something unconnected with the story'. Henry's sermon wouldn't be 'nonsense' but, if inserted, would surely be 'unconnected'.

In response to the comic notion that she may have purloined her nephew's 'manly, spirited' novel to help herself along, she makes the famous statement about her own literary work and practice:

> I do not think … that any theft of that sort would be really very useful to me. What should I do with your strong, manly, spirited Sketches, full of Variety & Glow?—How could I possibly join them on to the little bit (two Inches wide) of Ivory on which I work with so fine a Brush, as produces little effect after much labour?

This seems self-deprecating, ladylike modesty, but I find it also an aesthetic credo. Miniaturists were wonderfully skilled and the early nineteenth century, like the Renaissance, was a peak time for the art in England – an art in which, unlike prestigious historical painting, women were well represented.

On ivory in particular, the painter needed quick, deft strokes to gain effect. No room and opportunity for mistakes at the final point. Doesn't this sound like Jane Austen, how she differed and knew she differed from her baggy male (and female) competitors?

By the time she wrote the jaunty letter to James Edward with such kindly pretence that they were fellow authors, she was telling another white lie: that she was 'very well', when she could hardly walk to his half-sister Anna's house nearby.

This is how to behave. No complaints unless truly over-whelmed or communicating with one's close contemporaries. Write 'chearfully'.

January 1817 brought an improvement, so much so that Austen began a new novel, later named 'Sanditon'. To Alethea Bigg she wrote that she wasn't 'far from being well', convinced now she knew what was wrong – 'bile' of course. Then off she jumped from her ailments to Alethea's 'best Gown' and her recipe for making wine from Seville oranges. She was strong enough to walk to Alton – but not back.

She pressed on with her novel, that strange frolicking 'Sanditon' that might have become something new or just a reprise of the broad comedy of her teen years – or simply have been intended to amuse her carers. Fresh, funny and disconcerting.

There's some comedy of bile in the work. Indolent Arthur Parker declares:

'My sisters think me bilious, but I doubt it. … If I were bilious … you know wine would disagree with me, but it always does me good.—The more wine I drink (in moderation) the better I am.'

However, Diana Parker's complaint of 'spasmodic bile' resembles Jane Austen's own, mentioned in her letters:

> I am more & more convinced that Bile is at the bottom of all I have suffered, which makes it easy to know how to treat myself.

The energy Diana summons to attack her probably imaginary disorder is comical. Is it a wistful trivialising gloss on Jane Austen's own real suffering?

To the list of absurd medical jargon Austen gives to Tom Parker in puffing mode, she later added the term 'anti-bilious': 'anti-spasmodic, anti-pulmonary, anti-sceptic, anti-bilious and anti-rheumatic'. (Yes, she did write 'anti-sceptic', a rather fertile mistake.)

Even as she described fake illnesses and their exploitation by quacks, she hid her weakening state. Caroline remembered how her aunt glossed her actions to reassure those around her; how, when seriously ill, she lay uncomfortably on three chairs in the drawing room rather than on the sofa because, if she lay there, her mother who spent much time on it, would leave it for her daughter and be incommoded.

All those fictional sofas Jane had created! This is a poignant detail.

Brother Frank and his family were staying in Alton. When she managed to go there, Jane entertained the children with made-up stories. She took time to compose in mirror writing a funny little letter to Charles's young daughter Cassy-Esten, about to celebrate her third birthday (the Austens were a precocious family). She also wrote to Caroline Austen enjoying more word play – punning on 'better' and 'butter' – leaping from 'Mrs Clement's Cow' to Caroline's happiness at the return of a lost dormouse. Again, as with James Edward, she took seriously her niece's fictional writing, giving sound advice.

Such a compliment to read carefully what these young people wrote. Her relationship with her nieces and nephews on the cusp of adulthood is one of the warmest, most appealing aspects of Jane Austen's latter years.

Despite her failing body, she also wrote playfully to the niece who wasn't composing a novel, the 'inimitable' Fanny Knight with her 'queer little heart'. Jane advised her on her love life and its quandaries, then breaking out in girlish delight, exclaimed:

> You are the Paragon of all that is Silly & Sensible, common-place & eccentric, Sad & Lively, Provoking & Interesting … It is very, very gratifying to me to know you so intimately. … Oh! what a loss it will be, when you are married.

The last sentence was prescient. How one detests that Victorian married woman, Lady Knatchbull as Fanny Knight became, the one who considered that her loving aunt would have been 'very much below par as to good society and its ways' had she not been rescued from 'commonness and a lack of refinement' by her own rich father and his superior connections. It's insupportable.

Young Fanny was not this posh, snobbish old lady, and aunt Jane loved her youthful triviality – letting it bring out the youthful triviality in herself – as the narrator-author loves naïve young Catherine in *Northanger Abbey*.

Again she wrote to Fanny, declaring herself 'tolerably well', able to walk about by sitting down and taking frequent rests. When spring begins to show, she'll ride the donkey. Her delight in Fanny leaps from the page:

> You are all over Imagination.—The most astonishing part of your Character is, that with so much Imagination, so much flight of Mind, such unbounded Fancies, you should have such excellent Judgement in what you do!

Such enthusiasm, such involvement in the life of the young is a very high type of caring. The Fanny Knight of Jane Austen's vision recalls the vivacious description of Emma when suddenly elated by Mr Knightley's love:

> She was in dancing, singing, exclaiming spirits; and till she had
> moved about, and talked to herself, and laughed and reflected, she
> could be fit for nothing rational.

This is the penultimate letter to Fanny but, in the sudden spurt of
compliment, there seems – to me, knowing what I know and she
did not – something valedictory. The letter reads like a farewell
to Fanny as well as to that girlish part of Jane Austen herself that
lingered into adulthood.

Then it's Caroline's turn. Austen writes of her novel, praising
Caroline for 'bearing Criticism so well' (we don't hear Caroline's
reaction) and insisting that James Edward will find 'true fame &
his true wealth' in novel-writing. She has, she notes, this 'fine flow
of Literary Ardour' because she has just received near £20 from
the second edition of *Sense and Sensibility*. Then back she goes to
the ham from Caroline's mother and the 'extremely acceptable'
sea kale.

So she consoled herself in writing, in creating her fictional world
and almost fictionalising her real-life relatives. By mid-March her
relapse had accelerated. 'Sanditon' was broken off and the Parkers,
the formidable Lady Denham, addled Sir Edward, prim Charlotte
and mysterious Clara Brereton all fall silent.

Now even to Fanny she admitted:

> I certainly have not been well for many weeks, & about a week ago
> I was very poorly, I have had a good deal of fever at times & indif-
> ferent nights, but am considerably better now, & recovering my
> Looks a little, which have been bad enough, black & white & every
> wrong colour. I must not depend upon being ever very blooming
> again. Sickness is a dangerous Indulgence at my time of Life.

She pulled herself up and resumed her normal tone with the young.
She'd been, she declared, 'languid & dull' when she'd written so
personally. She was better. They were going to have rain but after
it 'very pleasant genial weather' and she would ride out.

This is her last letter to Fanny.

A WILL

There were problems besetting her beside physical weakness and it's distressing to find ordinary anxieties so close to death. The dying are said to remove themselves from the living as they approach the end, to cease concerning themselves with what has oppressed, harried or delighted them in earlier days. The deaths I've witnessed have not been like this – and the little we can see of Jane Austen's doesn't quite seem so either.

Mrs Austen's rich brother James Leigh Perrot and his wife Jane, who'd figured so often in Austen's life, were childless. It was understood (a frequent story in families) that James Leigh Perrot's estate in due course would come to his sister's children, the bulk to James, his namesake, with legacies to the younger children and, if he died before his wife, these legacies would still be paid: in the bleak circumstances of 1816, they were very desirable. The Leigh Perrots wavered when they suffered from Henry's bankruptcy, irritated at the family's kneejerk loyalty to their nephew, but James didn't change his will.

On 28 March 1817 he died, aged eighty-two. The Austen ladies put on the 'Old Black Gowns', and Cassandra went to console the widow and help with arrangements. Frank attended the funeral.

Then the will was declared. It was a shock. Back in Chawton it bewildered Jane and her mother, whose grief at losing a brother was compounded by what his death meant to her and her children. James had left everything to his wife for her lifetime, and from their experience with Jane Leigh Perrot over the years they had little hope of much generosity there. This despite Mrs Austen and her daughters standing by her during the murky incident when she was accused of shoplifting and faced transportation for the crime. Only after Mrs Leigh Perrot's death would the Austen daughters and younger sons get £1000 each.

When Henry Austen was seriously ill in late 1815, Jane had been astonished that he could begin to get better despite the worries over his failing business. It was different for her: 'I am ashamed to say that the shock of my Uncle's Will brought on a relapse,' she told Charles, 'I am the only one of the Legatees who has been so silly, but a weak Body must excuse weak Nerves.'

Those 'weak Nerves', ridiculous in Mrs Bennet or Mary Musgrove, but far less so in Jane Fairfax or Fanny Price, are real, yet so rarely complained about by Jane Austen. Indeed, the weak body and assaulted nerves excuse any 'silly' response. Even after two centuries it's impossible not to feel enraged by this uncle who gave such pain to the only genius in the sprawling family.

If she were suffering from Addison's disease, as many authorities suppose, this added stress would certainly have hurt her. We are constantly warned against stress by books and the Internet: Jane Austen knew that 'agitation' could be as harmful as fatigue in her weakened state.

I hope that by then she'd skewered Jane Leigh Perrot. The grasping and mean Lady Denham in 'Sanditon' had inherited much of her riches from dead husbands and is malevolent towards poorer relatives. There seems something more than light comedy in this predatory great lady who hopes to benefit from the sick of Sanditon. I'd like to think that Jane Austen rid herself of a little portion of her 'spleen' in this portrait.

There was more to worry her. Even wealthy Edward, the chosen boy who'd been whisked as a child out of the crowded Steventon parsonage into the rich snug fold of the Knights of Godmersham and would never need to go to sea or join the Church or struggle with uncertain times or, like his sisters, worry where they'd next have to lodge – even this lucky man was troubled.

From 1814 onwards he was involved in a lawsuit that threatened his ownership of the extensive estates he'd inherited from his adoptive parents. The Hampshire holdings included the great house at Chawton. It would also involve the cottage which had been such a haven for the Austen ladies and where Jane had lived the kind of life that perhaps, all in all, was the very best available to her at her time and for her art, in a household of supportive, busy women. The lawsuit was settled only after Jane's death.

When I turn on my computer screen or check some local news, I'm bombarded with advertisements telling me to make a will with this and that firm. If I don't, the greedy state will intervene and I'll be sorry. The ads are often accompanied by puffs for funeral plans. Somewhere in the data of these companies must lie my date of birth.

As a student of eighteenth-century fiction, I hesitate for I've learnt that no will pleases everyone. Think of the opening of *Clarissa*, where a will prompts envy that will destroy the whole family. Unlike Richardson, Frances Burney and Charlotte Smith, Jane Austen hardly uses wills as a plot device (as opposed to those entails so unfriendly to females). Only *Sense and Sensibility* opens with the reading of a will that instigates the action but doesn't feature again. After the disappointment of Uncle Leigh Perrot's will, however, Jane Austen might, had she lived, have found a place for a dramatic will in future fiction. Perhaps in 'Sanditon' Lady Denham could have died and made havoc with her 'young people' by perversely leaving her fortune where least expected or deserved.

Jane Austen made her will on 27 April. Unwitnessed, it was addressed to Cassandra who was the main legatee. She left two legacies of £50 each, not to the beloved nieces and nephew who had skills and family support enough to make their way comfortably in the world, but to those she valued and knew could benefit: Henry, now a poor curate, and Madame Bigeon, servant and companion to Henry's wife Eliza whom she'd nursed in her final illness. On London visits Jane had delighted in her company and fine cooking: 'M^{de} Bigeon was below dressing us a most comfortable dinner of Soup, Fish, Bouillée, Partridges & an apple Tart.'

TOWARDS THE END

Being 'a very genteel, portable sort of an Invalid', Austen was taken away for better medical help than was available from the Alton apothecary. She travelled the sixteen miles to Winchester to be treated by the surgeon of the County Hospital, Giles-King Lyford, nephew of the John Lyford of Basingstoke who'd looked after her mother in the Steventon days. Perhaps she sighed to leave her beloved home, but, as they all set out, she was suffused with gratitude:

> if I live to be an old Woman I must expect to wish I had died now, blessed in the tenderness of such a Family.

She was still her old self when it came to James's wife, Mary Austen, however. Mary had offered her carriage for the journey to Winchester; it was kind of her but, still, 'she is in the main *not* a liberal-minded Woman'.

They left on 24 May.

Later this became a significant date. It's Queen Victoria's birthday and we used to celebrate it as Empire Day. 'Responsibility, Sympathy, Duty and Self-sacrifice' were what we thought the day (and the Empire) was for. I remember in one of my temporary sojourns at the Welsh primary school being given a union jack on a stick to wave while an 'old' lady sang 'Jerusalem' in a wobbly voice.

It was also my mother's birthday, the only one in our little family on a useful date – I usually went back to school on mine. So we had a cake and a vase of sweet william. Despite the annual optimism for this floral month, it often rained – indeed I can hardly remember a 24th of May in England when it didn't. It rained on 24 May 1817 as Jane and Cassandra travelled to Winchester in the coach with Henry riding outside. He got wet.

She was deposited in College Street near the school she'd imagined the boy James Edward leaving to become a man at Oxford. From the sofa where she lay by day, she wrote her nephew a last letter grasping hold of that cheerfulness she tried to keep for the young – with them, as she'd noted, she did not grow older:

> Mr Lyford says he will cure me, & if he fails I shall draw up a Memorial & lay it before the Dean & Chapter, & have no doubt of redress from that Pious, Learned & disinterested Body.

A spinster aunt is always an entertainer.

ENDING WITH HUMOUR

Jane Austen was a comic writer, whose novels, tales, charades, funny poems and letters all aim to make existence for others a little lighter, quirkier and more bearable. Dying didn't preclude laughter or at least a smile.

The process of dying had been funny to young Jane; in 'A Beautiful description of the different effects of Sensibility on different Minds', a doctor offers puns to the dying Melissa, while her friend suggests hashing up 'the remains of an old Duck' to tempt the delicate appetite of an invalid. Melissa herself is simply too tired even to *think* of dying.

I was pleased to find that Jane Austen's last known letter ends with the hope that a naval captain's wife and daughters will wear 'longer petticoats' than they had last year. I was even more impressed when I learnt of her last creative words.

Perhaps to combat the self-pitying, maudlin feelings that overcome us all from time to time, she wrote a jolly poem, knowing or not knowing how close she was to the end. If you're moderately content with how you've lived your life, it may be as well to leave it on the same note. The copies of her Winchester poem that have come down to us aren't in her hand: maybe there's a lost original – or more likely she could now dictate but not write.

Like so many of her other funny verses, 'When Winchester races' was provoked by a newspaper announcement stating the time and place of the upcoming event. The Austens enjoyed a day at the races, which offered not only horses running, but betting, gambling, drinking and roistering; in *Mansfield Park*, Tom Bertram is nearly killed by excessive revelry at Newmarket. The races at Winchester (Roman Venta) were held at a steeplechase court about four miles out of town at Worthy Down. In July, that rainy month.

Jane knew how crucial the weather was to enjoyment. 'Poor Basingstoke,' she once wrote hearing of the miserable weather it suffered for its races.

In her Winchester poem she used the legend of St Swithin, the ninth-century patron saint of the city, who's able to control rain (as the novelist controls it in her fiction). His power is summed up in the popular ditty:

> St Swithin's day, if thou dost rain
> For forty days it will remain;
> St Swithin's day, if thou be fair
> For forty days 'twill rain nae mair.

St Swithin's Day is 15 July.

Jane Austen imagines the dead saint indignant at not being consulted by the townsfolk:

> When Winchester races first took their beginning
> It is said the good people forgot their old Saint
> Not applying at all for the leave of S^t: Swithin
> …
> But when the old Saint was informed of these doings
> He made but one spring from his shrine to the roof
> Of the Palace which now lies so sadly in ruins
> And then he address'd them all standing aloof.
>
> Oh, subjects rebellious, Oh Venta depraved
> When once we are buried you think we are dead
> But behold me Immortal.—By vice you're enslaved
> You have sinn'd & must suffer.—Then further he said
>
> These races & revels & dissolute measures
> With which you're debasing a neighbouring Plain
> Let them stand—you shall meet with your curse in your
> pleasures
> Set off for your course, I'll pursue with my rain.

As their aunt's literary reputation began to soar, Caroline and James Edward became guardians of the ladylike image the family wished to foster. Caroline deplored the notion that this poem might be made public after fifty years. As the great author's last creative words, it could only distress. Jane Austen would have torn up the verses had she lived, Caroline was sure.

Long before the now elderly Victorian pair sought to protect their aunt's reputation, however, Jane Austen's first biographer, her brother Henry, writing just after her death, had been delighted by the poem. He thought it 'replete with fancy and vigour': the stanzas were an example of his sister's 'truly elastic cheerfulness'. The poem was therefore impossible to hide.

Austen left intact much sillier things for her family to see and hear in her childhood notebooks, though never expecting quite so multitudinous an audience. And, if we do return to childhood in old age – or when dying – then why couldn't she return to that Steventon parsonage where the whole family revelled in word games and composed little poems for each other? To soak herself one more time in the magic of malleable words.

And that sentence: 'When once we are buried you think we are dead / But behold me Immortal.' Difficult to get it out of your mind once read.

I'm glad she wrote the poem, glad her last creative words were about English rain. It had played such a large part in her novels and letters.

My father's humour didn't leave him at the end; nor his (creative) telling of tales. He was in hospital for his hundredth birthday, having rarely before been there during his long life. A staunch royalist, he set much store by receiving the customary card for a subject on reaching his century.

Into the hospital we carried the large pile of cards and presents that had arrived for him. On the top of the pile of cards was one from Iain Duncan Smith, Secretary of State for Work and Pensions. My father gazed at it in dismay. Did this ordinary man now represent the state? What, he said with still a twinkle in his one rheumy eye, was the world coming to? He started opening the other cards, reading carefully the conventional words written on them, studying the pictures intently, assuming each had been chosen with care.

Then turning one big card over to put on the 'read' pile, he spied the special one: the glossy, properly royal image of the dumpy, smiling queen in full regalia wishing him a happy birthday. 'Right,' said my father, and it was.

A day or two later, he was moved to a hospice; then he was carted back to hospital having made it clear he wasn't ready to die. We were called to the bedside. My father began telling a comic anecdote about two bosomy ships' figureheads in the Bermuda dockyard called informally 'Yes, please' and 'No, thank you'. Then he stopped talking. We held his hands; they grew cold. We felt tears starting. We waited in silence. Suddenly the hands began to get warm again and take on colour. He opened his eye and continued where he'd left off with his funny story. He was always talking.

His optimism remained. He was sent back to the hospice, where he died. On his last day he asked if he could move into the bed with a view on the other side of the room once its present occupant died.

I described this death at the end of my book about cancer, *Radiation Diaries*. After all, I couldn't describe my own and even a diary needs a conclusion. Now, another decade on, I wondered about the truth of that interrupted story. Oh, yes, said the other witnesses, that's what happened.

DYING WITH PATIENCE

Jane Austen died in the early morning of 18 July 1817, near midsummer, the opposite end of the year from her birthday in December. The death was private and Christian, and we can approach it only through the letters of her nearest kin. Families and friends become properly pious and circumspect at this time, as Jane did when her own father died. But we can still hear a little of Jane herself through their words.

In those last weeks, she tried as much as possible not to give trouble to those around her. She could not refrain from grumbling completely, but when she did she stopped herself with a welcome asperity. Through their heroines, the novels had often stressed the need for mental exertion in suffering, for *fortitude*. In *Sense and*

Sensibility, Elinor begs her sister, 'Exert yourself, dear Marianne … if you would not kill yourself'.

Early in life Mary Wollstonecraft wrote, 'If I were to give a short definition of virtue, I should call it fortitude.' The older Wollstonecraft admitted, 'The fortitude of patience is the most difficult to acquire.'

Her husband's account of Wollstonecraft's death is one of the most detailed physical descriptions of a woman dying that we have from this period. William Godwin, married for only a few weeks, recorded every day and hour of his wife's long painful dying following childbirth. He tried to catch the heroism of a peculiarly female death, but couldn't avoid expressing his own views.

A lapsed Dissenting preacher, he'd become a confirmed atheist. Once a fervent Christian, with more anxious piety than Jane Austen revealed in her letters, Wollstonecraft had found her faith dwindling. But she retained a residue of Christianity, a sense of the numinous, of something after death or perhaps just around the edge of life. There's an anecdote that, under the influence of sedatives, she murmured, 'I feel in heaven.' Godwin responded, 'I suppose, my dear, that that is a form for saying you are in less pain.'

He might be right but it wasn't long since she'd written:

> It appears to me impossible that I should cease to exist, or that this active, restless spirit, equally alive to joy and sorrow, should be only organized dust.

More certain than this anecdote, which isn't in Godwin's *Memoirs* and may have been invented to reveal his po-faced literalness, is her knowledge that, with childbearing, there was always a possibility of death. A strong childhood memory haunted her – of her mother muttering just before she died:

> A little patience and all will be over.

The phrase imprinted itself on her daughter's mind. Wollstonecraft used it more than once in her books, including her last novel, *The Wrongs of Woman*, on which she was working at her death. Close to the end, she too used the word: the midwife told her she 'must have a little patience'; she relayed the fact to Godwin.

Patience: the word is all over Shakespeare, with characters failing to find it or finding it only after great trial. In *Twelfth Night*, it becomes embodied as 'patience on a monument, / Smiling at grief' (the phrase memorised by young Catherine in *Northanger Abbey*) and – I can't leave it out – in *The Pilgrim's Progress*:

> I saw in my dream the Interpreter take Christian by the hand and lead him into a little room. Here two little children sat, each in their own chair. The name of the eldest was Passion and the name of the other Patience. Passion seemed to be very discontented but Patience remained quiet and calm.

Cowper ends *The Task* with hope for patience and a life 'peaceful in its end', death from a 'gentle stroke'.

Patience strives for peace and gentleness.

Jane Austen suffered much pain in her last hours. Her body contorted so that her head no longer rested on the pillow but lay on the laps of Mary and Cassandra who took turns to watch and wait. Among her last words recorded by Cassandra were 'God grant me patience.'

Even as I quote this, I feel the unseemliness of intruding into the death scene. But it's what those who valued her most saw fit to record. The rest is intimate, familial and private.

For us who love the novels as much as any literature in the language, this death is hard to read about without tears or a lump in the throat.

Cassandra wrote to Fanny:

> I *have* lost a treasure, such a Sister, such a friend as never can have been surpassed,—She was the sun of my life, the gilder of every pleasure, the soother of every sorrow, I had not a thought concealed from her, & it is as if I had lost a part of myself.

Fortitude in life, patience in death, kindness and gratitude in both.

AFTERWORD

Jane Austen's novels have spread out and round me like rich mate-rial, a shot silk of rippling ambivalence, of passion and affection, temperamental undercurrents, neediness and intellectual solitude, confusions clarified, resilience, exertion and stillness – and love (however ironised). You can make sense of a life with many great writers – if there *is* such a sense – but Jane Austen is better than most for the business. She can't be used for divination, as some people use the Bible or Virgil's *Aeneid*, but if you open any page of her novels, you can find a good sentence – as well as a sign of 'delightful spirits, and that gaiety, that playfulness of disposition' she so admired.

You find beauty too.

I mention this because I've noticed that old age comes with a heightened sense of beauty in the natural world: a single heart-wrenching flower, a startlingly green hillside passed by when younger and healthier and able to stride more purposefully. The same with a ravishing literary work or piece of music. Like the primrose or peony, Jane Austen's novels (or Schubert's *Lieder*) have become more beautiful to me now that I take time with them than they were half a lifetime ago.

What have I learnt from reading Jane Austen and from think-ing and writing about her? I must look back over my chapters, memory being a little faulty. Probably I'm past loving the wrong people and worrying about the personal power one person, male or female, holds over another. I find it difficult to live in the present, to remember the past as it gives pleasure rather than dumping on me 'little zigzags of embarrassment'. Equally hard to avoid grumbling about ailments or stop seeking out wacky remedies for inevitable chronic pain. But I can find patterns and connections and give good words a 'second perusal'. Since I shrink from the modern mantra of learning to love myself, I can try to be more *patient* with myself – and others.

I can walk more, and keep walking even when my legs ache. I can feel more fully the body in motion and allow myself to become part of the world's life outside. I'll tell myself not to wait for the sun or to reject leaden skies, so missing Spring, the grass excitedly pushing up, flowers and blossom not hanging back for a decent day to bloom. If I need company, I'll take along Elizabeth, Emma or, though I may have given a critical impression of her book, my favourite walking companion, Anne Elliot.

What else? I think I've come to value home more than earlier in my life. I used to see myself as a rolling stone, a wanderer, both appalled and slightly proud I'd changed schools thirteen times. As I grew older, I continued putting down no roots, enjoying the open road, looking always for the exit sign on arrival, the way to a new north or south – a bit like Mary Wollstonecraft I think, also a product of a peripatetic childhood. I've stopped wandering now – perhaps because the road is jampacked with cars, scooters and fast bikes – and new destinations look the same as the old when I arrive. Mrs Elton's tourism has turned all the world into a theme park.

Jane Austen has helped me to this love of 'home'. She enjoyed going elsewhere, leaving Steventon and Chawton to visit the seaside, London and Bath, and a host of relatives and friends in mansions and parsonages throughout the South of England. But her least creative and contented period was the years she spent between those two fixed places, Steventon and Chawton. It's reported she fainted when suddenly told in the hallway of the rectory that she and her family would now live in Bath (the Austen daughters were always 'portable' commodities). In Florida I wrote my dissertation on the poet John Clare, who lost his reason when forced to move from his Helpston tenement to a better cottage only a couple of miles away. It wasn't and never would be 'home'.

Not quite relevant perhaps for Jane Austen who, though distressed at the move, soon described herself as 'reconciled' to Bath, although its 'putrifying Houses' would never be home.

When I first visited the dilapidated tenement in Helpston before John Clare became so celebrated that his cottage was prettified into a shrine, with gift shop and café, I couldn't think how anyone could be attached to such an unpicturesque place as the damp, flat countryside of East Anglia. I know better now, having been in Cambridge near sixteen years. Perhaps I chose John Clare to study in America because I was homesick even then, though I'm not sure where home was. Except, perhaps, in words.

Jane Austen was buried in Winchester's great cathedral. An honour, but she might have preferred to be in Chawton churchyard near the cottage where she'd now be lying with her mother and sister. It might have seemed more like home.

ACKNOWLEDGEMENTS

I have written this book hastily to catch the moment when we celebrate 250 years since Jane Austen's birth. I began compiling it just after I finished working on the new eight-volume Cambridge edition. It's more personal than my scholarly biographies and criticism, mainly because I've felt at liberty to tie in my readings with episodes in my life – a habit out of the question when I set out in academia in the 1960s. I've not returned to Austen criticism or consulted new books – old age is time-consuming – so I apologise if, in any remarks, I've inadvertently plagiarised someone unmentioned below; decent ideas may well have originated elsewhere, errors will certainly be mine. Not everyone will approve my desultory sort of writing. My two main mentors Marilyn Butler and Deirdre Le Faye are both dead but, were they alive, would probably have disapproved. To them now I can simply express gratitude. Both generously shared their remarkable learning.

Working with the editors of the scholarly Cambridge edition many years ago, along with my wise and meticulous colleague Linda Bree, I was fortunate to be exposed to details of Austen's cultural context through the annotations of Antje Blank, Barbara M. Benedict, Edward Copeland, Richard Cronin, the late Dorothy McMillan, Pat Rogers, Peter Sabor and John Wiltshire. Over the years I've benefited from reading the work of many other scholars. I'll list just a few whom I've valued, authors of academic monographs, trade books, talks and blogs: Janine Barchas, Paula Byrne, Robert Clark, Emma Clery, Irene Collins, Gillian Dow, Susan Allen Ford, Jocelyn Harris, Helena Kelly, D. A. Miller, Ellen Moody, John Mullan, Diego Saglia, Maureen Stiller, Kathryn Sutherland, Bharat

Tandon, Anne Toner, Clara Tuite and the 'Janeites'. I especially admire the recent scrutiny of material objects that helps make Austen's life feel a little less unknowable. To these scholars and readers, I must add appreciation of two friends whose enthusiasm and knowledge of Austen's work are unmatched: Devoney Looser and Diana Birchall.

In addition to his editing of *Emma* for the earlier Cambridge edition, Richard Cronin, a valued colleague from my years at the University of Glasgow, is responsible for encouraging me in this speedy project, and I'm indebted to him for any of its merit. He's been unfailingly patient with my doubts, as has the commissioning editor at Cambridge, Bethany Thomas. I have appreciated the astuteness of Maartje Scheltens as a copyeditor and the care with production of Ruth Boyes. Maud Ellmann and Hazel Mills both kindly commented on individual chapters.

The silhouettes which I have used to adorn this book were made with scissors and black paper by Jane Austen's nephew, James Edward Austen-Leigh. I admired them many years ago and always hoped for an occasion to use them within a book. I am extremely grateful to Ben Welland for photographing them so expertly.

Some of the material I have used here has been published in more academic form during the last thirty years: in the 'Annual Reports' of the Jane Austen Society (JAS) and in *Persuasions*, the journal of the Jane Austen Society of North America (JASNA). Some has been given as lectures at Chawton House; Gresham College; Jane Austen Study Days and JAS AGMs in Chawton and Winchester; JASNA AGMs in Vancouver and Denver; in Hull and Newington Green; in Bologna, Udine, and Calabria Universities, Italy; and Tokyo, Sophia and Doshisha Universities, Japan. I've also occasionally called on my fictional and autobiographical work written post-retirement, which was kindly published by Katherine Bright-Holmes at Fentum Press: *Radiation Diaries* and *Jane Austen and Shelley in the Garden.*

ACKNOWLEDGEMENTS

I could not have careered along through the wet weeks of an English spring as I did without the help of my daughter and the support and advice of my husband to whom the book is dedicated. And, having through those months ignored the patch of moss and clover I call a lawn, I am, finally, grateful to Newnham College for its beautiful well-kept gardens nearby.

In her *Letters to a Young Lady* of 1806, Jane West (the writer who amazed Jane Austen by composing so many novels and conduct books with household cares heavy upon her), declared that, in old age, authors 'seldom fail to diminish their reputation'. The old woman writer should fall silent, destroy any unpublished manuscripts, and use the remainder of her time on earth to correct the errors of her youthful works.

Jane West was in her late forties when she wrote this. She died age 94. It was a long time to be silent, however advisable.